Beauty and the Geek

by

I0687598

Roni Adams

Beauty and the Geek

Cover Art by *RJ Morris*

The Wild Rose Press
PO Box 706
Adams Basin, NY 14410-0706
Visit us at www.thewildrosepress.com

Publishing History
First Champagne Rose Edition, 2007
ISBN 1-60154-159-7

Published in the United States of America

...his gaze moved to her mouth. Oh no, what's he thinking? He's not going to, is he? Her heart accelerated, but she couldn't seem to make herself say anything.

Maybe the sudden impact of their fall had scrambled his brains. His gaze lifted to hers. Had his eyes always been that deep of a green? He leaned slowly towards her and she found herself meeting him halfway. His hand skimmed up her back and she tipped her head as their lips hovered Their lips hovered a mere hairsbreadth apart for the most incredibly long moment of her life.

When Louie's mouth met hers, her eyelids fluttered closed. She slid her hand up to wrap around his neck and kissed him back. His lips were warm and sweet and he tasted of coffee. He kissed her as if he was worshipping her lips, paying homage to them with his own. His fingers trailed over her cheek and he cupped her face in his palm. Their tongues touched, and a knot formed in her throat at the dreamy intimacy of the kiss. He tangled his hand into her hair and pulled her closer to deepen the kiss. A sigh of pleasure escaped her, and a really weird feeling washed over her. It was almost as if she'd kissed him before, like this. But that was impossible. She'd never kissed Louie, but it felt natural...not at all new or awkward.

Shifting so her breasts pressed into his chest, she raised both arms and linked them around his neck. Under her bottom she could feel his erection pressing into her and she moaned. Louie slowed the kiss, pulling back slightly and dropping the softest whispers of kisses on her lips, the side of her mouth, her cheek, and her chin. She arched her neck, loving the way tingles raced up her spine as his mouth fell to her throat. She didn't think she'd ever been kissed quite so perfectly. A burning need to roll to the floor and have him cover her roared up inside her. Somehow, she knew Louie was full of passion inside, but was holding it in check. What would it be like to help him unleash the tiger within?

His mouth caressed her ear and down her neck. Then he did what he never should have done.

He spoke.

Dedication

To RJ, my favorite geek, you are truly a beauty, inside and out.

To Alice, for the brainstorming, hair pulling, and edits. Thank you.

Chapter One

Louie Hanson's heart began to tap dance as the familiar yellow sports car slid to a stop in front of his computer repair shop. He drew a deep breath when the bell over the front door jangled, and willed his body to calm down. With his chin resting on his hand and the magazine open in front of him on the counter, he gave the illusion of nonchalance. Without looking up, he flipped the page as if he couldn't care less that she had just walked into the shop.

High heels clicked on the polished hardwood floor and the door closed behind her. Floral perfume filled the room and he drew a deep nostril full of the familiar scent. He looked up with his eyes, but didn't lift his head. The first things he saw were black, very high heels, that held up shapely calves. His mouth went as dry as first thing in the morning.

His pulse raced and adrenaline shot through his veins, making him edgy. Still he made himself look up slowly, dragging out the torture. A bit like a strip tease act, the moment was meant to be savored. He caught a glimpse of her knees, round, perfect and enough to make his own go weak. Where on earth was the bottom of her dress? Ahh, there it was. Short, flouncy, and black, his favorite kind. Very nice. He drew a deep breath knowing the next part was the toughest. Like ripping a band-aid off fast to get the pain over with, he looked up.

Damn. His groin sprang to life beneath his well worn jeans and he was grateful the counter hid his lower body. Need kicked him in the gut at the view exposed by the plunging halter-style neckline of the little black dress. It showcased her tanned shoulders. Her black hair glistened in the shop's light as if it was just washed and dried. It wasn't the length of her leg showing, or the bared shoulders that got to him. Becky Richardson's breasts

1

were the finest works of art nature had ever created, and in the cool air of the shop her nipples had turned as hard as popcorn kernels. His mouth, previously dry, now salivated as fantasies filled his mind.

But even while all this went on inside him, he knew that Becky had no clue that he was quivering mass of lustful need. He was the ultimate pro at hiding it from her. He should be; he'd been doing it for well over a decade. He dropped his eyes back to the high tech magazine.

Her slender hand settled on the smooth counter top. Her nails today were candy apple red, and on her index finger was painted a tiny white rose. The incredible detail of the drawing was amazing. Her slender hands were as perfect as the rest of her, and ring less. That's exactly how he liked them best. His worst fear was that one day she'd slide her left hand across the counter and a diamond would sparkle up at him. He didn't know if he'd live through that. He shut the magazine and looked up.

Wham! Eyes the color of cornflower captured his heart once again. They sparkled with mischief. She smiled. He melted. Annoyed at the way she could turn him into a pile of need without doing anything other than walk in the room, he turned around. On the shelf behind him he pulled down her laptop.

"Were you able to fix it?" Becky asked.

"Don't I always?" He set the silver notebook on the counter between them. Tenderly he stroked his hand across the top then pushed it slightly towards her.

Becky clicked the cover open. Her white teeth sank into her bottom lip as she studied the screen. "I don't know why it keeps acting up. It's only a year old."

Louie tore his gaze off her plump lip as her teeth released it. He shrugged. "It's a bad girl; it craves attention. A few strokes from me, and she's purring like a kitten."

Becky closed the cover. "Some kittens have claws you know."

Their friendship over the years had evolved into a pseudo-teasing banter that he loved even as it tortured him to pretend about his feelings. If Becky only knew how he really felt, she'd turn around on those mile-high heels of hers and be out the door so fast he wouldn't know what hit him. What kept him in his envied position of her friend was her trust in him. The trust that said he'd never try anything with her so she was safe to be herself. Few men in the world knew the real Becky like he did. He leaned across the counter and placed his hand on top of hers. Her skin felt like the petal of a rose and he smiled, touching the tip of his index finger to her nail.

"I bet these claws could do some damage to a man's back." He lifted her hand to his lips and kissed her fingers while looking at her from behind his glasses.

Her eyes sparkled. She tipped her hand over and cupped his cheek. Louie felt her touch send fire through his already incredibly aroused body. Thank God for counters.

"Nerdman, if I were ever underneath you the last thing you'd be thinking about was your back." She leaned closer. His body pulsed at the view of her cleavage. She dragged her index finger down his cheek and he forced himself not to tremble.

Then she laughed and Louie grinned and took a small step back. Her hand dropped and she tipped her head to study him.

"What?" He felt like a bug under a microscope. He touched his mouth. "Do I have something on my face?"

She shook her head. "What's with those nerdy glasses today? Where are your contacts?"

Self-consciously he pushed his dark glasses back up his nose. "I ripped one this afternoon."

"I thought we tossed those out last year."

Last year. When she'd decided to give him a makeover to try and make him more appealing to women. He'd gone along with her crazy idea because it had been great to have her focusing on him, but he couldn't care less about what he looked like. The only woman he was interested in would never see him as anything more than her friend. Louie the Geek—the guy who fixed stuff for her, but didn't do anything else for her.

"Well if some hot chick wanders in, take them off. Better not to be able to see than to be seen like that."

He rolled his eyes. "Whatever. You know the computer would work a lot better if you'd quit eating rice cakes while you're working on it." He didn't know why he wasted his breath; she never listened to his advice.

She nodded. "Thanks, Nerdman."

The nickname never was an insult. Only she called him that and she could call him whatever she wanted to. "No problem, Princess."

She smiled and spun toward the door. Her skirt twirled around the back of her thighs, and he silently prayed for some mercy. Who was she going out with tonight? More importantly, who'd be peeling that little black dress from her in a few hours?

He leaned back and crossed his arms over his chest. "Got a hot date?"

He hated knowing, but he couldn't help himself. It was his self-inflicted torture. Reminding himself that she would never be with him was supposed to help him cope with never having her. The only small consolation was his pretty firm knowledge that she'd never settle down with any of them. Becky went through boyfriends like he went through tea bags.

At the door she stopped and looked back at him. "Roger. He's a pilot for United."

He nodded. "Be careful, you know what they say about pilots."

She frowned and tipped her head. "What do they say about pilots?"

His mind went blank. Damn it. He knew there was something funny he'd heard. What the hell was it again? Good job, Hanson. Shrugging, he said, "I don't know. That's why I asked you."

Becky puckered her eyebrows and shook her head. "You're losing it. Too much time in cyberland again."

"Maybe you should rescue me."

"I've tried to help you, but look at you." Suddenly she came back, and set the computer on the counter. Before he realized what she was going to do, she'd removed his glasses. His mouth dropped open as her long fingernails sifted through his hair and mussed it up. He bit back a groan of pleasure that ripped through his body at her touch.

She stepped back and looked at him. "There, that's a bit better." She touched one finger to her chin. "You know," she paused and then nodded as if agreeing with herself. "You almost look like a young Harrison Ford with your hair like that. I think you should try for that look all the time. You never know, it might change your luck."

He grunted and shoved his glasses back on his face. The only one he wanted any luck with was completely clueless.

"You know, even Bill Gates managed to get married."

Louie shoved his hands in his pockets and raised his eyebrow. "You offering?"

She grinned and tossed her hair over her shoulder. The little bell over his door jangled as she opened it. "You know darn well I don't do marriage, or babies." She winked at him. "Or geeks! Have a good one, Nerdman." With a laugh and a red tipped wave she was out the door.

He refused to wish her the same. He watched her slide into the yellow sports car. It was the story of his life, she flittered in, brightened up his world, and left, leaving him feel like a balloon with all the air let out of it. He was pathetic. He'd wasted half his life worshipping her, hoping for something that was never going to happen.

He strolled to the large plate glass window of his shop and watched her turn at the four corners of town. Across the street Margaret Richardson waved to him from in front of her beauty shop. He waved back. Margaret's head followed the direction of her daughter's car, and she shrugged her shoulders and shook her head. Louie nodded in understanding. Margaret loved Becky to death but she'd never understand her.

The hardware store owner joined Margaret on the sidewalk, and the two began to laugh. Louie watched the interplay with interest. Two lonely people sharing a story at the end of the day. Too bad Mr. Smith was pushing 85; much too old for Becky's mother.

He stared at George Smith thinking yet again how incredible it was that he still worked six days a week. But then he had nothing else but his shop, why would he retire? The old man had never married; rumor had it that the woman he loved married someone else and moved away. He never got over her. It sent a cold finger sliding up Louie's spine when he thought about it. Was that going to be him someday? Not wanting to close the shop at the end of the day because there was nothing else to do once he locked up?

He turned from the window, flipped the front door lock, and the sign to CLOSED.

Bending down he picked up the newspaper that had fallen from the end table in his waiting area. He straightened the pile of magazines and looked around in satisfaction. The sitting area looked nice. Becky had argued with him when he'd wanted to just put a couple straight chairs on the wall for customers to sit on. She'd insisted the area needed cozy chairs with cushions, some bright curtains at the oversized window, plants and reading materials. She said customers would want to come in and talk about their computer needs. They'd hang around—and customers who stayed longer, bought more.

He'd told her to do whatever she wanted, just like he always did. He'd been amazed when people did exactly as she said they would. They came by and dropped off their broken computers, that was true, but sometimes they just popped in and asked his advice about the latest technology. They brought in articles they'd read and asked if he could get a certain item.

Business had more than tripled in the past year. It was his personal life that was stagnant. He flipped off the front lights and headed to his office in the back.

In the small break room, he poured a cup of hot tea. Becky's touches were here too. She'd forced him to make this room and his office, a home away from home. "You never know in our weather when you might be stuck in here for a while, Nerdman," she'd insisted.

All he could think about was getting snowed in with her, but that hadn't happened. He'd had the shop three years and he'd never even come close to getting snowed in. Still, knowing Becky cared enough about him to want him comfortable if it ever happened had him handing over his MasterCard.

Annoyed yowling at the back door brought him out of his musings and he pulled it open. His old beat-up looking tomcat strutted in with a look of disgust.

"I didn't tell you to go out there this morning." Louie glanced outside before shutting the door. Settling his hands on his hips he watched the grey tiger-striped beast plop down in front of his empty food bowl and look up at him.

"Coming right up, boss." He picked up the bowl and scooped some fresh food out of the plastic tub he kept in the cupboard. "Google" was another one of Becky's ideas. He gave the big old cat a pat and set his food down.

The cat ate greedily for a second, and then wound himself around Louie's legs. He crouched down to scratch behind the cat's ears, earning more rubbing and purring. "If Becky would stop spoiling you with that expensive cat food, you'd probably kill a lot more mice, which if I remember correctly is the reason she insisted that I needed to keep you to begin with."

With a sigh he stood up and brushed his hands down his pant legs, grimacing at the stray hairs that sailed through the air. He picked up his mug of tea and headed into his office. He took a drink and plopped his feet up on his desk.

As always his thoughts turned to Becky, and he smirked. She might be out with a pilot tonight but she was guaranteed to call him first thing tomorrow morning. She'd pop open her laptop, see his face, hear the joke he'd videoed and then she'd pretend to be mad and call to chew him out. And that would make it a good day in his book.

A slight breeze blew in the small window and he sighed. It was warm for September, but there wouldn't be too many more nights like this. Usually he loved the changing seasons of upstate New York, but for some reason, the thought of summer turning to fall and then the long cold winter made him think of how quickly the years were going by. He still spent every day wondering if he'd see Becky. He still went to bed every night cursing himself because he couldn't get her out of his head or his heart.

Setting his feet down he opened up a folder and picked up a photo. All that was going to change; it had to. He was going to focus on this new project and start focusing on the rest of his life whether or not that included Becky. After tomorrow's appointment, he'd have a huge reason to lock the shop up at night.

****

Becky pushed open the door to the beauty parlor and grimaced at the bright lights. She gagged at the smell of the hair product permeating the air and made a beeline for the coffee pot. Mornings came way too early.

"Good morning, sweetheart. How was your date last night?" Margaret Richardson spoke through the pins in her mouth as she rolled Mrs. Gregory's thin grey hair around tiny rollers.

Becky took another sip before moving to the front desk and peeking at the appointment book. As always, her mother's schedule was full until nine that night. She shook her head. For years she'd been trying to get her to cut down her hours at least a few days a week, but her mother wouldn't listen.

"It was fine. We went to that new Mexican place outside of Newdale," she murmured looking over the books. "Do you have the deposit ready?"

"It's all in the drawer."

Becky sighed, but didn't bother to comment. She'd done everything to get her mother to put the cash and checks in the safe at night, but Margaret had her own way of doing things.

She grabbed the large envelope from the drawer. "I'll write this all up on my lunch hour, and take it to the bank."

"Thank you, honey. Are you going to stop back after work then?"

"Not tonight. I'm going over to Callie's."

"Tell Callie to bring the girls in for a trim. I saw Jenna at church Sunday and she couldn't see through those bangs."

"I'll tell her." She finished off the coffee and set her mug in the small sink. Stopping at her mother's side, she kissed her cheek. "I'll talk to you later. Bye, Mrs. Gregory." She touched the older woman on the shoulder and met her eyes in the mirror. Mrs. Gregory smiled at her.

Becky headed to the door, already thinking about everything she had to get done today. Maybe she should stop at the bakery and pick up those chocolate éclairs Callie's girls' loved so much.

"I just can't get over the old Ryan place selling."

Becky froze at her mother's words. Snapping her head around, she interrupted them. "What did you say?"

Her mother frowned at her in the mirror. "The old Ryan place has been sold."

The air all whooshed from her lungs and shock froze her in her tracks. The old Ryan house? The house on the hill at the edge of town. The largest and oldest mansion in all of Oakdale. The house she'd loved since she was a little girl.

When had it gone on the market? She hadn't heard anything about it. Not that it would've mattered; she certainly didn't have that kind of money. Was she actually grieving for a house she'd never even been in? She shook her head to try and get back to reality. "Who bought it?" she managed to ask.

Her mother didn't look over as she continued to work. "No one knows, just that he's from out of town."

"Do you think he's going to live there?" What if the new owner turned it into a multi apartment complex? That would be awful. Maybe the owner had a large family and would renovate it and bring it back to its original condition. From the time she was a little girl, her mother had told of the dances and parties the Ryans used to have. The men always wore tuxedos; the ladies in elegant evening gowns and gorgeous jewelry. She'd made her mother tell her the stories over and over as she was growing up; she knew every inch of that house in her mind from the sweeping *Gone With The Wind* style staircase to the crystal chandeliers.

Mrs. Gregory handed up a bobby pin to Margaret who slid it into the last of the curlers. She shrugged and let the chair down with a push on the pedal. "I have no idea, honey. Why don't you ask Callie? I'm sure she'll have to do a story on it for the paper."

That was true. Callie might know who bought the place. There weren't many secrets her best friend couldn't uncover as Oakdale's one and only newspaper reporter. She nodded, "I'll call her when I get to the office."

Becky watched her mother help her customer into the chair of one of the Pepto-Bismol Pink hair dryers. How on earth could her mother do this, for twelve hours a day sometimes, and still claim to love it? She shuddered and walked outside.

She slipped behind the wheel of her sports car and tucked the deposit envelope into her oversized leather bag. Driving through town with her windows down she reveled in the warmth of the morning. The fresh air cleared her head and it was a short time later that she pulled into the parking lot of the law firm.

She was still feeling depressed as she unlocked the office door. She unpacked her laptop, opened the screen, and flicked it on before heading down the hall to make some coffee.

A few minutes later, she grinned at the sight of Louie on her opening screen mugging for the camera. It took a second for her to realize he was telling her a really dirty joke, accompanied by a video. Her mouth dropped open, and she slammed the top down glancing around as if someone was watching. She gave a short laugh knowing full well no one else was in the office yet.

"He's so dead," she muttered. The punch line struck her and she bit her bottom lip to not laugh.

"I hope he's sound asleep," she reached for the phone, but her second line rang before she could finish dialing. "Peterson and Peterson," she answered.

"Hey it's me."

Callie's voice came over the phone making her forget about killing Louie. "Hey, I was going to call you this morning."

"You heard already?"

"About the Ryan house? Yeah. Do you know who bought it?"

"Nope, and I've been on it all morning. The transaction is sealed up tighter than Mrs. Cole's girdle. All I could find out is that it was a cash sale."

Becky's eyes widened. "Cash? How much?"

"Don't know, but I bet it went for close to a million with all that land, don't you?"

"Yeah, I mean, even run-down the property is worth a fortune."

"I'll keep up the detective work," Callie promised.

"I hope whoever bought it takes care of it." The closest she'd ever been to being inside was a peek in the windows. Now someone else was going to have the right to walk in the front door.

"Unless they bought it as a tax shelter and don't intend to ever live there."

"I don't want to think about it anymore." Slumping against the back of her chair, she wound the phone cord around her index finger. Her nail polish was chipped, and she frowned wondering when she'd have time to fix it.

"I knew you'd be bummed."

Becky heard the concern in her friend's voice and sighed. "It's stupid. It's not like I was ever going to be able to buy it."

"I know, but it's your dream house. It makes sense that you'd be upset that it's gone."

"It's not like it was mine, but it sat there empty for five years. I guess I just always thought it would be empty."

"Well you know, maybe the guy who bought it is single, and you'll fall madly in love and marry him. Then you could live there."

Becky shuddered at the mere idea. "No thanks. Not even for the house of my dreams would I tie myself to one man."

"Someday, I think..."

"Cal, you know me better than that. Men aren't to be trusted."

"Not every man is like your father. Look at my Dad. You love him."

"Yep, but he's one in a million. Most of them are snakes, dirt crawling snakes."

She knew Callie was rolling her eyes even though she couldn't see her. It wasn't a new conversation. Callie still believed in love and happily ever after. She believed it was much better to love 'em and leave 'em.

"How was your date with Roger last night?"

Becky shrugged and twirled the phone cord some more. "Fine."

"Just fine?"

"Yeah, nothing to write home about."

"You still coming to dinner?"

"Chicken French with linguine?"

Callie laughed. "Yes."

"I'll be there. Oops, my other line's ringing, gotta run.

See you at six."

She hung up as one of the lawyers walked in. She waved good morning and picked up the second phone line.

It was several hours later before she was able to call Louie. Sipping a diet cola, she took a break, and waited for him to answer.

"Oakdale Computers."

"You're an idiot." The teasing tone of her voice softened her harsh words.

"Ahh, the Princess has finally gotten around to doing some work today. What is it noon? Tough life."

She shook her head at his jabs. For some reason Louie thought working in a law office was a piece of cake. "It was so busy this morning I never got my nails painted."

"No manicure? I'm horrified. You better keep those hands out of sight all day."

"No doubt. Now about your little x-rated joke. Do you know how much trouble I could have gotten in?"

"Only if someone was close enough to hear what I was saying."

"I opened it up and walked away to make the coffee."

Louie started laughing.

She couldn't help but laugh with him. "It's not funny; anyone could have walked in."

"Did you like it though, Beck?" His voice was low and seductive.

"I'm a hard sale, Nerdman. You'd have to do more than tell me a dirty joke to turn me on."

"I think that's a challenge."

"No, it definitely isn't. Now tell me how to delete this before I come over there and hurt you." She waited, knowing exactly what he'd say back to her.

"Ohhh baby, hurt me, hurt me. You know how much I like that."

"You're pathetic."

"Pathetically in love with you, Princess."

"Right." She rolled her eyes, ignoring his game of being obsessed with her. "Hey, did you hear about the Ryan house?"

Louie made a gurgling sound as if he'd choked. She frowned. "Nerdman, You okay? You swallow your tea the wrong way or something?"

He coughed for a few seconds, and cleared his throat. "Uh, yeah, it was hotter than I thought. What were you saying about the Ryan place?"

"Someone bought it."

"Who?"

"No idea. Callie's looking into it, but so far the deal is hush-hush."

"Weird."

"Yeah, that's what we thought."

"I got customers, gotta go."

He clicked off before she could ask him what the heck to do about her laptop. She frowned at the phone in frustration. Now she'd have to stop at the shop on her way to Callie's, otherwise his dirty little joke would be there when she turned the computer on again tomorrow.

****

Louie drove slowly up the winding driveway. He couldn't shake the feeling that he was trespassing. Trees towered on either side before he finally reached the horseshoe shaped turnaround at the front steps. He cut the engine. His old car sputtered for a minute before backfiring, and stopping. He gazed up at the four enormous white columns flocking the main entrance. He swallowed hard and paused to take it all in. It was magnificent.

Even with peeling paint and dirt, it rose stately up to the sky. He slipped off his sunglasses and climbed out of the car.

Gingerly, he climbed the steps, but found them steady under his feet. The porch floor didn't give a bit when he bounced on it. He ran his hand along the railing, some of the paint peeling under his touch. This was a house built to last and certainly had.

He looked up to the once brass knocker with the name plate Ryan on it. He drew a deep breath and pulled the single large key from his front pocket.

It took several tries, but finally it caught and turned and the old door swung open with a creak.

Chapter Two

As soon as the door opened, the musty smell of a house that had been closed up for years assaulted him. Louie stepped over the threshold, closed the heavy door behind him, and stood in the middle of the grand foyer. The afternoon sun streamed through the huge windows. The top portions were stained glass and the colors made a magnificent rainbow across the dusty wood floor. He walked to the wall where an old-fashioned push-button light switch rested. He looked up at the chandelier high in the center of the ceiling and pushed the button. The chandelier lit up and he grinned. It was absolutely stunning. The sweeping staircase would do justice as a backdrop for any beautiful woman to make an entrance. In his mind he saw Becky in a turn-of-the-century gown gliding elegantly down the steps.

Determined to not spend today thinking about Becky, he turned away and cupped the crystal door knob on the French doors. The intricate details in the house impressed him and he had a feeling he could spend a year just uncovering all the treasures this place had to share. The house was a work of art and he had no regrets about his impulsive decision to rescue it from the bulldozers.

He threw open the doors and stepped into the formal parlor. The room was bigger than the entire first floor of his own house, with ceilings that had to be at least fifteen feet high. The fireplace in the corner was flanked by built in shelves, completely empty at the moment, but he could easily imagine them full of treasured family heirlooms.

Slowly he made his way through every room—fifteen on the first floor alone. The second and third floors contained ten separate bedrooms, some complete suites with tiny sitting rooms and dressing rooms. Three bathrooms were the only real modern features to be found, and by modern that meant they were built probably in the 1950's. By the time he'd made his way to the kitchen, several hours had passed and the sun was almost down. He had taken so many notes on his palm pilot that his fingers were cramping. Louie rubbed the back of his neck as he looked around the kitchen. It was like stepping into a movie set. The appliances were what could only be described as vintage. He opened cupboards to discover several of them still contained dishes and glassware. Picking up one plate he flipped it over and let his breath out on a low whistle at the insignia. Even what must have been the family's every day dishes were of the best quality.

The lawyer had told him everything in the house was his. Outside there were three huge buildings and anything in there was his as well. For the first time, he felt a little overwhelmed by what he'd taken on. But he was also excited. For the first time in his life, something was going to consume his time and his thoughts and it wasn't a dark-haired, blue-eyed, ex prom queen. In fact, now that he thought about it, he hadn't given her a thought since he walked in the door almost three hours ago. That had to be a sign. A good sign. A sign that he was ready to grow up and move past his infatuation.

It took a bit of yanking, but he managed to open the back door and stepped outside to what would have once been the kitchen gardens. In the fading light he could just make out some of the overgrown plants and the path that once wove from the house to the formal gardens in the back. His cell phone chimed and he lifted it off his belt loop. His parent's phone number was displayed and a weird sense of guilt draped over him. He felt like they'd caught him doing something he shouldn't be doing.

"Hi," he greeted.

"How's the weather up there?' Harold Hanson's booming voice had Louie pulling the phone back from his ear. His father lived for the weather report from New York. He liked nothing more than to tell his son about the fantastic Florida sunshine.

"It wasn't bad today, but they're calling for the first frost tonight. How about there?" Louie played along knowing the answer already.

"It's eighty-five, and sunny. Someday I might get

bored with all this sunshine." His father chuckled.

Louie didn't bother to comment. "You guys coming home for Thanksgiving?" It was odd being an only child when your parents left home. The holidays weren't the same. Not that he'd be alone; no one in Oakdale was going to let him go turkey-less. Maybe he'd wrangle an invite from Becky's mother. He could handle carving the turkey for the lovely Richardson ladies.

"Why don't you come down here? I'll send you an airline ticket and you could come for the whole week."

He'd rather stick a hot fork in his eye and twist it around then spend Thanksgiving in Florida, but he wasn't about to hurt his parents' feelings.

"Actually, Pop, how about I make it for Christmas instead? I've got some plans with friends for Thanksgiving weekend." He crossed his fingers over his little white lie.

"I hope those friends are female for a change; your mother and I aren't getting any younger, and we should be enjoying grandchildren by now."

It was the same hint he got every time he talked to his folks. All he could do was ignore it.

"Everything okay at the house? You gotta get those ducts cleaned for the furnace. Don't wait until heating season, Son. Now if money is an issue—"

Louie laughed and cut him off. "Dad, I'm twenty-six years old; I own my own business; I can pay my bills. And yes, the house is fine and I've got food in the cupboards."

"Well the house isn't much, but at least it's yours. Free and clear. That's more of a start then your mother and I had at your age. Why I remember eating soup seven nights a week just to pay the mortgage."

As his father went on about the lean times they experienced, a story Louie had heard often enough over the years, he tried not to feel bad about deceiving them. There just was no easy way to explain to people who believed you only got rich after years of saving and penny pinching that their son had made millions almost overnight with tech stocks and dot coms before they fell apart. His folks would never understand that and would only worry that he'd done something illegal.

Last year, they'd gotten this idea to move to Florida and they gave him their house. He'd tried every way he could to talk them out of it. He was perfectly content in the apartment above the shop, but they had been so excited to give him this generous start on his life that he couldn't turn them down. Instead he managed to find a way to make sizeable deposits into their retirement funds, through their accountant, without them being aware of where it was coming from. His father just thought he was a genius at picking the right mutual funds.

A flock of geese squawked noisily as they flew overhead and his father immediately picked up on it.

"Aren't you at the shop? What if customers need you? That's no way to run a business, you know; customers are impatient."

His father's comment snapped him out of his thoughts.

"The shop phone automatically forwarded to my cell, Pop. My customers can reach me no matter where I am." His father didn't trust new technology. There was no point in getting in that conversation with a man who still had a phone with a rotary dial.

"Yeah, okay. Well, where are you?"

Louie looked back at the old mansion and wondered how to word this. "Believe it or not, I'm out at the old Ryan place."

"The Ryan place? That monstrosity of a house on the hill? What are you dong there? I heard they're finally going to bulldoze that thing."

"Actually someone came in at the last minute and bought it. He's a business acquaintance of a friend of mine and he's asked me to take a look around and give him a quote for some work."

"Work? What kind of work? You need me up there, son? I could come help you; you know you aren't set up to do the kind of work I did. I'd better get up there."

"Pop, it's not that kind of work. I'm doing the remodeling; I'm doing the high tech stuff—home automation, security systems, temperature controls. It's all stuff I can do, not a problem."

"Sounds like he's insane to me. Dumping money into that old pit. Make sure you charge him plenty. Anyone who can afford that old place has some deep pockets; you make some money on that job."

His father would never understand how much money this was actually going to cost, and there was no return on his investment, at least not in the near future.

"I will, don't worry about that. Listen, I better run. You guys are ok? Mom's fine?"

"Yeah. She'll be excited you're coming for Christmas. She's got some big New Year's Eve shindig planned. Now if you need me to get you the plane ticket..."

"I'll take care of it. Kiss Mom for me and I'll talk to you later."

Louie closed the phone and noted the time. He'd have to hurry to get back to the shop when Becky showed up with her laptop. He sprinted back inside, locked the back door and shut off the lights as he walked through it. The lock on the front door didn't work much easier than it did when he went in but he managed to get it secured and a short time later he was driving towards town.

As soon as he rounded the corner to Main Street he spotted the yellow sports car. Becky was leaning against it, looking impatiently up and down the street. His heart jerked at the sight of her and a big grin spread across his face as he hopped out of his car and half jogged towards her. She frowned at him, which made him smile even wider. Only Becky could look that good when she was annoyed.

She was dressed in one of her many business suits—the kind with the short narrow skirt that made her legs look even longer. Her heels were so high he wondered how she didn't fall off them. Her dark hair fell around her shoulders and her blue eyes glittered under the street light as she glared at him.

"Hey Princess, you really shouldn't hang around my shop like this, folks will talk." He winked and turned to open the shop door.

"I told you I was coming right from work. You said you'd be here."

He flipped the light switch on and turned off the alarm. "Miss me?"

"No, but it's not like you to not be here."

Louie glanced at her. Was she annoyed because she was worried about him? Nah, she was just annoyed he wasn't waiting around for her. "Why didn't you just call my cell?"

"I was just about to."

She followed him inside and handed him the notebook. "Take it off."

Louie reached for the laptop letting his hands settle over hers as he looked at her suggestively. "Now that's three words I never thought I'd hear you say to me."

The top three buttons of her white blouse were undone and her creamy breasts swelled into cleavage that was just made for staring at. He was kidding himself today, thinking that anything could take the place of her in his mind; certainly not a house, no matter how fantastic.

"Nerdman, I'm not in the mood."

"Ahh, now those are words I'm far more used to hearing." He took the laptop and set it on the counter. "Princess, your wish is my command. All you have to do is crook one of those beautiful fingers at me and I come running to do your bidding, you know that."

"I'll tell you what finger I crooked at you this morning when I heard that joke in the reception area of the law office. I could have gotten in trouble for that, you know."

"I had no idea you were taking it to the office, I thought you'd hear at home."

"I took it to the office to do Mom's books on my lunch hour. I opened it up and walked away to get coffee. When I come back..." she waved her hands in the air in frustration. "Anyone could have seen it!"

"Sorry." He hit a few keys and made sure it was gone completely, then shut it down and handed it back to her. "There you go, Princess. Your computer is as innocent and pure as..." he paused, looked at her and grinned. "Well, innocent and pure anyway."

A smile teased her lips but she pursed them again obviously not ready to forgive him quite yet.

She started to pick it up off the counter and he slapped his hand down in the middle of it.

"Don't I even get a thank you?" Pursing his lips he made a loud exaggerated kissing sound that he knew would make her laugh

He grinned as her eyes filled with humor and she let

herself smile.

"Someday Nerdman, I'm going to plant one on you and your heart is going to stop."

On the outside nothing about his expression changed, however, inside his heart was doing jumping jacks so hard it hurt his chest. "I would die a happy man," he said softly holding her gaze.

He stepped back from the counter and Becky slid the laptop off and tucked it under her arm before walking to the door. "Thanks."

Louie watched the sway of her slim hips and the way her skirt barely moved as it hugged her rear end. She spun around. She narrowed her gaze at him, but didn't comment on his staring.

"Callie and I are going to start working on the fifteen year reunion stuff tonight. We can count on you to handle all that...stuff, can't we?"

Anything technical was "stuff" to Becky. He nodded. "For you, the world."

She nodded. "You're the best—even if you are a nerd."

"And you're too beautiful for your own good. Hey, how was the date with the pilot? Did you get your wings?"

Becky tipped her head and looked up at him. "I never kiss and tell." She flipped her wrist over, looked at her watch, and frowned. "Callie's waiting for me. I gotta go."

"Tell her I'll call her about her computer. She said it was crashing again."

"Why don't you come by tonight and look at it? We could go over the reunion stuff."

Dinner with Becky, even if Callie and her two little girls were there, was more than tempting, but he was trying hard to not spend time with Becky. "Nah you two will sit there talking girl talk and I'll be bored stiff." He'd be stiff all right and that was another good reason not to go. He turned from her and took off his jacket.

"Ok, but you're passing up her Chicken French. Catch you later."

As always after she left the shop was cold and lonely. Outside most of the shops had gone dark and the cars were all heading out of town and not into town. His stomach rumbled. Maybe he'd head to the diner first. It was Chicken Pot Pie night. He loved Chicken Pot Pie night.

He shook his head. This new plan of his better work; he was tired of the highlight of his nights being the special at the diner.

****

"You sit right there." Becky ordered her blonde-haired friend. "The girls and I will do the dishes. Finish your wine and relax."

"Yes, ma'am." Callie didn't put up too much of a fight and Becky knew she was exhausted.

Becky stood up and looked pointedly at Jenna and Hannah who obediently got up and carried their plates to the sink. Becky took the plates and rinsed them, placing them in the dishwasher as the girls handed them to her. "Jenna, Mom said you should stop in after school this week and she'll trim up those bangs."

The dark haired twelve-year old blew at the wisps hanging in her eyes. "Can I go tomorrow?" she asked turning to her mother.

"That's fine. Walk there from school and stay there and I'll pick you up after work. Maybe you can help Grandma Margaret with the shop a bit."

"What about Emma?" Becky closed the dishwasher and turned the dial. A gentle hum started and she looked back at it in shock. "Hey, where's the horrible grinding this was doing last week?"

"Oh, Tom came by and fixed that." Two spots of color appeared in Callie's cheeks and she seemed to take an inordinate interest in her wine glass. "Emma's been going to an after-school camp three days a week."

Becky was dying to ask more about how Tom Jacobson had come to play handyman; last she knew the two weren't even civil to one another, but she wouldn't get anything out of Callie with the girls there. She looked over at the seven year old.

"Do you like going to the camp?"

Emma nodded. "We do projects and play games. A lot of my friends go there."

Becky was relieved and a quick look at Callie showed that her friend was relieved, too. Callie had made the decision to start working full time again when the girls

21

went back to school this month and it had been a big change for all of them. Jenna came home to an empty house, but seemed to handle it well, and with Emma settled in her camp, it seemed to be working just fine.

The girls scampered off to watch some television program and Becky poured them each another glass of wine and slid into the chair across from her friend. "Now you can tell me about this handyman." She slipped her stocking feet up on the chair next to her and laughed at Callie's red face.

"There's nothing to tell. He stopped by to pick up his daughter." Callie looked up from her wine glass. "His daughter Amber is in Jenna's class this year and they've become as thick as thieves already."

Becky nodded.

"Well, Amber was here after school yesterday. Tom came to pick her up and the dishwasher was running and making that horrible noise."

She nodded again waiting patiently for Callie to get to the good part.

"Anyway, before I knew it, he was in the kitchen and had it apart and told me what it needed. He left, came back with the part, and fixed it. Any of our neighbors would have done the same for me; it was no big deal."

"Uh huh, but I'm guessing you invited him to stay for coffee and your famous homemade apple pie for dessert just to show your thanks."

Callie looked indignant and guilty. "What else could I do?"

Becky loved having Callie on the spot like this. She knew that if Tom and Callie would put their pride aside, they could pick up where they left off the summer after high school. "So he had pie with you and the girls and left?" She was hoping no. She was really hoping he hung around and they talked.

"Well, there was a movie the girls had rented and Amber really wanted to see it."

"Oh, so it progressed into renting a movie." Becky laughed out loud when Callie glared at her.

"No, they already had the movie. They just hadn't had a chance to watch it yet."

"What movie was it?" She had a feeling Callie and

Tom hadn't sat around watching the latest pre-teen flick with their daughters.

Callie looked away. "You know that one with the blonde girl from their favorite show. It was out last summer, but we never got to the theater to see it."

"What did you and Tom do while the movie was on?" Becky leaned forward dying to know if anything more happened.

Callie pushed her chair back and stood up. "We had coffee out on the deck."

"Wasn't it cold out there?"

"A little."

Becky wiggled her eyebrows. "Did you sit close together on the glider and snuggle?"

"No. Well, not at first anyway, but it did get cold."

Becky grinned. "And I'm hoping he put his arm around you to warm you up and somehow you ended up kissing."

Callie glared at her and turned to the sink. "It was perfectly innocent. It didn't mean anything."

"I think whether or not you two want to admit it, there's still some zing between you."

Callie turned on the water and rinsed her wineglass. Becky waited, knowing her friend was replaying the kiss in her mind. "It doesn't matter how much zing there is. He'll never forgive me for what happened. He made that very clear when he moved back to town; our kids are friends and we have to get along because of that, but that's all. The kiss just happened, it wasn't any big deal."

Becky followed her to the sink as she heard her voice shake. "What happened after you kissed, I mean what did he say?"

Callie looked up at her and her eyes were full of pain. "He was really mad that it happened and he apologized. It was really awkward."

Becky slid her hand along Callie's back comforting her the way she would Jenna or Hannah. It would definitely take more than a kiss in the moonlight to make things right between Tom and Callie. "Well, until he blew it with his apology how was it?"

"How was what?"

Becky rolled her eyes and stepped away. "The kiss.

How was the kiss?"

Callie glanced towards the living room. "It made my toes curl," she said softly.

Becky laughed out loud. "Some things never change, huh?"

Callie dried her hands on the towel. "Did you talk to Louie about the stuff we need for the reunion?"

"Okay, I get it—change of subject. He said whatever we need, it's no problem."

Callie raised her eyebrow. "I'm sure he said, whatever YOU need, no problem."

Becky waved her hand in the air dismissing that nonsense. "You know Louie, he'll take care of all that technical stuff. By the way, he said to call him this week and he'll come out and look at the spare computer."

"He's such a sweetheart."

Becky snorted. "Yeah? Well, did I tell you what that "sweetheart" did to me today?" She went on to explain about the dirty joke on her laptop.

"Poor Louie, all these years and he's still infatuated with the prom queen."

"Oh, he is not. It's a game to him. If I ever turned the tables and started to chase him he'd run for the hills."

Callie gave her a pointed look. "I don't think he would. I think he's serious about how he feels about you."

"Come on, Cal. It's Louie. I mean, he's not exactly my type, and I'm not his either, you know? I don't have horn rimmed glasses and a subscription to Geek Monthly."

Her friend looked up from under the lashes. "Haven't you ever heard that opposites attract? Louie treats you better than any man you've ever known. Maybe you need to stop seeing him the way he was in high school."

"Maybe it's you who should be looking at Bachelor Number one. I could definitely see you and Louie together. He loves the kids, and you love to nurture so you could cook for him and fuss over him. He'd eat it up."

Callie shook her head. "No thanks. I like my life the way it us, just me and my girls."

"Uh huh, until Tom rolled back into town."

Callie glared at her before grabbing a pen and pad from the counter. "Let's work on the reunion and not my love life."

****

The sound of a car crunching on the stones in the horseshoe driveway made Louie race to look out the upstairs window. He frowned. What on earth was Becky doing here? She stepped out of her car and shut the door. Sliding her sunglasses off her face, she squinted up at the house. Louie leaned back so she wouldn't be able to see him at the window.

For over a week he'd been busy dealing with contractors, getting quotes, hiring firms for the renovation. He hadn't seen her since he took the joke off her computer. His pulse beat rapidly and his chest hurt as if he'd run a mile. He'd missed her. It felt like life was flowing back into his veins at the mere sight of her. What the heck was he going to say if she found him here? What excuse did he have for being inside the Ryan house?

He watched her walk towards the porch and then she was out of view. He should just stay up here until she left, but the desire to see her, to speak to her, was too strong. Then suddenly he knew why he was going to go down and let her in. He had an opportunity to give Becky something no one else could; the chance to walk through the house of her dreams.

His feet thundered down the staircase and he flung open the front door before he gave himself any chance to think about the repercussions.

He grinned when her hand hit her chest and she stumbled back. Her mouth opened in a shocked, short scream and he could tell she thought she was coming face to face with a ghost.

Louie grinned, "Boo!"

She slammed her hands on her hips and sputtered. "What are you doing here?" She looked past him as if expecting someone else there with him.

"More to the question, what are you?" He stepped onto the porch and crossed his arms over his chest.

She shrugged and looked up and down the wrap-around porch. "I don't know. Ever since I heard it sold, I felt like I needed to come out here and walk around it once more. I didn't see any other cars so I thought no one was out here. How did you get in?" She lowered her voice to a whisper as if he was doing something illegal.

"With a key. My car's around back." He leaned against the railing and watched the wind lift the black curl on her cheek.

"What? I mean, why do you have a key?"

"I got an email from the lawyer's office asking me if I'd give the new owner a quote on a complete home automation system. Wants it to rival Bill Gates' mansion or something." He shrugged. "Who else in Oakdale was going to do that kind of work?"

"So you got the job? Here?"

Louie nodded. "Yep. It's a huge project, probably take me a year to finish."

Becky glanced back at the open door. He knew what she was hoping for. Maybe he should wait until she begged, but he wasn't that cruel. Besides he wanted to show it to her just as much as she wanted to see it. He jerked his head. "Wanna come in?"

Her blue eyes lit up like his did every time he she walked into a room. "I'd love to."

He pushed away from the railing, "As I've always said, Princess, your wish is my command."

They stepped into the foyer, and he closed the heavy oak door behind her. She looked around in amazement and he shoved his hands in his pockets and let her set the pace.

The expression on her face was like a child on Christmas morning staring at the gifts beneath the tree and knowing that Santa was real and had come another year.

"It's incredible," she said softly. "It's just like my mother described. The chandelier, the staircase, the full length leaded glass mirror, it's breathtaking." She drifted into the room, touched the carved post of the staircase and ran her fingers lovingly along the now dust free wood. Her head tipped back to stare at the chandelier and Louie pushed the button to light it up. He heard her breath catch and her eyes grew wider.

Louie looked straight ahead into the long mirror that held both their reflections. Beauty and the Beast, or would that be Beauty and the Geek? They couldn't look more wrong together. She was gorgeous. The type of woman who'd been stopping traffic with her smile since she was a teenager. He was as plain as she was spectacular. From his brown hair to his jeans and t-shirt, there was nothing outstanding about him.

He certainly didn't belong in the same picture as her. Before that thought could depress him any further he cleared his throat. "Come on, I'll give you the nickel tour."

He flung open the French doors. "Look at that fireplace," he ordered sweeping his hand. Becky followed him into the room. "The hardwood floors should come back pretty easily. They're in great shape."

"They're amazing. Look at this hearth." She ran her hand along the enormous stone fireplace and mantle. "It's incredible." She looked around the large room.

Her reaction sent a thrill rolling through him. He'd give up a limb on his body if she'd ever look at him the way she was looking at this room.

"Wait until you see the dining room." He struggled to get the pocket doors to open, but eventually they revealed a cavernous space that could easily sit 50 for dinner. Her gasp was all the reaction he needed. Floor to ceiling cabinets for linens and china stood unused and a bit roughed up, but he knew she was impressed.

The long table had been covered with heavy dust cloths, but Louie had shoved them off a few days ago and they were piled on the floor. Most of the chairs were in storage but a few were scattered here and there.

"Think of all the meals that have been served in this room," she whispered.

Louie dragged one of the heavy scarred chairs to the table. He bowed and held the chair out for her, "Dinner will be out momentarily, Lady Rebecca."

Becky smiled and pretended to lift a long elegant skirt as she slipped into the chair. For just a moment, Louie rested his hands on either side of the chair arms behind her. Her perfume filled his nostrils and her dark hair tickled his nose. She glanced up at him with a smile.

"Are we having the pheasant or the quail this evening?"

Louie stepped back. The sight of her sitting at the head of his table, in his dining room, made his head reel. If only... He swallowed hard and looked away. "Both of course."

Becky smoothed both hands over the wooden table. "I can see the china and the linen napkins. They would use the finest crystal glasses," her voice trailed off as if she was dreaming.

"Come on, there's lots more to see." He went on ahead through the swinging door to the kitchen. He wondered if she'd notice the small microwave and coffee maker he'd brought in and question it. What difference did it make? He was going to be working here; he needed to be able to eat.

Becky's hand trailed along the ancient stove. "Does this still work."

Louie nodded. "Yep, but it needs to be re-glazed or painted or something." He walked past her and opened the doors leading to other rooms. "There's a full laundry room down that hall, and a walk-in pantry over there. That room over there is what looks to be the servants' room or maybe a maid's quarters." He pointed towards another door and Becky opened it and peeked inside at the tiny bedroom.

He watched her brush aside some spider webs. "I think the first thing the owner should have hired was a cleaning crew." She brushed her hands together and turned her attention to the door at the far end of the room. "What's out back?"

"That goes to small mud room, a little sitting porch, and then the back yard. There's a kitchen garden, and then a path that leads to a gazebo and what must have been some really beautiful formal gardens. I found some pictures at the library; I have them in the den; you can see exactly how they once looked." The excitement built inside him at sharing his visions for how he was going to bring everything back to the way it once was. "The gardens are a mess but there's a gazebo and a greenhouse and two carriage barns. It's going to take me months to get it in shape."

"You?" she turned wide blue eyes on him.

Louie stopped talking, realizing he'd said too much. He'd gotten carried away. Turning from her confused look he picked up a rag he'd been using earlier. He ran it under the water so he wouldn't have to look her in the eye. "Yeah, actually the new owner asked me if I'd take over the entire renovation project, from start to finish."

"You're kidding? You don't have experience with a project like this."

The idea that she thought he was a complete dolt when it came to anything physical burned in his gut. He laid the rag out on the sink board to dry and turned around. "I did all the work at the shop, remember."

"I know you did, but this is a bit more than painting the walls." She must have realized she insulted him because her eyes softened and she walked across the room to his side. "Well, you do have all those typing muscles." She wrapped her hand around his arm and squeezed.

He flexed his bicep under her hand and she grinned before dropping her hand. He'd give anything to have the nerve to pull her into his arms right now. Kissing Becky in his mansion—what more did he need for true happiness?

But she was across the room already and peeking out the large picture window that overlooked the side yards.

"It doesn't matter what work I can or can't do; I'm going to be overseeing the project. I'll have contractors handling every aspect of the physical work."

"Do you have time for all this? What about the shop?" She moved back across the kitchen and opened up the cupboards. She lifted out an old china bowl. "This is pretty, are there more?"

He watched her flip it over to read the maker. "No. There are just a few odd pieces here and there. The attic has a bunch of stuff in it that I'll have to go through eventually, and there's three huge outbuildings full of stuff."

He took the bowl as she handed it to him and set it on the counter. She began to pull other pieces out of the cupboard and he automatically took them from her. "As for the shop, I forwarded the phone to my cell. I can work over there at night if something comes up. It's been pretty quiet anyway."

"Yeah, no one has put nasty things on my laptop lately, either." She stretched to reach a glass.

Louie watched her sweater slide up and a band of bare skin appear above her low slung waistband. She twisted and handed him a glass and he took it from her and then another. She emptied the cupboard, wiped her hands down the back of her jeans and Louie bit back a groan at the sight of her slender hands rubbing against her jean covered rounded bottom. He practically raced to the door. "Come on, don't mess with those dishes; there's lot more I want to show you."

At the foot of the stairs he waited for her. "Never thought I'd see the day when I'd be leading Becky Richardson to the bedroom."

"Ahh, but it's not your bedroom so it doesn't count." She pushed past him and ran the rest of the way up the stairs.

Like a kid in a candy store, she raced from room to room. Her cries of excitement echoed with every door she opened. Louie didn't follow her; he waited outside the master suite. The heavy double doors were closed and he didn't open them until she was by his side. He'd started work on this room already, and he couldn't wait to get her thoughts on it. As soon as she was ready, he flung open the doors dramatically and let her enter first.

She didn't say anything as she walked through the room. Louie had shoved the enormous four poster bed against the far wall to give him room to work, and although it was uncovered at the moment, he'd eventually have to put the drop cloths back on it. The bed was the largest he'd ever seen, far bigger than a standard King size bed. He imagined the mattress would have to be custom made. He couldn't help but think about Becky waking up in the middle of it. He shoved his hands in his pockets as she ran her hands around one of the posts.

When she moved towards the French doors to the outside balcony he cautioned. "Don't go out there, it's not safe."

She looked back at him, but didn't argue.

Louie turned the key in the lock and opened the doors. "I haven't had that balcony floor tested yet."

"I don't even have words to describe this view," she sighed. "Can you imagine waking up to this every day of your life?" She shook her head as if it was too much for her to even dream about.

Louie stared at her. In his mind he saw her in a white flowing gown. The sun would shine through making it transparent and he would join her on the balcony for breakfast. He'd feed her strawberries and kiss the sticky juice off her mouth. He would cup her breasts and lift them to his mouth as the morning sun warmed them. Then he'd lift her into his arms and carry her back to bed.

Becky snapped her fingers in the air and he blinked.

"Where'd you go?" she asked

"See those buildings out there?" He pointed and she turned to follow his direction. "They're full of stuff. I have to go through every one of them. Sometimes it's almost too much to figure out how it's all going to get done."

"You need help, that's all."

"It's not something I want a bunch of contractors doing. Decisions will have to be made about what stays and what goes."

"I could help you," she said softly looking up at him.

He frowned. Immediately an image of the two of them covered in dirt and dust climbing around the old stuff popped into this mind. Did she really want to do that? "You want to help me?"

She smiled and settled her palms on the front of his t-shirt. A jolt went through him as if someone had placed cardiac paddles on him and yelled "Clear!"

His body jerked and certain parts of him sprung to life. He lost his breath at the pleading in her eyes.

"I could help. I can paint, and I could help you do that inventory. I mean with two of us, it would go so much faster. Oh come on, Louie. It would be fun. Let me help you."

Becky Richardson was begging to spend time with him? Lots of time? Working side by side, mostly alone? He swallowed hard. Wasn't buying this house a way for him to spend less time with her, not more?

She took a step closer, and his mouth went dry.

Chapter Three

"Come on Nerdman, I'm bored. I need a project. This is my dream house, you know that. Someone else is going to live in it forever let me play here for a little bit."

So let me get this straight? Becky Richardson is standing in a bedroom with her hands on you, asking you to let her play house? Yep, you're dreaming, Louie old man. This is definitely some type of dream.

"How come you're not saying anything?" She slammed her hands on her narrow hips. "I know what it is. You really do think I'm a princess. You don't think I can get down and dirty do you? You think I can't handle it."

Becky down and dirty? Sweaty and hot? He blinked to rid himself of that particular image. "No, Princess," he said purposely using her nickname. "I don't think that at all. I'm just wondering how you're going to help when I'm here days. You have to work at the law office."

"You work days, and I'll work nights. Two shifts mean it'll go faster."

Like hell! If Becky was going to be here at night so was he. "Actually I was thinking of spending a few nights a week here to move things along. Maybe you could help those nights that I'm here. I wouldn't want you out here alone."

Before he knew what hit him, she flung her arms around his neck. Those breasts he'd only felt in his dreams smashed into his chest. He wrapped his arms around her to keep from stumbling backwards. His heart pounded so hard he feared it would explode.

"You're the best friend in the world." She squeezed him tight once more before dropping back to her feet, but Louie couldn't seem to make his arms let go.

She plastered her palms on his chest and pushed. "Okay, back off, Nerdman. Don't go getting all excited just because I hugged you."

He quickly stepped away hoping she wouldn't notice exactly how excited she'd gotten him. He was pathetic. An innocent hug and he was on fire. To cover his reaction he cocked his eyebrow, "I don't know how you're going to work around me every day and keep your hands to yourself, Beck. You really have to stop treating my body as an object of lust."

She rolled her eyes. "I'll restrain myself. Now where do we start?"

Closing the balcony doors and turning the key he swept his arm to indicate the walls. "I've been working in here a bit." He hesitated and tipped his head to look at her. "You know what you could do for me?"

"Anything, just say it." She looked up at him her eyes glowing with anticipation.

Ohhh, don't tempt me, angel. Immediately an image of her spread on the settee in front of the fireplace popped into mind. "The uh, owner, gave me free choice with paint colors. I know you're good at that kind of thing."

"You want me to pick the colors for the walls in here?"

"The whole house. Every room is going to be completely redecorated. As long as you don't go crazy and do hot pink or something weird, you can help me with the interior decorating. I've got a master sketch downstairs you can use to jot down color thoughts."

Her eyes were wide with excitement and she tucked her hair behind her ear in a gesture he recognized. She was eager to get started. "I'm going to walk through the house quickly again; then maybe I'll go the paint store and start getting some chips, and bring them back, and..."

Louie held up his hand. "Whoa, one thing at a time. I have to go to the hardware store, too, so we can do that together, but don't you have something else you need to do today?"

She shook her head. "Nope, Callie and her parents took the girls to New York City for the weekend. I have no plans this whole weekend."

"No date? Becky Richardson home on a Saturday night?"

"Don't be so shocked; it's not like I didn't have

invitations. I just wasn't in the mood."

She was out the bedroom door and heading down the stairs before he could question her. His brain kept coming back to one thing. It wasn't even noon on Saturday, he had Becky all to himself for the entire day and the evening.

Oh man. Oh man, oh man. He felt like a motherboard that had just received new ram.

****

"I never knew it was possible to spend three hours in a hardware store." Louie grumbled around the food in his mouth.

Becky watched in amazement as he used his chopsticks to eat rice, shoveling it in as if he hadn't had a meal in days. The man had the most voracious appetite. She took a nibble of her spicy chicken and then set it aside. "It's not a hardware store. It's a home improvement store and it takes time to select the right things."

"You were just getting paint samples, how long can that possibly take?" He took a huge bite of his egg roll and held it out to her. She shook her head and he popped the rest of it in his mouth. "Our little field trip showed me just how lucky you are I agreed to help you on this project."

Louie laughed shortly. "Yeah, I asked you. I keep forgetting that I had to beg you for your assistance."

Becky looked around the bedroom where they sat on the floor eating their Chinese take out. Already in her mind she could see the way the room would one day look. The colors would be bold and rich. The furniture was dark cherry and she wanted to keep it, giving it an old money feel. All over the floor she'd spread paint samples and as she nibbled at her dinner she discarded choices she knew weren't right. Mostly ones that Louie had picked out, she noted with delight.

"I'm thinking of red and gold in here. With a lot of brocade. Possibly even drapes that could close around the bed, but would be drawn back with heavy cords during the day." She brushed back her hair and looked at the bed shoved against the wall. In her mind she saw it taking center place in the room with a small settee at the foot facing the fireplace.

Louie nodded. "There's a program I can get for interior design. I'll load it on your laptop and you set it up however you want it."

Becky wrinkled her nose. "Can't we just draw it on paper?"

Louie grinned. "Trust me you'll love this program. You can move pieces around and change the colors; I promise I'll show you."

She glanced down at his empty cartons, and shoved her own towards him. "I'm done, if you want this."

He eagerly reached for it but then stopped, "You sure?"

She nodded. "I'm going to eat this egg roll and then I'm done." She dipped it in sweet and sour sauce and took a large bite. Bits of filling oozed out, and she lapped them up with her tongue. Louie was consuming the rest of her chicken as if he hadn't just eaten two other servings.

This was nice. It was so relaxing being with Louie. What other guy would sit cross-legged on the floor with her, in a bedroom, and not be trying to get her into bed? There weren't any other men she trusted the way she did him. Being around Louie was like putting on a pair of comfy old slippers. He knew her in a way no one except Callie did. And now he'd given her something no one else ever could. He'd given her a chance to fulfill one of her biggest fantasies. For a year she was going to be a part of the Ryan mansion.

With a sigh she set her egg roll down and lay on her back on the floor. She bent her knees up and rested her hand on her stomach and stared at the ornate ceiling. "Have you ever seen anything more beautiful?" she sighed.

Louie didn't comment. After a few seconds she turned her head to see why. The look in his eyes made her heart melt. She knew Louie appreciated her friendship. It was going to be so great to do this project together. She lifted her hand and held it out to him. He took it and lifted it to his mouth in a friendly kiss before releasing it.

"Back in high school, did you ever for one minute, think we'd be like this?" she asked.

"Like what? Friends?"

She shook her head. "Still friends. I mean after all

these years."

"I guess I never thought much about it."

She looked back up at the ceiling and sighed. "I always thought by now I'd be living anywhere else but Oakdale."

"I always imagined you'd be married to some high powered executive by now and have a couple kids."

She laughed and sat up. "Hardly. No to the marriage; definitely no to the kids."

He scoffed, "You love kids."

"I love other people's kids. I can't stand it when someone needs me too much. I freak out."

She started to get up and Louie reached his hands down to pull her to her feet. "What should we do next?"

"Next? I figured we'd just stop for the night." He scooped up the empty containers and dropped them into the paper bag they'd come in.

"It's not even eight o'clock." She planted her hands on her hips.

He didn't look back at her as he gathered the rest of the things. "I've been here since early morning. I'm ready to pack it in."

He moved so quickly around the room that she got the feeling he couldn't wait to get rid of her. Then an idea hit her, maybe Louie had a date and needed to get rid of her quickly. He didn't say anything, but why else would he suddenly be rushing her out of here? Neither of them had anyone waiting at home for them. She tipped her head and continued to watch him. He wasn't going to bring her here was he? That would really annoy her. She swept out of the room and down the stairs.

She yanked her leather coat off the antique coat tree in the hallway. She heard Louie come down the stairs and head down the hall to the kitchen, probably to dump the garbage. She pulled open the front door and stepped out onto the porch without waiting for him.

"Wait, I'll walk out with you," he called from the hall.

She didn't answer him, but kept on going down the stairs to her car. She reached for the handle to her car door, but his hand covered hers before she could open it.

"What's the matter?" he asked.

Without looking at him she shook her head.

"Nothing. You said it was time to go so I'm leaving."

"Beck?" He took her shoulders in his hands and turned her around until she faced him. "Are you mad because I was staring at you?"

She furrowed her brow in confusion, "What are you talking about?"

He dropped his hands from her and looked uncomfortable. "When you said the ceiling was beautiful and I was, well, staring at you."

Was he nuts? She lifted her hand to touch his cheek. "You always look at me as if I'm beautiful. Even on my worst days I can count on you to make me feel like a supermodel. I'd be crazy to say I don't like that."

The look on his face was serious. "You're always beautiful to me, even on what you call "bad hair" days. So if that's not it, what are you ticked off at me about?"

She let her breath out, watching it form a cloud in the cold night air. Leaning back against her car she crossed her arms on her chest. "Are you racing me off because you have a date?"

He frowned and looked at her in confusion. "A date? No, I don't have a date, and if I did, why would that make you so angry?"

Becky brushed her hair back. "I guess I was thinking you were going to bring her here, and I didn't like the idea."

Louie laughed. "Princess, for as long as we're on this project, I promise you will be the lady of the house. Okay?"

Becky felt like an idiot. "It's not like I don't want you to have a date, or anything, I mean if you have a girlfriend or whatever..."

"I don't."

"I'm just saying,"

Louie reached out and touched her cheek. "You are the only woman in my life, Princess."

"Well now I just feel bad. You deserve to find someone to be with. You deserve to be happy."

Louie stepped back and shoved his hands in his pockets and she wondered what she'd said to annoy him. "I'm happy."

"No you're not."

"Yes, I am."

She opened her mouth to argue with him again, but he shook his head. "Beck, stop it, I don't want to talk about it anymore."

She nodded, knowing she shouldn't push him. "Are you coming out here tomorrow?"

He nodded. "Yeah."

He didn't say anything else and she slammed her hands against his chest. "Why do you keep making me ask?"

He chuckled. "You want to come out here on Sunday? Don't you have to get your nails done or lay around in bed until noon?"

She swatted at him and he caught her hand.

"I don't lay in bed until noon, unless someone gives me a good reason to." She pulled her hand back and batted her eyelashes at him. "I have nothing to do tomorrow except dinner at Mom's."

She yanked open her car door and Louie stepped back. "I'll be out here at nine; come whenever you want."

"Why don't you pick me up on your way here? Then you can come over for dinner. You look like you need a good meal." She scaled his body with her eyes, noting how his jeans always hung baggy on his lean hips.

"Dinner at Maggie's house? That's an offer no smart man passes up," he said.

"You come get me in the morning and I'll tell Mom to set another place."

She turned the key and the car roared to life. She pressed the button to lower her window. He looked dejected and she frowned. "You ok? You look weird."

"Weird? I always look weird, I'm the Nerdman remember?"

She tipped her head. "Maybe it's the lack of time you've had in front of your computer; withdrawal, or something."

"I'll be sure and put some time in on the old computer tonight."

She opened her mouth to tease him about what kind of websites he might be visiting, but then decided she didn't want to know.

She blew him a kiss then followed the long winding

driveway back out to the road. Ten minutes later she pulled up to her dark house. It looked uninviting, but with a click of the remote on her keychain the porch light came on and the living room lit up. As she walked up the steps, she pressed another button and the door unlocked for her. When Louie had insisted on putting in the home security system, she'd argued that they lived in the safest town in the world, but she had to admit it felt great to come home and never feel nervous.

Inside the front door, she pushed the buttons to set the alarm system and kicked off her shoes. She grabbed a can of diet cola out of the refrigerator and padded into the living room. Louie had told her all about the security system he'd put in at the Ryan house; it would make the White House look inadequate. She grinned; the owner had no clue that giving Louie a blank check for technology was like giving a chocoholic the keys to Hershey Park.

She sank to the couch and hit the blinking button on her answering machine. The first caller was her mother, nothing important, just saying hello and that she'd see her tomorrow evening. The second call was from Roger. Becky grimaced as his smooth voice came across on the tape.

"Hey sexy lady, I'll be in town this week, and was wondering if you'd like to get some dinner."

She knew what he meant by "dinner", and she wasn't interested. Not that Roger wasn't a good date and more, but she'd lost interest. Part of his appeal was that he was out of town more than he was in town. She'd just seen him last Saturday; enough time hadn't gone by for her to want to see him again.

She flipped on the TV and looked around her small living room. It was hard not to compare its tiny size to the grand parlors at the Ryan House. In her mind she could picture herself sinking into a deep leather couch, her feet up as she watched the enormous plasma TV Louie was going to have installed. She grabbed a throw pillow and pressed it to her chest as a wave of longing came over her. Was she going to be able to be a part of that house for a year and really be able to walk away from it forever when it was done?

It wasn't as if she didn't love her own house, she did.

Now. At first she'd been completely against buying a house. It was Louie who had convinced her she had to do it for financial reasons. When this one came on the market, so close to Callie's, Louie had pressed her to look at it. She'd liked it ok, but it was the realtor's insistence that she could easily sell it if she wanted to that made up her mind. She didn't want anything that tied her down.

It was barely nine at night on a Saturday and she was heading upstairs to get her pajamas on. She flipped on the TV in her room just as the phone rang. The caller ID relieved her mind that it wasn't Roger and she grinned as she picked it up. "I made it home safe and sound."

Louie chuckled. "I'm just looking after my hard working staff. You sure you know how to get up at nine on a Sunday morning, Princess?"

Becky grinned. "I get up every day at six and you know it." She cradled the phone between her shoulder and neck and unzipped her jeans before shimmying them down her hips and off.

"Ahh, but this is on a weekend, a Sunday morning. Prime time for beauty sleeping."

"Hang on a sec." She set the phone down and whipped her shirt over her head before putting the phone back to her ear. "Okay."

"What are you doing?" he asked.

"I'm changing my clothes."

He groaned. "Why do you tell me things like that? To torment me?"

"Oh knock it off. It's not like you're here and can see me."

"It's worse, my imagination is going nuts right now." He lowered his voice, "Are you standing there in your bra and panties?"

She grinned and lowered her voice to a sexy tone. "I'm wearing a bra, but no panties; a thong."

"Oh God," he moaned.

She giggled.

"What color?"

"Remember the color I picked for the trim in the bedroom?"

"Uh, huh."

"That color," she whispered.

Sinking to the side of her bed she slid one of her bra straps down her arm.

"Now what are you doing; describe it to me."

"I'm sliding my bra straps down my arms so I can unhook it."

"Take it off really slowly," he whispered.

"Okay." As if he was there watching she slid each strap down her arm carefully.

"Front or back hook?" he asked.

Her fingers flicked open the catch. "Front." Her breasts sprang free of their confinement and she drew a deep breath. She flung her bra on the floor and shivered in the cool air of the room. Her nipples hardened and she glanced down at them critically.

"So, they're, I mean your—" He couldn't seem to speak

Becky laughed. "Do you know what I'm doing now?" She asked in her best sex kitten voice. "I'm plucking my nipples. It feels so good, ooh they're getting hard as little pebbles, mmmmm." she moaned and tried not to laugh at how ridiculous she sounded.

"You're killing me," he growled.

"Hmmm, I'm tingling all over and aching." She stood up and headed to the bathroom looking at one of her hands as she walked. That's what she'd do, her nails. They desperately needed a manicure. "You know what I need?" she said softly into the phone.

"What?"

"A good, long…" She paused at his growl through the phone. He sounded like he was in agony, but she knew it was more teasing. She'd never have the guts to play this game with any other man. Anyone else would take her serious and come racing to her house to see if she'd follow through. But not Louie; they both knew they were only teasing the other.

"A good, long what, Princess? Want to tell me all about it?"

She laughed and turned on the faucet. "Bath. A good, long, hot bath with bubbles all the way up to my chin like they do in the movies. That's what I need."

He groaned and she smiled into the phone. Lifting her leg to the side of the tub she examined it. Maybe she'd go all out tonight, wax her legs, and give herself a manicure, a regular girly pampering night.

"You're all talk, Richardson. You're sitting there in those horrible blue sweatpants you love and your rattiest sweatshirt eating a pint of Ben and Jerry's and making this all up."

Becky glanced down at her half naked self and decided to let him keep his fantasy. "Yeah, you're right Nerdman. I just wanted to give you a Saturday night thrill."

"You're a mean woman, Becky Richardson."

"So I've been told, so I've been told."

"Hey, Beck?"

"Yeah?" She grabbed a clean nightshirt out of the drawer and walked back to the bathroom.

"Thanks for your help today. It's going to be a lot more fun working with someone rather than alone."

She smirked and looked at herself in the full length mirror. "Ahh, Nerdman, I've been telling you for years it's not good to play with yourself."

He choked and she could picture his tea spilling all over the place. She laughed. "Sweet dreams." She clicked off before he could answer.

****

For as long back as Becky could recall, Sunday dinner was a big deal. Her mother was notorious for having guests over. When she told Margaret that Louie would be joining them, her mother had reached into the potato bin and added a few more to the pot.

"Pot roast?" Becky asked lifting the cover.

Margaret wiped her hands on her apron and nodded. "They had them on special at the grocery."

Becky reached into the refrigerator for a diet cola. "I'll get the table set."

"Tell me about the project." Her mother paused, and threw her hands up shaking her head. "No, no wait; tell me about the mansion." She clasped her hands looking for all the world as if Becky was about to tell he she'd found the Hope Diamond.

Becky smiled at her excitement. She flipped the tab on her cola and took a long drink. "It's exactly as you remember. The hallway is..." she looked around. "I bet it's as long as the apartment, at least. And the mirror at the end of the hall, I can't even guess how tall that thing is, and beveled, with etchings in the sides." She paused trying to recall all the details. "The staircase is like something out of Gone With the Wind; it sweeps up and when you walk down it you can't help but go slow as if you were a true princess."

Her mother gazed at her, but she seemed focused somewhere else.

Margaret turned back to the sink. "What kind of condition is it in? I have to imagine after all these years it's falling apart a bit."

Becky nodded and slid into a kitchen chair. "Some parts of it are in need of major repairs, but really most of it is in good shape. Louie and I took careful inventory of everything that has to be done. It's a big project, that's for sure."

"Sounds like it."

"Louie's going to get me a computer program so I can draw it all out, then I'll show you."

Her mother turned back around and smiled warmly. "I haven't seen you this excited about anything in a long time, Rebecca. Maybe interior design is your secret passion."

Becky nodded. "I love it, and I think I'm good at it; well, Louie says I am anyway." She stood back up and joined her mother at the sink. Grabbing the vegetable peeler she worked on the carrots her mother washed.

"Where's Callie and the girls tonight? I thought maybe they'd be here."

"They just got back from New York City. I think Tom's over there for dinner tonight." Becky paused and waited for her mother to look at her.

Margaret's eyes widened. "You think maybe the two of them?"

Becky nodded and crunched off the end of a carrot. "I more than think, I know it."

"Tom is such a nice boy, always was. Why I remember his parents giving the most incredible card parties."

"Card parties? You didn't play cards."

"No. But I heard about them from some of my

customers. Not that they didn't invite me, mind you, but—" Her mother paused and glanced over at her daughter. "I would rather be with you."

"You couldn't afford a sitter." Becky stated. She felt the familiar burning in the pit of her stomach when she remembered how rough her mother had had it as a single parent.

Margaret touched her hand to Becky's shoulder. "I wasn't going to leave you with a sitter so I could play cards, honey. I was away from you enough. Anyway, my point is they were good people. So sad about his Dad; I heard his mother moved to Florida to be with her sister."

"Yep, and Tom's living in the family house. His daughter is the same age as Jenna."

"Yes, I know. She was in for a haircut the other day. She was so determined to get rid of her waist length hair."

The doorbell rang and Becky pushed away from the counter. "I'll go buzz him in."

Another of Louie's gifts was the buzzer he'd installed on Margaret's door years ago. This not only enabled her to unlock the door from the safety of her upstairs apartment, but it was less stress on her legs going up and down the stairs.

Becky hit the buzzer without asking who it was. The buzzer timed out and then the doorbell rang again. Again she hit it. Nothing. Finally she pushed the intercom button and spoke into the box on the wall. "What are you doing?"

"What are you doing? You're supposed to ask who it is first. I could have been a psycho."

"You are a psycho. Now get up here." She hit the buzzer again, and this time he opened the door.

She stood in the doorway as he came up the stairs. "If you were a psycho I could have just put the chain on and not answered this door."

"Knowing you, the chain wasn't on."

He held an armful of flowers, and she reached for them, but he shook his head. "These are for the cook, Princess."

She gave him a pretend pout, and from underneath the bouquet he pulled out a computer cd. "This is for you."

She took it from him. "Oh! Will you put it in for me

tonight?"

He raised his eyebrows. "That's all I ever hear from you, Louie, will you put it in? But somehow it's never in the way I'm hoping."

Becky shut the door behind him. "You couldn't handle it, Nerdman. Stick to your own species."

But Louie was already down the hall. She could hear him greet her mother in a fake thick Irish brogue.

"Ahh if it isn't the lovely Maggie O'Riley Richardson. 'Tis sure an honor I'd be havin' to share this meal with such a fine Irish lass."

Her mother giggled like a schoolgirl as she took the flowers from him. Becky loved how Louie made her mother feel special. He lifted the pot on the stove, completely at home in the small kitchen. He inhaled dramatically, and slapped his hand over his heart. Rolling his eyes he drawled, "To a starving bachelor, that's a pot of heaven right there."

Kissing Margaret's cheek soundly, he patted her on the shoulder. "Thanks for having me over, Maggie. A home cooked meal is hard to come by."

Margaret took the flowers and moved to the sink while Becky reached into the small broom closet for a vase. "You need to find yourself a good girl to share that nice home your folks gave you."

"I've been trying to get your daughter to marry me since the second grade, you know that." He picked up a carrot and chomped on it while Maggie handed him a beer from the refrigerator. "She claims she's not the marrying type."

"Yes, I know, she tells me that too. I can only hope someone comes along some day to change her mind."

Becky stuck her tongue out at Louie behind her mother's back, and Louie waggled his eyebrows at her.

An hour later, the meal was cleared and the remnants of coconut cream pie sat in the middle of the table. Becky's eyes widened as Louie reached for a third piece. He looked at her and winked.

"Where on earth do you put all that?" she asked shoving the pie closer to him.

"Louie, you have as much as you want; ignore her. You work hard and you don't get a good meal often enough."

Louie shoveled more pie into his mouth. "You'll have to come by the Ryan house and I'll show you what we're doing."

Margaret lowered her eyes and set her cup down. "Perhaps," she murmured.

"What's wrong? I thought you'd be excited at the thought of seeing it again." Becky glanced at her mother wondering why she looked so uncomfortable.

"I am, Rebecca. I have wonderful memories of that home."

Becky turned to Louie. "She used to attend some of the parties they had there." She looked back at her mother again. "Did you know the Ryan boys? Did you go to school with them?"

Margaret stood up abruptly and began to clear the table. "No, I didn't go to school with them. I didn't move to Oakdale until I was already out of school. My folks were from further downstate." She said the last part to Louie who nodded as he picked up his plate and carried it to the counter.

"If you didn't know the Ryans how did you get invited to the parties?" Becky pressed on.

Margaret laughed strangely. "Honey, I don't know. I was young. I don't remember."

Becky narrowed her eyes, knowing her mother remembered everything. Why was she suddenly reluctant to talk about the Ryans?

****

Several hours later, they walked out in the cold dark night. Louie unlocked her car door and Becky slipped around him and climbed behind the wheel. It was so chilly out, she could see his breath as he stepped back.

He glanced down at her, one hand leaning on the door frame. "Thanks again for inviting me to dinner. My week always goes better when it starts out with one of your Mom's meals."

On the crisp air she got a whiff of the deodorant soap he used. She glanced up at him, wondering how many years he'd had that same brown leather coat. It was impossible to think of him in anything else, though. Her eyes met his and for a long moment they clung. She furrowed her brow, wondering why she wasn't eager to leave. "Thanks for the project. I had a good time this weekend." She tucked her hair behind her ear and bent to turn the key in the ignition. When Louie didn't step back and shut the door she flipped her head back around.

Something weird zinged in the air and if it was any other man, she'd think he was about to lean in and kiss her. Wow. She'd definitely been in Louie's company too long if she was thinking about that. Frowning, she laid her hand on the door handle, hoping he'd get the hint. "Thanks for the computer program. I'll work on those drawings this week."

"Call me if you need help."

Still he didn't step back. She fiddled with the heat controls, sending a blast of still-cold air pouring into the car. "So I'll see you at the house on Wednesday night, right?"

He nodded. "I'll make a bunch of calls between now and then and we'll have a solid plan in order."

Becky nodded. "Sounds good." All of a sudden, he leaned towards her and kissed her cheek. She blinked in surprise and he stepped back from the car. "What was that for?"

He shrugged and shoved his hands in pants pockets. "No reason. Drive careful, Princess."

****

"It's amazing what money can do." Tom Jacobsen threw his hands up as if he couldn't quite believe what he was seeing.

Louie glanced up at his friend but didn't stop typing. He grinned around the pencil in his mouth. "Yep."

His buddy looked around the makeshift office set up in the dining room of the Ryan house. "It's unreal how this has come together in just a month."

Louie hit the 'send' key, and yanked the pencil from between his lips. "This is just phase one."

Tom wandered the room. "The owner hasn't been out here to see it yet?"

Louie busied himself with papers on the desk. He hated lying to his friends, but he wasn't ready for them to know yet. "Nope. He's away for the winter. He said he might not get here until sometime in the spring."

"You think it'll be done by then?"

Louie yanked another drawing off the oversized printer and scanned it. This one was ready to go to the crew working on the third floor. "Done? Nah. But we'll have a good handle on it, and we'll have started on the grounds too." He looked to the left and out through the French doors that led to the formal gardens

"So how's it been working with Miss High Maintenance? She driving you crazy yet?"

Driving him crazy? Yes, but not in the way Tom meant. Working alone with Becky, day in and day out, sometimes long into the night, was enough to send him to heaven and hell in the same hour. He'd been surprised and impressed at how hard she worked and how dedicated she was to this project. In all honesty, he thought she'd give up the first time she chipped a nail. This mansion had become a passion for both of them. He wasn't about to say any of that to Tom. "Becky doesn't bother me."

"She doesn't throw a tantrum when she breaks a nail or spills something on one of those cashmere sweaters?"

Louie tried to remember the last time he'd seen her in anything but worn jeans and an old sweatshirt. He smiled, thinking about yesterday when she'd slipped on one of his old flannel shirts. It was something out of his wildest fantasy. Only in his mind, she was naked under the shirt, not just protecting her sweater. "We both keep a change of old clothes here."

Tom wandered to the far side of the room and looked at the blueprints taped to the wall. "Tell me again how this home automation stuff works. It looks complicated."

Louie set his pencil down and walked over to Tom. "It's not hard once you understand what all those codes mean. Come on, I'll give you the tour, it's easier to explain that way." He led him out the door of the dining room and gestured to the foyer and living room beyond. "Every room is controlled by the computer. Every room is, or will be, fully equipped for internet, phones, security and fire alarms." He picked up the remote in the den. With the push of a button, a wall slid open to reveal a room beyond.

"This was originally a walk-in safe. I took out most of it, but left the shell intact. Then I added a regular door and it becomes a panic room." He watched Tom's look of shock. He couldn't blame him. No one in Oakdale had a reason for a panic room. He shrugged "It seemed a shame to have all that steel and not use it for something."

They both stepped inside and he was struck again by Becky's touches in what should simply be a serviceable hiding place. "Becky had a field day with this room. That's what all the 'coziness' is about." The room held a futon, small table and refrigerator as well as a pile of books in all genres. A battery operated flashlight, a couple of radios, first aid kit, and some shelves stocked with water and nonperishables. "Two people could live in here for about a week, maybe longer, if they had to."

Tom grinned. "I think I should show this to Callie, and maybe you could accidentally lock us in for about four hours."

They stepped back out, and Louie hit the button to hide it again. "Anytime, not a problem. I'll pretend the computer locked up and I can't get the signal."

"Don't tempt me. With three young daughters between us, privacy is scarce."

"Things are going good then?"

The look on the other man's face changed radically, all amusement leaving his eyes. Louie realized he'd hit a nerve. He put up his hand as if in surrender. "Hey, man, no big deal. We'll talk about something else."

Tom raked his hands through his dark hair and shrugged his shoulders. "There are a lot of issues and it makes things complicated."

Louie wasn't sure how to answer. He knew all about the 'issues', but they weren't as impossible to overcome as Tom seemed to think they were. It was old history, and shouldn't have anything to do with the people they were today. Personally, if he thought there was even a chance that he'd get a shot at the type of love his friends seem to be fighting against, he'd grab it with both hands. Images of Becky laughing with him, moving room to room, painting, or struggling with the computer flashed through his mind. He'd give anything for it all to be more than a platonic friendship.

Tom glanced at his watch. "I better get going and pick up Amber. I told Callie we weren't staying for dinner.

I know the girls will argue with me, but it doesn't do any of us any good to spend even more time together."

"Why?"

Tom looked back at him with a frown. "What?"

Louie shrugged. "You got two families that fit together like matching socks, and you seem intent on not letting it happen."

Tom glared at him. For a second Louie figured he'd overstepped, but maybe it was time someone kicked him in the proverbial rear end.

"I can't just forget everything that happened."

Louie shrugged. "Speaking from someone who's been alone most of his life, get over it."

Tom's face reddened. "Get over it? Do you know the hell I went through?"

Louie nodded. "Yep. But it was fifteen years ago. You were a couple of kids. Why waste the rest of your lives being miserable when you've been given this second chance? You've changed, she's changed, but you both seem to click."

Several seconds went by before his friend's posture relaxed. He looked confused, as if he was used to having all the answers, and it was new for him to not know what to do. "I love her daughters as if they were mine. Sometimes I forget they aren't."

Louie clasped him on the shoulder. "Then make them yours, pal. Pull out that Visa card, get that diamond on her hand, and make sure this time it's you she marries."

Tom looked like the thought had never occurred to him. "You really think it's that easy, don't you?"

Louie grinned and nodded. "Hey, I'd even loan you the money, but I know you high school principals make a ton off us taxpayers."

"Oh yeah, sure, we're loaded. How'd you get to be so smart about love anyway?"

"I'm always on the outside looking in. I see a lot. If I had your chance, man, I wouldn't waste a second. She'd be mine before she changed her mind."

"Becky?" Tom asked pointedly.

Uncomfortable at the change in the conversation, Louie turned away and headed back down the hall.

"Oof." He collided with a soft body at full speed

"Oooh!" Becky cried out.

His arms reached out and caught her. Her body pressed into his and all his senses flared to life. Not wanting her to feel how quickly she affected him, he jerked back. "Princess! We have company. Save that for later." He jerked his head towards Tom.

Becky swatted him on the chest with her open hand before turning to their friend. "Did he show you all we've done?"

"All we've done, she says, like the crew of forty-five workers have been sitting around watching her hang sheet rock." Louie rubbed at his chest as if her smack still stung.

He leaned against the door jamb and stared at her. Her jeans were worn and old and hugged her hips like a second skin. Her sweatshirt was an obnoxious color of orange and she'd torn off the sleeves. On her, the whole get-up looked like it was fit for the Paris runway. Her breasts jutted against the material and he could see she'd decided to go braless. Great. Like working around her wasn't hard enough without that image in his mind.

"You could probably rent that safe room out by the hour." Tom teased.

"I'm telling Callie you said that."

Tom winked. "Maybe she'll be your first customer." He glanced at his watch. "I gotta run or I might miss dinner."

After he left, the room was quiet. Becky looked around. "Everyone gone already?"

"Already? It's five-thirty. Quitting time for normal folk."

"Well, no one ever said we were normal." She headed down the hall to the dining room and he followed. She picked up the drawing he'd been studying earlier. "Is this the one for the kitchen?"

"Yeah."

"Give me your pencil." She held out her manicured hand, and he took one from his pocket. He wondered why her demands never grated on his nerves. He was always excited to see what she was going to add to his ideas, and what thoughts she had drifting around in her head. When she added her thoughts to his, the results were incredible.

If only he could figure out a way to make her realize they could be incredible in other ways too.

Becky was making fast work of his drawing, her pencil flying as she crossed off things and made notes on others. "This needs to be longer and larger," she murmured.

Her words had an unwelcome effect. Leaned over the drawing, with her backside lifted into the air and her sweatshirt revealing a band of skin around her back, she looked way too enticing. In his mind, he stepped behind her and slid his hands up to cup her bare breasts. Her nipples would harden at his touch and she'd moan with pleasure while he pressed into her backside.

The conversation he'd had with Tom about taking chances replayed in his head. Pretending he was looking over her shoulder, he stepped directly behind her. Her hips were right in front of him, almost touching but not quite. He closed his eyes to keep from losing control. Acting casual, he laid his hands in the middle of her back and rubbed in big circles. It wasn't unusual for him to give her a back massage, so he wasn't surprised when she didn't complain. He knew how hard she liked him to press, where the muscles were that she liked kneaded. He swallowed hard and slid his hands up to her shoulders and massaged her neck. Her dark hair was loose today and he brushed it aside. Leaning forward, he inhaled her fragrance. Her perfume filled his nostrils and made him a bit foggy. He lowered his mouth towards her neck, but didn't kiss her. He simply inhaled deeply and pressed slightly into her backside.

She rolled her shoulders back and scrunched her neck as if he was annoying her.

"Is this a new perfume?" he pressed his nose against her neck.

"I'm not wearing perfume, cut it out." She jerked away from his nose. "Now, look, see this window? That's not what I pictured. I think it should have a huge bay window with a large seat. It could have storage inside it and huge cushions on top. Outside the window, we can hang a long flower pot for annuals. It would be the perfect place to curl up on a rainy afternoon for a—"

"For a little afternoon delight maybe?" He was

intoxicated, not responsible for his actions. He kissed her neck and slid his hands down to cup her slender hips.

Chapter Four

Becky's head twisted around and her eyes were wide with shock. "Were you and Tom hitting the beer today?"

She shoved back hard with her hips and Louie's breath whooshed at the instant pain. He stepped back. "No, we didn't have any beer. He wasn't even here an hour."

She looked at him through narrowed eyes. "Well keep your hands to yourself or I'll have to file some sort of sexual harassment suit against you."

He couldn't believe he'd done that. What had gotten into him? Maybe he had low blood sugar? "All I did was smell your perfume."

She didn't look for a minute like she bought that story, but she didn't say anything else.

She set the pencil down on the table. "Come on, I picked up sandwiches; they're in the kitchen. Let's take this in there and look at it while we eat." She grabbed the oversized drawing and sashayed through the door before he could agree or disagree.

"Just crook your finger, Princess," he muttered, but followed behind her without arguing.

What had he done? He'd have to watch himself. It was fine to joke around with Becky and pretend to lust after her body, but he knew her well enough to know that if she though for one second he was serious she'd walk out the door and not look back.

In the kitchen, Becky stood on tiptoe, reaching into the upper cupboard. Her breasts rose and Louie forced himself to look away. She brushed past him on her way to the refrigerator and pulled out cans of pop. "What's going on with you tonight? You're acting weirder than usual."

He took the can and flipped the tab open. "I think I'm burning out. Maybe I need to take a break."

"Really?" She lifted one perfectly arched brow in

surprise.

"I think I'm going to tell the workers to take off until after New Year's."

"What will Mr. M. say to that?"

Several weeks ago, Becky had casually started to call the owner, "Mr. Mystery" and shortened it even more to "Mr. M". Stupid thing was, now he did the same thing. Sometimes he even forgot there was no Mr. M. Yeah, it was definitely time for a break.

Louie drained his drink. "He doesn't care as long as it's done on schedule."

"I'll stay and keep it going. I'm not burned out at all."

Leave the beauty here with a crew of forty workers? Not on his life. "No way. The workers deserve the time off anyway. Don't you have Christmas shopping to do or parties to go to or something?"

Becky shrugged. "The law firm's too small for a holiday party. They give each of us a very nice Christmas bonus which is far better."

"Which you will immediately invest, right?"

Becky pulled a face. "Did you decide if you're going to Florida?"

"I guess, although sunshine and eighty-five degrees on Christmas morning doesn't do it for me."

"It wouldn't me either. I like the snow and the traditional stuff."

"It's really too bad that old sleigh out there isn't in better shape. Callie's kids would love that." It wasn't really Jenna and Hannah he was picturing in the sleigh, though. He thought about having Becky there under a blanket, snuggling against the cold.

"Do you think we could get it up and running?" Her eyes sparkled.

He should never have mentioned it. She'd hound him to death if she decided she wanted that sleigh to work. "Where would we find horses in Oakdale trained to pull a sleigh?"

She twisted her lips and nodded. "That's true."

He was relieved to see she was going to let it go. Maybe next year he could surprise her with it. "What about you and your mother? You going to Callie's folks?"

She nodded. "I'm sure this year Tom and Amber will

be there too. Did he say anything to you when he was here? About the two of them?"

"You know I don't gossip." He stood up and put his glass in the sink.

He heard her scrape back her chair. "Since when? You love gossip almost as much as I do."

He turned to face her, twisting his fingers against his lips as if turning a key. "I do not spread gossip."

"No?" She raised her eyebrow and walked towards him.

He eyed her suspiciously.

"Ve 'ave vays of making you talk," she said with a very bad German accent.

"Ahh you may have 'vays', he played along. "But you would never waste them on a geek like me."

"You never know how desperate I might be," she said softly.

He leaned against the kitchen sink. Becky put her hands flat on his chest and looked up at him from under her eyelashes in a move he knew usually got her whatever she wanted. "I think you know more about what's happening with our two stubborn friends than you're telling me."

She toyed with the top button of his shirt, her fingers searing the skin she touched. How far would she go with this teasing? How long could he hold out before he cracked under her persuasion? "I know nothing."

"Tom was here for an hour and nothing was said about Callie?" she stepped even closer until their bodies were touching.

Louie breathed deeply again, smelling that sweet fragrance she insisted wasn't perfume. "I didn't say nothing was said. I said I didn't know anything."

Her hands slid over his shoulders. "Ohh, Nerdman, I think you're getting some muscles. Must be all the physical activity I've been putting you through." She kneaded his shoulders as if feeling the new strength in them.

He knew some physical activities he'd like her to put him through. Right here, right now. On the kitchen counter, on the floor, it didn't really matter.

She linked her arms around his neck and pressed

against him. Her face inches from his own, she whispered. "You sure there's nothing you can tell me about Callie and Tom?" She wet her bottom lip with her tongue and he bit back a groan.

Her blue eyes sparkled. This was another part of the game to her. It didn't bother her to be this close to him. It meant nothing to her. He spanned her waist with his hands. He wanted to slide under that sweatshirt and touch her skin, but he wasn't about to do that. This was enough. She was in his arms. He could fill an entire month of daydreams with this.

She tossed her head back and looked into his eyes. None of what he was feeling showed in her gaze. He knew she felt safe. She felt safe to tease and press against him because she knew he'd never take advantage. She probably never even though about it. Maybe the time had come to show Becky Richardson that he wasn't quite as safe as she thought. His gaze flicked to her wet pink lips and he lowered his head.

She immediately stiffened in his arms. In her eyes, he saw alarm. He was an idiot. She didn't want him to kiss her, not now, not ever. Embarrassment and anger filled him and he jerked her arms from around his neck. "Cut it out, Becky."

She looked confused, like she had no idea what had just happened or why he was mad. He moved away from her, turned his back and jerked his hands through his hair. His erection throbbed painfully behind his jeans and he wished she'd just leave.

"Louie, I'm sorry. I wasn't thinking."

Something in her voice had him turning around to look at her. Her face was flushed, and he wasn't foolish enough to think it was because they'd almost kissed. She was embarrassed. "What are you talking about?"

She looked away. "I shouldn't toy with you like that, it might confuse you."

His jaw fell open. Did she think he couldn't handle a little bit of flirting? "Look Miss 'I-think-I'm-irresistible', it may come as a surprise to you, but I am not overcome by your body and unable to control myself. We're friends and friends shouldn't be feeling each other up like that."

She slammed her hands on her hips and glared at

him. "Oh, like you were with me in the dining room? Enjoying feeling my butt pushed into your..."

"I was looking at the drawing over your shoulder," he yelled. Why the hell didn't she just leave?

"You were not!" she yelled back

"Was too!"

Becky opened her mouth as if to argue again, then bit her bottom lip. He watched her struggle not to smile.

He shook his head and grimaced. "I think this just proves that we've been stuck together much too long and I'm right about the Christmas break."

She sighed. "Maybe you're right. I mean, for a minute there I was going to—" She broke off and gave a half short laugh

"You were going to what?"

She waved her hand. "Nothing, nothing. It just got out of hand, that's all. I'm sorry I used you as an object of lust, Nerdman."

"I'm sorry your butt was offended by my being too close, Princess."

She held out her hand. "Friends?"

He took her fingers and lifted them to his lips. "Forever and ever," he murmured then dropped her hand. "Let's finish this drawing and call it quits tonight."

****

Becky grimaced as she gingerly picked her way over the snowy sidewalk to Callie's parents' house. With a sigh of relief, she stepped onto the porch and stomped her feet to get the snow out of her shoes. She'd no sooner grabbed for the storm door, when it was swung open wide.

"Missy, if you'd put on some boots, you wouldn't ruin those pretty little shoes of yours." Robert Murphy swept her inside and into his arms for a big bear hug. "Merry Christmas, sweetheart. You're looking beautiful as ever."

Becky kissed the cheek of the only man she loved as a father. Growing up in Oakdale, Callie's parents' house was her second home. She swiped the red lipstick off his cheek. "Boots are the ugliest things ever invented."

"You women are all alike. You won't look so good in a cast, either."

Becky handed him the bag of gifts she'd brought with her. She'd been dropping off presents all week so she wouldn't have as many to carry today. "Where's everyone?"

"Where else? In the kitchen." He took her coat from her and moved to the hall closet. "What can I get you? Wine? Eggnog?"

Becky crinkled her nose at the eggnog.

He patted her shoulder. "Wine it is."

She kicked off her shoes, leaving them in the hall before heading to the cramped kitchen. Callie's mother was at the sink and smiled as she walked in. "There's my girl."

Becky wrapped her arm around Helen's shoulders and leaned her head against hers. "Merry Christmas."

"Your mother just called and said she'd be over in an hour."

Becky took the glass of wine from Bob with an appreciative smile. "You know why, don't you? Did she tell you?" She couldn't keep the disgust out of her tone.

Helen shook her head and sighed. "I know, honey, but you have to understand your mother."

"She's doing Mrs. Martin's hair! On Christmas!"

"I know, but Mrs. Martin is very old and she wants to look her best."

"Yeah, because 'every Christmas might be her last'; I've been hearing that for ten years. That woman has no intention of ever dying."

"Rebecca!" Helen scolded and shook her head again. "Your mother enjoys making people happy. It only takes her an hour. She doesn't mind; it makes your mom feel like she's doing something special for someone else. She loves that. Besides, as much as you resent them, customers like Mrs. Martin adore your mother and they're very, very kind to her at the holidays. She likes to repay them for their generosity."

"I heard Tom and Amber went to his Aunt's house this morning. Are they coming here later?" Becky changed the subject, knowing she'd never agree; she'd had enough Christmas's where her mother had to take care of one more customer.

Helen handed Becky the potato peeler. "Finish these vegetables while I check the ham. Yep, he promised to bring Amber over. I have a few things for her."

"They looked great together at church last night didn't they?"

Helen nodded. "They did, but I'm not getting my hopes up."

"Who's got hopes up?" Bob asked coming back into the room.

"No one, honey. Can you get me those folding chairs out of the garage? And I'll need that other table cloth that's upstairs in the linen closet. Oh never mind, you won't know which one I mean. I'll get it myself."

Becky finished peeling the vegetables and set them aside, looking around for what else she could do. A sense of peace came over her as she worked around the familiar kitchen. Growing up she'd spent as much time at Callie's house as she had her own. It wouldn't feel right to spend Christmas anywhere but here.

All of a sudden she thought of Louie. He'd left two days ago for Florida and he wasn't too happy about it. He'd grumbled and groused when she dropped him at the airport. She hoped once he got there he'd stop complaining. Although she had to agree with him, Florida wasn't where she'd want to spend Christmas. Not that it was a bad place, but it wasn't home.

She smiled, thinking how strange it felt not to see him for two days in a row. Since October they'd been practically living together. It would be a shame when the project ended and life returned to normal.

The front door banged open and she heard little girl voices. She dropped the dish towel on the counter and headed down the hall as Emma came charging in. Dark brown curls bouncing and her huge eyes sparkling, she threw her arms out. "Aunt Becky, Aunt Becky!" Becky caught the pint sized girl up into her arms, smoothing her beautiful green velvet dress carefully.

"Oh my goodness, baby girl, what are you so excited about?"

"Santa Claus came and he brought me my very own bike!"

Becky widened her eyes appreciatively. "Well Santa must know what a big girl you are now and how much you wanted a big girl bike."

"Jenna got one too but a different color. Where's

Grandma?" She wiggled and Becky set her down.

"She went upstairs to get a table cloth."

The young girl was gone in a flash and her footsteps pounded up the stairs like a mini elephant.

Callie came into the kitchen, balancing foil wrapped trays and a couple of bowls in her arms.

Becky grabbed for them. "Why didn't you let me help you bring those in?"

"Oh, trust me, there's more out there. I don't know what I was thinking making all this stuff. Like my mother wouldn't have enough food to feed a third world country."

Becky set the bowls down on the counter and opened the refrigerator. "See, I was smart and brought mine over yesterday."

"Hmmm, well I was trying to get things done yesterday at the house."

Becky glanced over her shoulder at her friend. "Did any of those things you had to do include lighting Tom's fire?"

Callie's face flared and Becky laughed. "You too looked pretty cozy during mass. I said to myself, there's going to be a little mistletoe action at that house tonight."

Callie got a dreamy expression on her face and leaned against the counter. "It was definitely a magical night." Her face twisted. "But I hate it when he has to leave. I mean, I know he has to, we have young daughters and all, but still nothing is worse than when he gets up and leaves."

Becky shut the refrigerator and moved to the sliding glass door, shivering as the cold December air hit her. "These are going to have to sit out on the deck. There's no room in there."

Several minutes later, she slid the deck door open again, but this time to let the cool air in. The small kitchen had filled up and was busy and happy but also stifling hot. The girls sat at the kitchen table drinking special non-alcoholic Christmas drinks their grandfather had put together. Becky stole a sip from Jenna's, remembering how grown up she and Callie always felt drinking from the crystal wine glasses when they were kids. Wow, what was with her today. Normally she hated the 'remember when' conversations, preferring to live life today and not in the past.

Margaret had arrived and taken up her post beside Helen at the sink. Becky watched the two women work side by side in perfect harmony. As they giggled together, Becky could almost see them as they must have been when they were young. She glanced at Callie but her own best friend was staring out the window with a dreamy expression on her face.

"I think everything's done." Helen declared, poking a fork into the roast.

Bob clapped his hands together, rubbing them gleefully. "My favorite part of the day."

Callie looked at Becky and grinned. "Doesn't he say the same thing at Thanksgiving?"

The dining room table was set with the good holiday dishes. A Christmas tree that Becky knew the girls had decorated took up one corner of the room, and a chair that had been moved from the living room to make room for Christmas gifts was pushed against another wall. When everyone was seated, they bowed their heads and Bob gave the blessing.

"Amen!" Bob said solemnly.

"Amen." Everyone repeated.

Huge platters of food and bowls began to pass around the table as everyone talked at once.

"When's Louie due back?" Callie asked, taking the bowl of potatoes from Becky and helping Emma scoop some on her plate.

Becky took one of the steaming hot rolls out of the basket and set one on Jenna's plate next to her. "Right after New Year's. Personally, I don't think he'll survive that long down there."

"How're his folks doing? I can't imagine living in Florida. I mean, I enjoy our time down there in February, but not permanently," Helen said.

Becky shrugged. "They like it. I guess they told Louie that since he didn't seem to be in any hurry to make them grandparents, they had nothing holding them here."

"I know how they feel." Margaret murmured and looked pointedly at her daughter.

Becky wagged her fork at her mother. "Callie gave

you two surrogate granddaughters and if she plays her cards right you could have a third."

"Beck!" Callie scolded and glanced at Jenna and Emma who suddenly took a huge interest in the conversation.

"What's Aunt Becky mean? Are you having a baby, Mommy?"

Callie's face flamed.

Becky grinned and looked over at Hannah. "Would you like Mommy to have another baby, angel?"

"Only if it was a girl. I don't like boys." Emma shivered as if they were the worst things on the earth.

"Oh, boys have their good points, honey."

"Well if that's the case maybe Auntie Becky can have a nice little boy baby," Callie declared, lifting her eyebrow as if to say touché.

Becky laughed. "Now Callie, you know I can't have a baby because I'm not getting married and only married ladies get babies."

"You could marry Louie and have babies," Jenna spoke up with the knowledge of an almost teenager.

Becky felt her face flame. Louie and her? Having babies? The incident in the kitchen several days ago sprang to mind. She'd been as shocked to find his shoulders powerful and muscular as she had by the way she'd responded to being in his arms. Her heart had sped up, she'd lost her breath, but when he leaned down to kiss her she'd pulled back in shock. She'd wondered often in the past few days what would have happened if they'd kissed. Instead of being completely turned off by the idea, it intrigued her. Her and her nerdy friend? How weird was that? Or was it?

More than likely, she would have given him a heart attack on the spot. Never before could she have spent so much time with one man and not get bored, but with Louie every day was different. She missed him right now. It didn't feel right not seeing him every day anymore.

What was going on? She was Becky Richardson. She didn't need any man on a daily basis, certainly not her nerdy buddy. She'd known Louie since the second grade, so why was she suddenly thinking of him so much? The room was quiet and she realized everyone was looking at her.

She laughed self-consciously. "Hey, you want me to lose my appetite and not be able to eat your grandma's dinner? Louie needs to find a nice little rocket scientist to hook up with and produce some more brainy nerds."

"How are the renovations going?" Helen asked.

Becky was grateful for the subject change. "Amazing. It's almost like the old house is glad someone's taking care of it again."

"You must be in your glory over there. You've always loved that place so," Helen said.

Becky nodded. "Sometimes Louie and I forget it isn't our house."

"Our house? Is there something more going on then you're telling us? Could Jenna be right about a possible romance?" Bob spoke up.

She felt a flush creep into her cheeks and she busied herself with her roast beef. "Are you kidding me? Unless I have a microchip inside me, Louie's not interested. Don't forget you're talking about the King of Geeks."

Immediately she felt a pang at thinking like that. Louie wasn't a geek, at least not in the way most geeks were. There was so much more to him than what appeared on the surface. He could do everything. She'd watched him do plumbing and electrical work. He'd helped the contractors with drywall and painting.

He really was a guy who could handle anything.

Fortunately, the conversation had turned to Santa and the presents waiting in the living room. The adults finished their dinner and didn't dare linger over coffee with the girls wiggling impatiently.

Helen and Margaret stood up and began to clear dishes and Becky rose automatically. Bob took the girls into the living room. It was only a few minutes before the table was cleared and the dishwasher was already humming.

Helen wiped her hands on her apron and took it off. "I'll put coffee on, but we better start on those presents or these girls will go crazy."

Walking into the living room, seeing the enormous Christmas tree and the decorated fireplace reminded Becky of every Christmas she'd ever spent here. The pile of gifts under the tree was just as large as it had always been when she and Callie were little.

"Beck?" Callie touched her shoulder as she tried to get past her into the living room. "What are you thinking about?"

Becky blinked. "How many years do you think we've been doing Christmas together?"

Callie looked at her as if surprised that her usually tough friend was being nostalgic. She twisted her lips with thought. "I think the year your grandparents died was the first year we did Christmas together. I think we were eight maybe? Why, you getting sick of us?"

Becky laughed and slid her arm around Callie's waist and hugged her. "Never. It wouldn't be Christmas without being in this house."

Hannah and Jenna stood by their grandfather, waiting for him to distribute the gifts.

Becky settled in a wing chair opposite from her mother and Helen. Emma ran over to Margaret and handed her the ribbon from her hair. "Will you fix my bows, Grandma Maggie?"

Becky watched as her mom tenderly readjusted Emma's hair and hugged her tight. She'll make a wonderful grandmother. Becky blinked and straightened in the chair. Wow, where'd that thought come from? She's never going to have grandkids because I have no intention of having kids. My mother should have had more kids. That's what she should have done. Of course, it would have been a whole lot easier to do that if her husband hadn't left. Becky set her coffee down on the end table. One more thing he'd ruined in her life.

Every holiday, whether she wanted to or not, she wondered where her father was. Did he have another family? Did they sit around a table full of food and a tree full of presents? Or was he alone, in an apartment with no one to share the holiday with. When she was little, she used to have fantasies of him walking through the door and shouting Merry Christmas. In her mind, Margaret slammed the door in his face. In reality, Becky always suspected if the man showed up on her doorstep, she'd let him in.

It seemed like only minutes later the gifts were

distributed and Callie's dad attempted to put together the various new items Barbie had accumulated this year.

Becky's big gift to the girls had been an enormous dollhouse. Louie had wired it and it came complete with a remote control that turned on lights and made the fireplace glow.

"Where am I supposed to put this huge thing?" Callie asked.

Becky smiled back at her. "Not my problem that you live in such a small house." Becky put her finger to her chin as if a sudden thought occurred to her. "I bet Tom's house would be able to hold ten dollhouses."

"Shhh!" She glared at her.

The girls were bouncing around the room, trying on new sweaters and eating way too many Christmas cookies. "Is it done yet, Papa?" Emma asked clinging to her grandfather's back as he leaned over the project.

"Nope, not yet pumpkin. Don't you worry though, they haven't invented a toy yet that your Papa couldn't put together."

The doorbell rang and Callie lunged across the room and through the door before anyone else could move.

"Jeez, you think that might be Tom?" Helen smiled knowingly.

Becky listened to the murmured greetings in the hall, and then Callie walked back into the room holding Amber's hand. Tom followed behind with his hand on her shoulder. It struck Becky how they were already a family. All that was left was for the two of them to accept it.

"Merry Christmas, Tom." Becky stood up and hugged him. "Can I get you a glass of wine or a beer?"

"A beer would be great, thanks." He moved into the room and shook hands with Callie's father, kissed Helen and Margaret and then joined Bob on the floor with the pink plastic.

"This looks more complicated than the space station," he said, glancing at the half put together toy

"Cost about the same, too," Bob muttered.

Becky handed Tom a beer. "Bob says after a few of these, the pieces go together a lot easier."

"Thanks, Becky. How're the renovations to your house going?"

"If only it were my house. Can you imagine?" She moved back to the couch and picked up a glass of wine.

"What I want to know is why it's such a secret? Why is this man keeping it so quiet and what's he plan on doing with that place?" Callie sat on the arm of the chair, her eyes never leaving Tom.

"He's sinking a fortune into it, that's for sure," Margaret added.

"Becky, you have no contact at all with him? How do you do the work? How does he pay the bills?" Tom asked.

She shrugged. "Louie handles it all, mostly through email. I don't even think he's spoken to him on the phone.
"

"I'm kind of surprised that Louie's the one heading this project, aren't you? I mean, he's never done anything like this before, has he?"

Becky shrugged. "I wondered that too, but after working with him, there's a side of Louie we never knew about. He's a natural at this. He's got all these ideas and he's so passionate about it."

Helen leaned forward. "His mother is hoping he gets passionate about something entirely different this season. I guess she's invited the niece of one of her neighbors over and she's hoping something clicks. Bernice says the girl is an actual honest to goodness rocket scientist, works at the space station at Cocoa Beach."

Louie was spending Christmas with a geek girl? The words she often flung at him haunted her, 'find yourself a nice geek girl and have some geeklings'. What if he did? What did that mean to her? And their project? Was that the only reason she was upset? The project? She stood up, feeling the need to get out of the room. "Maybe this will turn out to be the best visit to Florida he's ever had."

"Now if somebody else could only meet someone nice," Margaret said, looking pointedly at her daughter.

Becky rolled her eyes. "I'm going to get more Christmas cookies," she said over her shoulder as she walked down the hall.

Images of Louie smiling at some other woman, taking her hand, and fussing over her, spun through Becky's mind like a movie in fast forward. Suddenly, she remembered last week at the sink when he'd almost kissed her. Was he kissing this geek girl? Did his eyes light up when the rocket scientist walked into the room? Did he call this other woman princess, too? If Louie fell in love this weekend with this female version of himself, where did that leave her?

Oh my God. Am I that selfish that I want him miserable and alone? Even though I don't want him romantically, I want him to want me?

Not liking what she was feeling, she slid the glass door open to the deck and took a deep breath of the arctic wind. It only took a few seconds for her head to feel clearer.

The afternoon slid into evening. Becky stretched out on her stomach, playing with the Barbie mansion with Emma and Jenna. Finally, Callie started making excuses for why they should be leaving. Tom stood, too, apparently ready to leave if Callie was.

Becky sat up and grinned at the two of them. They were already as good as married, what was their problem?

All of a sudden, Tom grabbed Callie's hand and pulled her to the wing chair. He settled his hands on her shoulders while everyone in the room watched with curiosity. When he dropped to one knee, Becky grinned and Helen said, "Oh my God!"

Becky saw Callie's face go pale.

Tom pulled a black velvet box from his pocket and opened it, holding it out for Callie to see. "Some people might do this in a more private setting, but since everyone here is a part of our family, I think it's fitting that I ask in front of everyone. Callie, will you make me the happiest man in the world and marry me?"

The entire room was silent. The three little girls seemed to understand how significant this moment was and they didn't utter a word. After what seemed like forever to Becky, and had to be a lifetime to Tom, tears slid down Callie's cheeks and she nodded. Tom pulled the ring from the box, slipped it on her hand and scooped her up into his arms. Everyone cheered and the girls flung themselves at their parents, laughing and shouting about being sisters forever.

Bob yelled that he was going to get the champagne. Tom and Callie kissed in the middle of all the commotion and seemed to only see one another for that moment in time. Finally, Helen forced them apart so she could hug them both.

When Becky finally got her friend in her arms she squeezed her tight and clung to her. "I'm so happy for you, sweetie, you know that." She pulled back to look at Callie. "You two deserve this and you'll be great together."

"Will you be my maid of honor, again?" Callie laughed.

Becky nodded. "I do have experience in that department, don't I?"

"Who's going to be your best man, Tom?" Bob asked.

Tom looked at Becky. "I think I'm going to ask Louie, think he'd do it?"

Becky grinned. "Let's call him and ask him."

"I'll go get the phone number," Helen said, wiping her tears away. Bob popped the champagne and began pouring. A few minutes later Helen walked in with the phone to her ear. She wiped at the tears on her face. "Thank you, Bernice. Yes, we're all thrilled. Oh, I have no idea when, they've only just got engaged, but we'll be sure to let you know."

She handed the phone to Tom. Becky listened as he asked Louie to be his best man. He gave the thumbs up and everyone clapped and drank their champagne. After Callie talked to Louie she handed the phone to Becky.

"Louie wants to say Merry Christmas," Callie said.

Warmth and excitement raced through her. She wished he was here to share in the celebration. "Merry Christmas," she said.

"Merry Christmas. Princess. What fantastic news, huh? About time too. I heard you're my date for the night," he said.

"Unless you end up bringing someone else," she said, half fishing for information on the Christmas guest.

"Wouldn't that be in poor taste?"

Becky wandered away from the noise in the living room, heading to a secluded corner in the kitchen. "No. You could bring a date. I mean, if you have someone special."

There was silence at the other end and then she heard rustling and figured he was also walking somewhere more private. "Ahh, my mother's little matchmaking scheme has made it all the way up north."

"Did you think it wouldn't? So spill it, how is she? Should I plan on buying an outfit for the wedding?"

"I wouldn't say that. She's very nice. We have a lot in common."

"That sounds great. I'm happy for both of you."

"Yeah, you sound it. You wouldn't be a tad bit jealous would you, Princess?"

Becky smiled at the usually hated nickname. "Why would I be jealous of a geek like you? She probably lives and breathes that techno stuff you love. I'm sure you two have had long intimate conversations about the home automation system."

"Actually, I may invite her up there to get her opinion."

"Great, that'll be cozy, me and two geeks."

Louie laughed. "So did they set a date?"

"I think Tom would like it to be yesterday, but I heard Callie mentioning May. She doesn't want to get married in winter boots."

"She's got a point. The mansion will be done by then; maybe our infamous Mr. M. would let them use the garden for photos."

"That would be awesome with the gazebo and all. That's a great idea. Hey, maybe they could even get married out there."

"Whoa there, don't go getting ahead of yourself. We don't even know for sure if he'll let us use the gardens. Let's take it one step at a time."

"Yeah, you're right. I'm thinking of going out to the house sometime this week."

"No. We agreed on a two week break. Besides, I don't like you out there alone, it's too secluded."

Becky couldn't tell even him how much she missed the place already. It was too weird to be this obsessed about a home that wasn't hers. What on earth was she going to do when she had to leave there for good?

"All right, Nerdman. You better get back to your new friend and I've got to get back to the party. Have a good night."

"Thanks, you too. Talk to you later."

Becky stood there for a minute holding the phone after he hung up. She imagined Louie and some woman in ugly glasses laughing with his parents. Maybe this was the year Louie was going to have a date on New Year's Eve and she wasn't. For Christmas, she'd given Callie New Year's Eve as a gift. She was going to sleep at Callie's house with the three girls so she and Tom could have privacy. When she'd made the offer, she'd hoped that Tom would take advantage of the night alone to propose. Obviously, Tom didn't want to wait that long.

****

Louie bounded up the porch stairs, taking them two at a time. It was so damn good to be home. Not just to Oakdale, but the mansion. He'd missed it. He missed the snow, the cold, the house, and of course, he'd missed his princess. It had taken every bit of willpower he had not to call her on New Year's. He didn't want to know what she was doing or who she was doing it with.

He knew it had disappointed his mother, but as much as he enjoyed talking to the niece of their neighbor, he wasn't interested. New Year's Eve he'd played cards with his parents and their friends and was in bed before midnight. All he could do was obsess over who was kissing Becky at midnight.

While he tossed and turned that night, he'd had this wild idea. Becky wanted to meet the owner of the mansion. She was growing impatient of the Mr. M game and had built up an entire fantasy around the man. What if somehow he became the mystery owner and introduced himself? How could he do that and not have her know it was him? Then it hit him. An old fashioned masquerade ball and he had the perfect time to do it. Valentine's Day. The theme could be famous lovers in history.

It was ingenious. As himself, he would act annoyed by the whole idea, but reluctantly go along with it if that's what the owner wanted. Then he could disappear and reappear dressed in costume. He pictured himself as the Phantom of the Opera, something that completely obscured him.

He even imagined what type of gown he'd have Becky wear. He pictured her in a Victorian gown with the plunging neckline and tight waist. It would be blood red with a full skirt, probably made of velvet or some other really heavy material. With her hair up, she'd be the belle of the ball. He spent all of New Years' day on his laptop searching for the perfect gown on costume web sites. He'd found not only the gown but the mask he needed as well. He knew he could do this. He could pull this off. Finally, he sent himself an email from the infamous Mr. M. announcing his interest in having this masquerade party.

He glanced around the porch. It was so good to be back. He hadn't told Becky he was in town. She wasn't expecting him until tomorrow. He needed to get out here and get his head together before he was with her again. In the two weeks he'd been gone, he had come to the conclusion that Becky was his addiction. The only way he was ever going to get over her was to eventually stay completely away from her. Something that wasn't going to happen until this project was finished. He also realized that for Becky, he was never going to be anything more than her geeky friend. He had to learn to accept that for his own sanity.

He punched in the keycode on the security panel, disguised as a picture on the porch wall, and the front door clicked open. He stepped inside and closed it. Immediately, his senses were on full alert. He sniffed the air. There was no mistaking that perfume. He looked down and sure enough, her shoes were on the boot tray and there was water in the bottom.

His heart leapt at the idea that he was going to see her, she was here. He was annoyed that she'd ignored his orders about coming here alone. He didn't hear any sounds coming from the kitchen or anywhere else on the first floor, so he raced up the staircase. The door to the master bedroom was half closed and as he moved towards it, he heard the bed springs squeak. He froze. She wouldn't have brought someone here with her, would she?

Chapter Five

Anger filled him at the thought of her in bed with someone else in their house.

Without thinking any further, he pushed open the door and steeled himself for whatever was happening inside.

The room was dark and it took several minutes for his eyes to adjust before he went any further. The curtains were closed around the bed. Listening carefully for any type of sound, he crept closer. His hand shook as he reached out and grabbed the heavy material and slowly pushed it aside. Louie let his breath out in a whoosh. The only one in bed with Becky was his big fat cat, Google, who blinked up at him.

Her hand tucked under her cheek, and her black hair splayed on the pillow, she looked like an angel. She wore one of his flannel shirts over some worn thin lounging pants and on her feet were slouchy wool socks. Louie smiled and his hand reached out, but he pulled it back before he touched her. His princess, he'd missed her so much.

She stirred and shifted in the bed. He sank to the side and watched her sleep. How was he going to live without her? When the project ended and the truth came out, she'd hate him for lying to her. The last two weeks, not seeing her, had been hell and only a small taste of what the rest of his life would be like without her in it. He used to think what he had for Becky was infatuation, or obsession, but now he knew better. It was far worse than that. He loved her. He honestly loved her and he knew damn well she'd never love him back. Happily ever after only happened in fairytales. In real life, princesses didn't kiss frogs or geeks. Her eyelids flickered and opened. He watched her smile softly and pull her hand out from under her cheek. Her skin showed the impression of her hand.

"Hey," she said.

She arched her back and Louie's pulse raced. He envied that old shirt of his.

"Hey," he said softly

She lay back on the pillow and looked up at him. "Did you just get in?" She yawned. "What time is it?"

"It's almost nine. I came right from the airport, but why are you here?"

She looked up from under her lashes. "I couldn't stay away. I was bored and I missed the house."

He knew the feeling but it was far more than the house he missed while he was away. "Anything new in Oakdale? Besides the engagement, of course."

She frowned and sat up. "Oakdale? Nah. How 'bout you? How was the geek woman?"

Louie laughed.

She narrowed her eyes. "What's so funny?"

"The way you call her that, it almost makes you sound jealous."

She frowned. "Of what?"

"Maybe you're jealous because I met someone who might take my attention off of you."

"You're joking, right?" She ran her hands through her hair and tried to sit up but Louie wouldn't move out of the way to give her room.

He leaned closer, letting his gaze take in the v neck of the black checked flannel shirt. She smelled warm and sweet and his heart raced. "You have nothing to be jealous about, Princess. You're my one and only."

She lifted her hand to lay it on his forehead. "I think the Florida sun fried your brain cells."

Disappointment surged through him, but he smiled as if he was teasing too. He pressed his lips to her cheek. "Someday, you're going to believe me."

She sat up and pushed him away. "And someday pigs will fly too."

He shifted and watched her climb off the bed. "You haven't been coming out here every day have you?"

"No. I came out here this afternoon, but then I got a rotten headache and came up here to lie down. I can't believe how long I've slept."

"How's the happy couple doing?"

Becky shook her head. "If I didn't love both of them so much, I'd say it's revolting how in love they are. It's all 'Honey, whatever you want is fine with me,' and then she says 'No, I want to make you happy'. Gag."

"Well, I have something else to make you gag. I got an email from our friend, Mr. M. while I was gone."

As always, Becky's attention was caught at the sound of the mystery owner's name. "What did he say? Is he coming to town?"

Louie slid off the bed. "No. Calm down and listen. He wants to have a Valentine's Day Ball."

She furrowed her forehead. "A ball here? In February?"

Louie nodded. "It gets worse. He wants it to be a masquerade party where the guests have to come dressed as famous couples in history."

"Famous couples?"

"Yeah, you know like Scarlet O'Hara and Rhett Butler or Miss Piggy and Kermit?"

"You're kidding, right?"

"I wish. Then he said that anyone without a date would be paired up when they got here."

"What's he trying to do? Play cupid?"

Louie shrugged, trying to look nonchalant about the whole thing. 'It doesn't matter to me. I'm not dressing up as anything."

"How do you intend to get out of it?"

He grinned. "Just like I got out of the high school dances. I'm the AV guy."

He was fascinated by the changing expression on her face as he knew her mind was already putting it all together. He shoved his hands in his pockets. "He asked me to find out if you'd handle all the details for the ball."

Her eyes widened. "Me? He doesn't even know me. Why would he trust me with such a project?"

Louie looked away. "I might have told him you'd be the best person for the job."

"You're kidding!" She flung herself at him and wrapped her arms tight around his neck. "You're the best, you know that?"

Louie closed his eyes and held her tight, but all too

fast she jerked away again.

"That's only a little over a month away. There's so much to get done; I need to start a list. Did he say anything about what he wants? How about the food? I have a million things to do. I have to start a list; I have to figure out what kind of food he wants. Did you say anything more? Did he..."

Louie held up his hand. "I'll get you the email."

Several minutes later, they were in the den and Becky was scribbling on a pad of paper. "I definitely think a cocktail party, as opposed to dinner. A live band. We'll have some door prizes too. He says he wants it to be a benefit for the children's hospital. Now for the invitations, we don't want it to be just the upper crust of town, we want to include everyone so the best way to do that is to sell tickets. I know, I'll ask Callie to write a story on it. She can interview me."

Louie sipped his hot tea and watched her excitement. He pictured her in the gown he'd already ordered. Mr. M. would have to send her an email and invite her to be his date for the night to ensure she didn't bring anyone else. As Becky chattered on about the catering company and the type of wine they needed, he was thinking about the costume he'd found online. If it was as good as it appeared to be, no one would suspect who was really under the mask.

"The gazebo will look so romantic with soft red and white lights."

He blinked. "What? The gazebo? The snow will be waist deep out there."

She smiled that smile that he knew so well. It was the smile that said this was going to cost a ton of money. "We'll have the snow removed and we'll have heaters installed out there. It'll be perfect for couples to stroll hand in hand. We'll have the music piped out there too."

"Strolling outside in February?"

"My poor Nerdman, don't you know love will keep you warm?"

Louie rolled his eyes. "I thought you didn't believe in love?"

She shook her head and went back to her note scribbling. "I never said I didn't believe in love. I'd be a fool not to; look at Callie and Tom, Callie's parents, your parents too, for that matter. I said I don't believe in love for me."

"Your whole theory on love is that men leave. You've just given three great examples of why that's not at all true."

She looked directly at him. "It's not for me." She looked down at her notepad again and shrugged her shoulders. "I've always believed that variety is the spice of life."

Louie pushed back from his desk and walked around to stand in front of her. He leaned his hip back against the desk and crossed his arms. "Don't you think there's something to be said for familiarity? For knowing another person inside and out? For knowing that person will be there for you no matter what? Don't you believe that everyone has a soul mate out there?"

Becky looked up and he waited while she searched his eyes, looking for what, he had no clue. Finally, she shook her head. "I think all this talk of famous lovers and weddings has gone to your head." She stood up. "I'm going to head out. I'll take this with me." She waved her steno pad.

Louie didn't answer and he didn't follow her to the door.

She looked back. "Can all this be done by then?"

"If that's what the Princess wants, it'll be done. I'll get a crew started this week. That gazebo is a mess and I don't even know what we'll find in the greenhouse."

She smiled. "I know you can do it."

Yep. He would. He'd walk barefoot on hot coals if she wanted him to. "I live only to please you."

Becky rolled her eyes and walked out the door to the hall. A moment later, she came back. Her bright red ski parka was zipped up and she yanked on the matching gloves. "How late are you staying tonight?"

"I don't know. I'm too keyed up to sleep."

She nodded, "I'll see you tomorrow after work."

He pushed away from his desk and followed her to the front door. He watched her head down the stairs to her car. "Good night," he called.

She turned and looked up at him. "I'm glad you're

back, Nerdman, I missed you." She blew him a kiss and climbed inside her car.

Louie's chest constricted. If only she really had missed him; had welcomed him home with a real kiss. He watched as her car disappeared into the dark. The cold January air went right through him and he shut the heavy door. The staircase reminded him of her snuggled in the bed upstairs. Maybe instead of waking her up, he should have climbed in beside her and gone to sleep. He raked a hand through his hair and headed to the kitchen for more tea.

****

Becky twisted around in the chair at her mother's shop. "Hold still, Rebecca." Margaret's hand settled on her shoulder, halting her nervous twirling.

Callie laughed at her in the mirror. 'Stop worrying so much, everything will be fine."

"Easy for you to say, all you're planning is a wedding. This is the biggest social event to hit Oakdale in a hundred years or more."

Callie pulled a face and Becky laughed. Her mother clipped away with her scissors, making Becky incredibly nervous. "Not so much, Ma," she said, chewing her bottom lip.

"You do your job and let me do mine, Rebecca." She combed through her daughter's thick black hair.

"You know how I want it, right? Swept up, but not in a tight bun. I want some wispies coming down." She scooped up her still damp hair and tried to show her, but Maggie swatted at her hands.

"I'm trying to cut, will you stop it." Her mother shook her head. "I'm going to need a hundred bobby-pins to hold that up like that. You've got that thick hair of your father's."

Becky caught Callie's eye in the mirror and her friend smiled. "I can't believe you won't tell me who you and Tom are coming as."

"It's a surprise. Have you seen your dress yet?"

Becky smiled. "No, all I know is, it'll be there tomorrow afternoon for me to try on. If it doesn't fit, I don't know what I'm going to do."

"Do you want me and Tom to come out early? Do you

need help with anything?"

"I don't think so. You know, I love you for that article you put in the paper. Louie said he mailed it to Mr. M."

"I can't believe you're finally going to meet him. Are you excited?"

"I'm a nervous wreck. I hope he likes the house, I hope the decorations and the ball are what he expected." Becky's stomach fluttered thinking about meeting the mystery man, but also out of worry that he wouldn't like all she'd done.

"Is Louie nervous?"

"I don't think so. He acts like this is no big deal."

"He told Tom he worked all night Saturday."

"Well, he's got some new fangled automatic system that pipes music and lighting out to the gardens. Wait until you see the gazebo. It's so romantic looking!"

"Do you really think Mr. Mystery will let me do the wedding pictures there?"

"I don't see why not. He's never there anyway."

Maggie unclipped the plastic cape, and shook it out. The dark hair fell all around her and she swiped at it. "There you are. You can dry it yourself or sit under one of the dryers."

Becky stood up and Callie took the chair. "Are you sure you don't mind doing highlights?"

Margaret pushed the pedal and the chair lifted. "Have I ever minded before?" She snapped the plastic cape around Callie and fluffed out her hair.

Becky turned on the blow dryer on the counter and bent from the waist, blowing her newly trimmed hair. She was so excited and yet so nervous; she had no idea how she was going to wait until tomorrow night. This was worse than waiting for Christmas when she was a kid. Everything was done, and she felt good knowing it was the best it could possibly be. The mansion was decorated in a red and white Valentine's Day theme right down to the heart shaped appetizers that were coming from the best caterers in the area. She'd used this particular company several times for the law firm and they did a classy job. Yep, she was confident that the food and the decorations and the music were top notch.

A tap on her shoulder from her mother had her

turning the blow dryer off. "Your cell phone's ringing," she said.

Becky grabbed her phone off the shelf in front of her. "Hello,"

"Hey, it's me."

She smiled and sank to the chair. "Hey you. What's going on?"

"Your dress is here."

"Is it gorgeous?" she shrieked. "Tell me it's gorgeous!"

"I haven't opened the box. It's addressed to you."

"I'm coming right out there."

"Good, bring me food."

"Food? The kitchen is overflowing with food." She sighed, knowing he wouldn't touch anything that was reserved for the party tomorrow. "Ok, fine, how about Chinese?"

"I'm sick of Chinese, and no subs either."

"Well what do you want? It's not like we live somewhere with a lot of take out choices."

"They sound like an old married couple if you ask me," Margaret said, pulling strands of hair through a cap on Callie's head.

"It's been like this all month while they've been planning this party."

Margaret leaned down to whisper in Callie's ear. "Poor Louie."

"Hey! I heard that." Becky pulled a face at her mother. Into the phone, she said, "I'll think of something for dinner and bring it. See you in an hour."

"I'll be waiting, drive safe."

Becky clicked off. What the heck was she going to pick up for dinner? Then she remembered her dress. She looked at Callie and her mother. "My dress arrived."

"So we heard."

"Louie wants dinner."

"So we heard."

She reached for her coat and gloves. "Have you guys tried that new barbecue place yet? Maybe I can get some take out from there."

"Why don't you get fish fries from the diner?"

"Louie doesn't like fish."

The two women smirked at one another in the

mirror. Becky looked at them with her hand so her hips. "What's so funny?"

"Nothing, dear. You have a nice evening with Louie. What time are you coming by tomorrow so I can do your upsweep?"

Becky sighed. "I wish you'd come out to the party." It was a huge disappointment that her mother refused to come. Half of Becky's excitement at the idea of a ball was thinking that her mother would once again dance at the Ryan Mansion in a fancy gown.

Margaret finished pulling Callie's hair through the cap and patted her shoulder. "About thirty minutes and we'll rinse." She handed her a magazine and turned to look at her daughter. "Parties are for the young, sweetheart. I really am not interested in putting on a costume. However, this shindig has brought me some extra business and for that I'm thankful."

"So you'll be here doing hair until closing while the rest of the town is having fun?"

Margaret sighed and walked to her daughter's side. "Honey, someday you'll figure out that the things that make you happy aren't the same things that make me happy." She kissed her cheek and patted her shoulder as she walked over to her desk.

Becky saw her mother grimace as she sat down. The hours on her feet were getting to her. How much longer did she think she could keep up this pace? Somehow this year she was going to convince her to not work as long or as hard. Margaret needed to learn how to enjoy the rest of her years.

"I'll come by around noon. I'll bring you lunch and you can put my hair up."

"Ok, dear. You have a nice evening. Give Louie my love."

Becky nodded. "Cal, I'll see you tomorrow night."

Callie waved absently without looking up from the gossip magazine.

Driving through town, she couldn't help but be impatient to get out to the Ryan house and see her gown. She spied the diner and pulled into the crowded lot. Louie would just have to deal with whatever the special was tonight. A half hour later, she hauled the bag of fried chicken dinners with her as she mounted the porch steps. She hit the security code and pushed open the door.

She pushed it closed with her hip. "Hey, I'm home," she yelled. Screwing up her face, she realized what she said. "Come on, food's here!"

Louie mumbled something from upstairs. Kicking off her shoes, she headed down the hall to the kitchen. They hadn't done any work in the kitchen yet but it was sparkling clean and would definitely be up to the challenge of the catering crew. The counter tops were already lined with china and crystal and trays that the company had dropped off earlier in the week.

She plopped the dinners on the table and grabbed a beer out of the refrigerator. There wasn't a spare inch of space.

"I'm starved."

She turned around as Louie came into the kitchen. Her heart did a funny flip flop at the sight of him and she wondered why he looked so cute and rumpled. It was obvious he'd been out here all day working.

"Did you even go to sleep last night?" she asked, setting his beer in front of him.

He looked up. "Who has time to sleep, woman? There's a ball tomorrow night. Us worker bees have a lot to get done."

He dug into his chicken like a starved animal. "Mmm, this is perfect. Thanks."

"Yeah, well don't get used to it. I realized today, this is becoming way too domestic for me." She handed him a napkin and he winked at her.

Louie wiped his mouth. "I appreciate it. I really do." He reached out and covered her hand. "You've been fantastic through all this and when it's all over with, I'm going to take you out for the best dinner you've ever had. Your choice of restaurants, too."

Becky's eyes met his and she wondered why the thought of a night out at a restaurant with Louie sounded so appealing. Six months ago, she would have scoffed at the idea of such an intimate outing. Now it sounded perfect. She didn't dare let him know, though. He'd definitely take it the wrong way. "You'll have to take a number. You know how many dates I've turned down since we started this project?"

The sparkle in his blue eyes disappeared and he pulled his hand away. 'I've heard the hearts breaking all over town. I have to tell you it doesn't hurt this geek's pride any to know the Princess has been spending her nights with me, and not some stud."

"I'm working; it's a project, that's all."

"Oh that's all? That's why you yelled, 'I'm home' just now?"

She felt the red creep into her face. "That just came out. It's natural. I yell it when I walk into Callie's house too."

"Uh huh." He picked up his second piece of chicken and bit it like a ravenous dog.

Becky picked off the crispy skin from her meat and wiped the grease on her napkin. "I'll be able to walk away from this project without any further thought. How about you?"

He picked up the crispy part that she'd set aside and tossed it into his mouth. "Sure. It's just another job. A big job, but still just another money making adventure."

Becky knew it was more than that to him too, but she decided it was time to change the subject. "I'm so curious about Mr. M. I can't believe we're finally going to meet him tomorrow. Aren't you excited about that at least?"

"I guess."

"I wonder what he looks like."

Louie tipped his beer back before answering. "Probably a rich geek."

She ignored his jab. "I bet he's tall, dark, and handsome. That's how I picture him."

"That's how you picture all rich guys. They aren't all handsome you know."

"Hmm, well it's my dream and I think he's handsome." Suddenly remembering her gown, she pushed away from the table. "Where's the dress?"

He jerked his head towards the hall. "In the master suite. I laid it on the bed so it wouldn't get wrinkled."

"I thought you said you didn't open the box? That cat better not be sleeping on it." She raced up the back stairs to the second floor.

Every time she came in here, she marveled at what a

beautiful room it was. The rich colors she'd chosen were a perfect compliment for the heavy dark furniture. It had a richness that was hard to describe but easy to appreciate. The room was straight out of a home and garden magazine. She couldn't help but be a bit proud of it.

The curtains surrounding the four poster bed were all drawn back and tied with the gold cord. The settee and lounging chair were placed by the fire with a book and cashmere blanket set in place to give the illusion someone had just gotten up from reading.

On the bed lay a dark garment bag. She quickly removed it, gasping at the gorgeous gown. The crimson color was bold and she immediately knew it would be a great color on her. Lifting it, she was amazed at how heavy the dress was. Turning to the full length mirror, she held it up in front of her trying to picture how it was going to look on.

"Why don't you try it on?"

She looked in the mirror to see Louie lounging in the doorway watching her. Looking back at the gown, she ran her hand over the crushed material and shook her head. "I know it'll fit. I'll try it on tomorrow when my hair is done so I can see the full effect."

He pushed away from the door jamb and came to stand behind her. He gathered her hair in his hands and held it up in exactly the type of sweep she planned on. "Does this help?"

He met her eyes in the mirror. They both looked down at the gown and then their eyes met again. Something crackled in the air and Becky felt her mouth open as she needed to breathe. Louie was directly behind her, his hands holding her hair. But it was the look in his eyes that made her breath catch.

It wasn't just desire she saw there. Desire she could handle, she was used to men wanting her physically. This was something far, far deeper. This was almost a need, a hungry devotion. Her eyes widened as she saw what she should have known for years.

She'd always taken his talk of worshipping her for granted; it was a joke between them. But suddenly it wasn't. The look on his face was raw and open and she realized with a sick feeling in her stomach that Louie really did believe he was in love with her.

In a rush of images, their friendship rolled through her memory. From as far back as she could remember, he'd been telling her he loved her; telling her he wanted her. She thought it was a game. She'd teased back, even lead him on at times, all the while believing it was just a silly game.

But to him it wasn't. It was all too real.

She whirled around to face him, her eyes scanning his urgently as his hands fell from her hair. "Louie..." she had no idea what she was going to say but she needed to break the incredible tension in the room.

He immediately stepped back and shoved his hands in his pockets. "I think the gown will look fine. Hey, thanks by the way for the chicken. How much do I owe you?"

He pulled his wallet out and began to sift through the bills while she stared at his face, wondering what to say to him.

"We need to talk."

"Yeah, well listen, I'd love to but I have hours of work left to do. So I'm going to get to it. Is twenty dollars enough?"

Becky shook her head as he handed her the bill. "I got it."

"No, no, that's not right; you're always bringing me dinner here." He pressed the bill in her hand and she wrapped her suddenly cold fingers over it. He jerked away as if her touch burned him. "If you're finished here, I could show you what they've done in the dining room. I think you'll be impressed."

Becky had to get out of there. "Actually, if you think it looks ok, I'm going to take off." She turned to the bed and carefully placed the gown back in the bag. "Roger actually is in town and wanted to meet for a drink. You know I can't resist those pilots." She gave a nervous laugh.

He didn't answer her and when she turned to look back at him, he was gone. She sank to the side of the bed and closed her eyes. How could I be this blind and stupid? All the times she'd teased him and flirted, she'd thought they were both playing the same game.

Dropping her head into her hands, she thought about the project they'd taken on. There were still months of work to do; she couldn't just walk away. The ball tomorrow night was the easy part, they'd be surrounded by people. No, it was the alone time that was going to be tough. How could she act as if everything was fine when it wasn't? She would feel awkward and uncomfortable. The easy friendship she enjoyed suddenly was gone, as if it never existed. Had he only pretended to be her friend all these years? Had he really been hoping that one day she'd fall in love with him?

Growing angry at what she viewed as his deception, she stood up resolutely and tossed her hair. It wasn't her problem. She'd been upfront with him. He knew how she felt about love and all that. If he got hurt it was his own fault, not hers. She didn't ask for him to love her or think he was in love with her.

****

Louie had never been more nervous in his entire life. For the fifth time he glanced into the hall mirror and straightened his collar. Becky had insisted he wear a tux even if he refused to wear a costume. He'd let her talk him into it but only because it really fell in with his plans for his other costume.

Hearing the door upstairs shut, he moved to the bottom of the sweeping staircase. He heard her footsteps reach the top landing.

"Are you ready?" she yelled down.

"Yeah, just hurry up. It's only an hour until the first guests arrive." He hoped she thought he was impatient for her to help him and not that he was impatient to see how she looked.

She came into view and then stopped at the same time his heart did. He stared up at her as if looking into one of the portraits hanging on the wall in the library. She was without a doubt the most beautiful woman in the world.

He reached his hand towards her, and she lifted the hem of her gown with both hands as she descended the rest of the way, stopping three steps from the bottom.

She held her head high, her blue eyes full of confidence. She knew damn well she looked good. He could only smile and nod, his voice caught in his throat. The deep red of the gown was a perfect backdrop for her jet black hair and white skin. It rested on her shoulders, scooping low and revealing a large amount of her breasts. He swallowed hard, realizing that there was more revealed than was concealed.

She laughed and he lifted his eyes. "It plunges kind of low doesn't it?"

"Uh huh," he muttered like an idiot.

Placing her hands on her waist she smiled. "It really makes my waist look tiny. I love that." She looked up at him but his tongue was still tied and he couldn't speak.

"Say something!" she demanded.

Lifting his hand, he took hers and brought it to his mouth. "You will be the belle of the ball." He kissed the back of her hand and tucked it into his arm to escort her the rest of the way down the steps.

Holding her full skirt up with on hand and clinging to him with the other, she let him lead her into the ballroom.

"How about a drink before all hell breaks loose?" He started towards the bar but she grabbed his hand.

"In a minute. Let me look at you."

She wandered around him, checking him out from every angle until he was flustered.

"Well do I pass inspection? I told you I'm going to be in the background, way in the background, all night."

"You can't hide in the kitchen the whole time, but you look great, Nerdman. Really. The single ladies will go crazy."

Moving to the corner where the bartender would soon be, he poured them each a glass of wine and returned to her side. "Every unattached person is already spoken for due to the game. I've got all the cards as to who will be who."

"When's that dance supposed to happen?"

He took a long drink, trying hard not to keep staring at her or the bodice of the dress. "Around eleven o'clock you can make the announcements for everyone to pair up."

"What about you? Who's your other half?" she asked over her wine glass.

You. Only you. His mind screamed. Outwardly, he shrugged. "I don't dance so I'm not playing."

"What do you mean you don't dance?" she asked.

"I don't dance. Never learned. In school I was busy running the AV equipment, speakers, etc. Remember?"

"What about at weddings?"

"Nope."

A look came into her eyes that made him very nervous. Setting her wine down, she reached for his glass.

"What are you doing?"

"Teaching you to dance."

He couldn't resist as she placed one of his hands at her waist, rested her hand on his shoulder and clasped his fingers in hers. "There's no music," he protested.

"Where's the remote?" she asked, moving out of his arms again.

She snapped it up off a nearby table and handed it to him. "Find something slow."

He stared at her for a minute but she pressed the controller on him and he knew she wouldn't leave him alone until they danced. It was all a ruse, of course. He could dance. But for his charade to work tonight she had to think he was Klutzy, Nerdy Louie.

He hit the button while he looked into her eyes and '*Lady in Red*' began to play. He smiled at her as her cheeks turned pink and she glanced up at him from under her lashes. His temperature rose at her look.

"Thank you," she said softly, understanding that it was meant for her.

The sultry words filled the quiet room, and she slipped into his arms. "Now just follow me. It's very easy to dance. Sometimes some songs you barely even need to move, others have really simple steps."

Looking at their feet, she led him through a few steps, and he pretended to stumble before finding his rhythm. It was hard at first to let her lead and pretend he couldn't do it, but watching how pleased she was at thinking she taught him made it worthwhile. He shifted until they were closer, and while she looked at him knowingly, she didn't pull away.

"Ok, but what if it's a song that you can only barely move to? What do you do then?" he asked.

She hesitated before removing her hand from his. Lifting both her arms she linked them around his neck and her body made full contact with his. "Put both your arms around my waist," she instructed.

Louie couldn't think. At all. Her breasts pressed into his chest, their thighs met. Impatiently, she reached down and pressed his hands to her waist before returning to her position.

"Like this?" he asked, pulling her closer still. He lowered his head to her neck. "Hmm you smell good."

She giggled and shifted as he tickled her neck with his nose but as the music drifted over them, she relaxed against him. The singer sang about the lady in red and how much he loved her. He closed his eyes and took over the dance, leading her very slowly in a tiny circle on the enormous dance floor. In a few hours, he'd be sharing her with five hundred people, but this one moment in time she was his. His lady in red. Her gown was crushed velvet and he petted it in the back, not even realizing that his hands had crept down her waist to her shapely rear. Her face was buried in his neck; her breath hot on his neck. His pants grew tighter as he hardened. He didn't care if she knew how affected by her he was. It didn't matter to her anyway.

The music ended and another slow song started. Neither seemed to notice at first, then he felt her move her head. He looked down into her eyes. From under her lashes, she looked up as their bodies moved together. He caressed her cheek with the back of his hand; her skin was like the petal of a rose. "Princess, I..."

She shook her head and placed one finger over his lips. "Don't say anything."

She settled her head against his shoulder and he wrapped his arms around her. He could die tonight and be a happy man for having had this dance with this woman.

Chapter Six

It was hard to believe that only four hours earlier, Louie had had her all to himself. There were so many people in the mansion that it was impossible to move. All he saw of Becky now was a glimpse of the ruby red dress as she flitted here and there. It was enough to keep him going. That and playing 'Lady in Red'. He played it so often people began to groan when it came on but he couldn't care less.

A glance at the clock made his stomach clench. It was almost eleven; that was the agreed upon time when Mr. Mystery was supposed to show up. His plan would either be the best idea he'd ever had or he would be embarrassed for the rest of his life. As the grandfather clock chimed eleven, Becky appeared as if by magic and swooshed to the front of the room. A small dais had been set up and she reached for the microphone he'd set there.

"Ladies and gentleman. This is the time of the night when I would like to call out our famous couples and have you come to the dance floor. If you don't have a partner, we've chosen one for you." She smiled and picked up the index cards. "Our first famous couple simply goes to show that opposites attract. Kermit, would you please bring your lovely Miss Piggy to the center of the floor?"

The group laughed and clapped as Tom and Callie hurried to the front of the room and began to dance.

"The next couple on my list is Scarlett O'Hara and Rhett Butler."

As everyone watched the couple dance, Louie slipped out of the room. He raced through the kitchen as the staff scurried around getting things ready for the midnight dessert buffet. He slipped into the pantry and flipped the lock he'd recently installed. He ripped off the tux jacket and replaced it with another one and a long black cape. Then he stepped up on a small stepstool and reached into the box on the top shelf. He'd slipped the mask on enough times that he could do it expertly and was confident it completely concealed his identity. He kicked off his shoes and stepped into another pair complete with lifts to give him more height. His buddy in Hollywood had sent him everything he needed to completely transform his image. The mask had a special transmitter installed to disguise his voice. Not even his own mother would know him in this costume. He picked up his top hat and walking stick and the outfit was complete. Not completely Phantom of the Opera, but close enough.

Conscious of the time, he took a deep breath and slipped the lock off the door. He stuck his head out, but no one was around. He moved back through the kitchen, listening to the laughter from the guests. Becky was still calling out couples. He had to keep this appearance short; one, maybe two dances and he had to disappear again. He couldn't risk sticking around too long. Slipping through one of the back hallways, he made his way to the back of the ballroom and inside the door. Lucy VanPelt was dancing with Schroeder and his piano as the band played the famous music from Peanuts. The floor was a sea of lovers, some comical, some of historical importance. Becky was coming to the end of the list and he knew it was going to be his turn next. He watched her face as she read the card. Oh no, he wasn't going to have an asthma attack was he? His heart beat so loudly he thought it would come right out of his chest.

Becky lifted her eyes and he moved across the room. He forced himself to walk slowly, to appear as if he was completely in control. The room went quiet and the music ended as he stopped in front of her. He inclined his head and held out a white gloved hand. "I believe this is our dance."

She hesitated for a moment before taking his hand. Louie searched her eyes looking for any sign of recognition, but all he saw was curiosity and if he wasn't mistaken, interest. Her hand settled against his and he nodded to the band. A waltz began and the couples on the floor backed away to give them room. Louie could hear the whispers, but he never took his eyes off her. Unlike his klutzy attempts at dancing earlier that night, this time he led her smoothly across the floor. As his hand enfolded hers, he led her to the dance floor and into a waltz. They glided across the floor effortlessly as if they had practiced for years. Louie held her the proper distance away from him; his body barely touching hers. All too soon the music ended. He took her hand and brought it to his mouth.

"Thank you, Rebecca."

Becky's cheeks flushed and he was shocked. Her blush? That was a new one. "My pleasure. You are a very smooth dancer."

He let her hand go. "Would you join me for a glass of champagne or punch?"

She nodded and he crooked his arm for her to slip her hand through. At the bar area, she asked for an ice water and lemon. Louie ordered a scotch. He never drank scotch but it seemed like the type of drink Mr. Mystery would drink. He handed Becky her water and watched her watch him.

"It's so good to finally meet you. I'm very impressed with everything you and Louie have done so far."

Becky's eyes lit up, and once again he watched her cheeks flush pink. "It's all Louie. He's amazing, he can do anything." She took a sip of water. "Well except dance. I had to give him lessons earlier, but I don't know why I bothered, he hasn't used them."

"I'm sure Louie appreciated the lessons." He set his drink on the bar.

Becky smiled. "Thank you for the dress, it's breathtaking. I couldn't believe it fit."

Louie inclined his head. "You have your friend Louie to thank for that. I sent him the picture and he ordered the proper size and made sure it was the right color."

Becky smoothed her hand down the skirt of her gown. "It's like it was made for me."

The conversation dragged and Louie picked up his drink and took much too big a swallow. It burned going down and he struggled not to cough.

"What are you going to do with the house? I mean when it's done," she asked.

The band started playing again before he could come up with an answer. Once again, he set his glass down and held out his gloved hand. "Would you walk with me and show me the gardens?"

She nodded and set her glass down on the bar. Louie folded his hand around hers and led her across the front of the ballroom and over to the French doors. The cold air hit them as soon as he slid the doors open and he glanced at Becky as she immediately hugged her arms to her. Louie unhooked his cape and settled it around her shoulders. The ground was clear of snow and her high heels clicked on the path.

He watched her hook the cape and pull it around her. "I can't believe how cold it is."

"Yes, but at least the snow held off. Louie mentioned you were concerned about that."

She nodded and they walked towards the gazebo. "I wanted the guests to be able to walk out here."

The path was lit with tiny lights. They passed several couples embracing in the shadows before reaching the secluded greenhouse. Louie pulled the door open for Becky to step inside. Warmth enveloped them and the electric candles placed strategically among the hothouse flowers gave off a soft glow.

He latched the door closed.

"You never answered my question. What do you plan on doing with the house when it's finished?" Becky asked as soon as he turned around.

Louie wasn't sure what to tell her. He wanted to tell her his dreams for it, his real dreams, but that would never happen. "I bought it because it was recommended to me by my accountant as a good investment. I should be able to make a nice sum from it when I sell it."

He saw the disappointment in her eyes before she lifted her chin and hid her reaction. His poor princess, he wanted to take her in his arms and promise her he'd never do such a thing, but he couldn't.

She turned away and plucked at a leaf. "That's what we figured you were going to do."

Louie leaned against one of the pillars and crossed his arms over his chest. "You sound like you don't approve. You didn't think I was going to live here did you?"

Becky shook her head. "Not really. It's too big to be a one family home. It's not economical."

"Especially for someone by himself. It's not like I have a wife and children, nor will I have any. I'm not the marrying type."

"No?"

"Does that surprise you?" He lifted one eyebrow, anxious to hear her answer.

"Not really. I don't believe in any of that nonsense either."

"Now that's a surprise. I have met very few women who weren't looking for a wedding ring and picking out nursery colors."

She laughed. "Not this woman. I would think it would be tough for you to know if a woman is with you for you or for your money."

"Most of them I can see through. But I'm surprised that you don't want the white picket fence. You are a beautiful woman, Rebecca. You should have a man who treats you like a princess, someone who sweeps you off your feet."

Becky dipped her head. "I've got my feet firmly planted on the ground and I like it that way."

Louie edged closer until he was directly in front of her. "Maybe you just haven't met the right man yet."

"I'm not a big believer in romance." She looked at him warily as if she thought he might pounce on her.

The music drifted in from the hidden speakers.

"May I have this dance?" He held out his hand.

She hesitated before taking it. Louie drew her into his arms and began to sway. He looked down into her eyes, loving the way it felt to have her in his arms again. She was so beautiful. In his mind he could pretend they truly were this couple from the theatre. He was the Phantom of the Opera and she was the woman he adored. She had no clue that he was her nerdy friend. For tonight he was as suave and confident as they both imagined Mr. Mystery to be. In disguise he was everything he wasn't in real life. He had promised himself he'd only dance one dance with her and then disappear and ditch the disguise, but now he couldn't leave. He wanted this moment to last. Worse, he wanted to kiss her. Just once, to know what it would be like to have Becky kiss him like he was any other man. His heart jerked at the thought. He couldn't do that, could he? The mask left his lower face open, that wasn't a problem, but would she figure out who he was? How could she? They'd never kissed. His palms inside the white gloves began to sweat as considered that this could really happen.

Becky looked up at him. She looked at his mouth. She wanted him to kiss her! Didn't she? Was that the look of a woman who wanted to be kissed? It sure looked that way to him. What should he do? His heart raced so fast he feared he'd have a heart attack right here and now. Wouldn't that be his luck?

With a confidence he didn't feel he lifted the hand he held in his own and set it on his shoulder. The movement brought their hips in contact with each other and he tried his best to ignore how incredible that felt. He cupped her chin in his gloved hand and lifted her face for his kiss. Her breath caught and he lowered his head as her eyes flickered closed. Becky tipped her mouth upward, inviting him to keep going.

A million cells in his body exploded at the feel of her soft warm lips. He forced back the groan that bubbled up inside him and pulled back a fraction. He wet his lips, tasting her on them and kissed her again. This time he didn't hesitate, he tilted his head and meshed his mouth fully with hers. He wrapped both his arms around her and pulled her against him.

Her arms slid around his neck and she lifted up on her toes. Her tongue tangled with his and he didn't stop the moan that escaped him at the desire that raced through him. His hands itched to roam her body, but he couldn't. He had to be satisfied with this. He plundered her mouth and she whimpered with pleasure, sending him soaring to the heavens with satisfaction. He drew his hands up her bare arms under the cape and settled them on her shoulders before sliding back down again. Her skin was like satin to his touch.

His fingers traced along the delicate bones at her neck, and then he cupped her face between his palms. He shuddered as she arched even closer into him. Kissing Becky was everything he'd ever imagined it would be and more. The fact that she thought she was kissing another man was of little consequence. He knew exactly who he was kissing. After all these years of wondering what it would be like, he now knew and it was all that and then some. He wanted more, he needed to touch her. At the same time he weighed the consequences of whether he dared go any further, Becky pulled back. She slid her hands from his neck to flatten against his chest in a tell tale sign.

Reluctantly he lifted his head. His breathing was fast and shallow and he noted she was struggling with hers too. He forced himself to drop his hands and step back from her.

"You should slap my face, Rebecca."

"For kissing me?"

He nodded. He pulled a handkerchief from his breast pocket and wiped at his mouth knowing it would be covered with her red lipstick.

"I never do things I don't want to do."

She walked a few paces away.

What should he say? Would it be lame to mention how hot that kiss was?

She lifted her head and he watched her look out at the moon. "Have you ever wondered what it would be like..." She paused, laughed slightly, and shook her head. "Never mind."

Louie knew what she was about to say. There wasn't much about Rebecca Richardson he wasn't privy too. He stepped behind her and wrapped his arms around her middle. He dropped his mouth to her delectable neck and loved the way she shivered. "Have you ever wondered what it would be like to make love with a masked stranger? Hmm, is that what you were thinking my little Countess?"

Her light laugh, and the way she tipped her neck, inviting him to nibble further was all the answer he needed. Becky loved excitement. She craved it. It made her feel like the bad girl she really thought she was. His mind raced. Could he do this? Could he give her what she wanted? He kissed her neck again, her collarbone and the slope of her bare shoulder. Knowing she wanted him gave him a confidence he earlier didn't think he could find. He slid his arms around her and rested his hands just beneath her full breasts. If Becky wanted to fulfill a fantasy, he was more than happy to combine it with one of his own.

His fingers brushed the undersides of her breasts and she shifted in his arms. Her hand reached up and behind her to stroke his bared chin. Louie cupped her breasts in his hands and literally had to bite his tongue not to moan out loud as they filled his palms.

His knees trembled and he forced himself to believe he was as confident as she thought he was. He stroked the pad of his thumb across her nipple. The material of her gown was thick and he couldn't feel much beneath his hands, but the soft sigh of pleasure let him know she felt it. It wasn't as if he'd never touched a woman, he'd been with women. But none of them mattered like this one. In fact, of the few women he had made love to over the years, he'd always had to pretend they were Becky in order to satisfy himself. He kissed her ear, drew his tongue around the delicate shell and she stretched her neck allowing him full access. He squeezed her breast gently and nibbled at her shoulder. In the soft light he could see the deep cleavage he created when he lifted them together and he shuddered.

He traced the collar of her gown where the creamy swell of her breasts threatened to spill out. Dipping his finger into her cleavage and pulling it out again he groaned at the action. Becky whimpered and he laid his open mouth on her neck being very careful not to leave marks on her. He'd seen those on her creamy skin before and it made him see red that someone could manhandle her in such a way. Now he knew how tempting it was. He longed to put his mark on her, to shout to the whole world that she'd been with him. When his fingertips reached inside her bodice and finally touched her velvet and very erect nipple he shook.

So soft! So perfect! Her softness filled his hand and spilled over. She moved backwards pressing herself against his hardness. It was more than obvious she was enjoying this. He had no problem standing there all night caressing her, stroking her. If there was anything else on earth he was an expert on it was Becky's breasts. He'd made love to them in his mind half his life. He knew exactly what he was going to do when he got a hold of them and he put all of his imagination to work. He molded them in his hands, plucked her nipples with a light touch until her breath sped up and she all but purred.

He wanted to see her bare in the moonlight. He wanted to turn her around his arms and pull her gown down so he could feast his eyes on her and then lift them to his mouth. His mouth dried at the thought of taking her nipple between his lips and suckling. He should have locked the door to the greenhouse. As it was anyone could walk in on them right now and he wasn't going to take a chance of some idiot seeing her half dressed.

All of a sudden it ended. Becky twisted around and since he still had his hand down her gown it was a bit awkward to get disentangled. His cufflink caught on the material, but she efficiently snipped it free and took a step away.

"Hmm it's a bit warm in here now don't you think?" Her eyes sparkled and there wasn't a single sign of regret or embarrassment in them.

His body wasn't ready to stop holding her. He reached out and pulled her back into his arms. "I was thinking it was just about right."

She let him kiss her again, but when he would have gone further she slid her hands up between them and rested them on his chest. "I have to get inside. If Louie saw me leave with you and we don't get back in there, he'll be out here looking for me."

"I don't think he saw us leave," he protested.

"You don't know Louie. He's very protective. If I'm out here too long with you, he'll think you're doing pure evil things to me." She slipped out of his arms and over to the door. Brushing at her gown she tipped her head and looked back at him. "I doubt I'll be able to sleep much tonight. I may end up taking a walk later, maybe wind up here again."

She was inviting him to meet her here later. To continue. Wasn't she? Stay cool. James Bond cool. He forced himself to act nonchalant about the whole thing. "I doubt I'll be able to sleep much myself, jet lag and all. I think I might enjoy a stroll myself."

She winked at him and was gone with a swoosh of

her gown. Louie let his breath out slowly and waited for his heart to calm down. Somehow he had to get back to the house without her knowing it, and then become himself again. He waited until he knew she had enough time to get halfway up the path and then he raced around the other side of the mansion and slipped through the servants' entrance to the basement.

****

Becky didn't go immediately back to the ballroom, she headed to the kitchen instead. It was a flurry of activity as men and women in black and white hustled to replenish trays of food. The atmosphere was fun, even among all the hard work, she heard the flirting of the waitresses with some of the staff. Must be something in the air tonight. She grinned, thinking about her moonlight meeting. A quick look around assured her Louie was nowhere around and she slipped into the powder room in the back hall. Inside she didn't bother to flip on the bright overhead light, instead she used the small nightlight that was burning. Her body tingled and a heavy ache pooled between her thighs. She turned on the tap water and shoved her wrists under it forcing her body to cool off.

She'd been kissed by a lot of guys in her life, but never had one been as amazing as he was. When he'd caressed her ears and cupped her breasts she'd all but melted. She wanted to rip her gown down and force his hands on her, his mouth on her. It was like nothing she'd experienced before. It had been a long time since a man had turned her on so quickly. He knew exactly how hard to stroke and he had the touch of someone who knew what he was doing and her body responded to it immediately.

She wasn't a fool. Part of the excitement had been the whole disguise thing. She loved that. As a kid she'd always found Spiderman and Batman to be fascinating. When she was a teenager, she'd seen the movie Zorro and used to imagine him coming to her in the dead of night and making love to her. She'd seen the movie at least a dozen times. What could she say? Masks turned her on. Some women liked a nice butt, or hard thighs, those were good things too, but hide the guy's identity, make it the mystery of the unknown and she was a goner. Mr.

Mystery had chosen to dress like the Phantom of the Opera with the black cape and white mask. That alone was enough to make her want to jump him. The fact that she'd fantasized about him for the past six months only heightened her excitement.

The mirror revealed her cheeks were flushed and her eyes were bright. She looked like a woman who'd been getting some action. Louie would be looking at her like a bug under a microscope when she got back. He had to have seen her dancing with Mr. Mystery. He was probably right now getting ready to put the place in lock down if she didn't get out there and show herself.

She didn't have her purse, she couldn't freshen her lipstick. Grabbing a tissue she wet it and did the best she could with the smeared lipstick. Shivering she remembered her invitation to Mr. Mystery to meet her later back at the greenhouse. She hadn't been thinking straight. Did she really think she'd be able to get away from Louie at that hour? If he even suspected she'd been doing what she'd been doing with Mr. Mystery, he wouldn't let her leave his side until dawn.

She had to meet him. She pressed her hand to her stomach. Her entire body was coiled tight with need. It had been a very long time since she'd looked forward to anything as much as she was this. "You're a bad girl," she scolded her reflection. She wanted him and she was going to do this whether or not Louie liked it.

With determination she yanked open the door and stepped into the hall. Louie stood there, his arms crossed over his chest.

"Where've you been?" he asked.

Heat filled her cheeks and she lifted her chin. He didn't own her. He had no right to question her. "I've been dancing. Where've you been?"

He narrowed his eyes. "I haven't seen you on the dance floor for well over an hour. In fact, the last time I saw you, you were heading out to the gardens with the Phantom of the Opera. That wouldn't be our Mr. Mystery would it?"

She crossed her arms over her chest noting that his eyes zeroed in on her cleavage. "He wanted to see what we'd done with the gardens."

She pushed past him and entered the kitchen. Louie followed and she closed her eyes wishing he'd stop questioning her.

Louie picked up a piece of chicken from a tray, and popped it into his mouth. "It's kind of hard to show someone gardens under four inches of snow."

"The path was clear and I showed him the greenhouse. It wasn't snowing in there."

"Uh huh." He looked at her with narrowed eyes.

"Whatever." She walked away and headed back to the ballroom.

The crowd didn't look as if anyone had any intention of leaving for hours yet and she scanned the sea of black and white, desperate to find the Phantom again. The only one she saw constantly was Louie. Everywhere she looked. It was like there were five of him and they all were watching her like a hawk. She watched him talking to Callie and Tom. Maybe Callie would distract him if Becky shared her plans with her. Nah, she couldn't tell even Callie what she was up to, she'd never understand.

The party continued and the hours slid by. Just as she had given up being able to escape without him, she looked up and Louie was gone. She walked around the ballroom and out into the hall, but no Louie. Laughter from the den caught her ear; maybe he was showing some of the guests the blueprints for the rest of the renovations. This would be her chance. She stood in the middle of the hall. She couldn't do it. Two hours ago, she never wanted someone as much as she wanted that masked man, but now that it was put up or shut up time she couldn't go through with it.

Her heart sank. Damn it. She couldn't do it. She didn't know him. He was a complete stranger and under that disguise he could be a complete toad. Looks didn't matter that much, but if he was a toad inside, well, she wasn't about to have her fantasy fulfilled only to find out she'd been an idiot. The door to the den started to open and she flew up the stairs. She didn't want to look at Louie or anyone else. She was shocked at herself. In all her years she'd never had an issue with physical relationships. Men were good for only a few things in life, and sometimes they were really good at one of them. She had no doubt Mr. Mystery would be good. But even she had scruples. Making out was one thing, going further with a complete stranger wasn't the smartest move to make in this day and age.

In front of the master bedroom door she pulled the key from the vase on the table in he hall and unlocked the door. Louie had told her that for some reason Mr. Mystery wasn't staying at the mansion while he was in town; he was checked into a hotel. Weird, but not her problem and right now she was thrilled to have the room to herself.

She didn't turn on the lights but shut the door behind her and rested her head against it. Her head snapped up when she heard the bathroom door open. She turned around ready to tell whoever was there that this suite was off limits when her breath caught.

Mr. Mystery stood outlined in the doorway. The light from the bathroom spilled into the bedroom giving him a surreal profile.

Chapter Seven

He seemed as surprised to see her as she was to see him. "Rebecca?"

"I'm sorry. Louie said you weren't staying here. I, uh, left my purse in here."

"Were you leaving?" he asked quietly. He reached out and clicked off the light in the bathroom, sending the entire suite into moonlit darkness

"No. I won't leave until all the guests leave." She swallowed as he moved across the room towards her.

"I was just on my way to meet you in the greenhouse. Is that where you were heading?" He stopped in front of her.

"The greenhouse? Oh, you mean for our, um, talk. No, actually I wasn't. There's a house full of guests and Louie, and, well I didn't think I should just walk away." Her words came out in a rush. She hated the way he affected her.

He reached out and tucked a tendril of hair behind her ear and she trembled. He must have put on fresh cologne; the musky scent brought the memory of his earlier kisses back to her.

"There're so many people here, I doubt anyone will miss us for some time."

Her eyes widened but she didn't step away. "Louie will. He'll wonder where I am. He'll actually probably be up here any minute looking for me."

He chuckled lightly. "I sent Louie on a little errand."

"What kind of errand?" Oh God he hadn't done something to Louie had he? Was he a madman? Was she alone in the dark with a psycho?

"Don't worry, he'll be back. There's a document I wanted to see, but he left it at his shop. He said he'd be back in about an hour. I figured that would buy us plenty of time to, well, be alone without worrying about him."

He slid his hand down her bare arm and took hers. He lifted it to his lips.

"Oh." Her voice came out like a sigh at his touch.

"But since you're here, we don't have to go outside in the cold. Will you sit with me?" Without waiting for her response he led her across the room to the old fashion fainting couch she'd placed by the large windows. When she first bought it, she'd flopped on it several times teasing Louie about it making her feel like royalty. Now as Mr. Mystery settled her back on it, she had a feeling that it had an entirely different purpose altogether.

He sat down next to her. She shifted over, and moved her gown so he wouldn't crush it. She'd never been nervous around a man before. It was time to stop being nervous around this one. She lifted her chin. "What kind of papers did Louie need to get? I thought everything was here in the den or in the safe."

"You don't need to think about that right now." He leaned forward and brushed his knuckles down her cheek. "Rebecca?"

She wet her lips and drew an unsteady breath. "Yes?"

"These past few hours, all I could think about was how it felt to hold you in my arms." He brushed his thumb across her bottom lip. "To kiss you and touch you. You have the most kissable mouth. Your lips are so full and warm. Just staring at them brings a man to his knees. I want to kiss you again," he whispered and moved closer.

Becky closed her eyes and tried to control her breathing. "What if I say no?" she whispered back

"If a lady says no, then it's no." His tongue flicked out, and he drew her lower lip into his mouth.

Oh God. Her insides melted like snow in late April. She was turning to mush in his arms. She'd never experienced a time when a man was able to seduce her so easily, make her want him so effortlessly. He kissed her hard and her head fell back against the lounger. He loomed over her and framed her face with his hands. He caressed her cheeks with his fingers as his mouth took full possession of hers. Her head spun. All thoughts of wrong or right flew out the window. His tongue thrust against hers and mimicked actions that made her squirm. Like a match to a flame, her body erupted in fire and she lifted her arms to wrap them around his neck pulling him closer. All thoughts of the party going on downstairs, of Louie, or the fact that she really didn't know this man fled from her head.

Her body had never responded like this before. Nothing that felt this right could be bad, could it? Or was that why it felt right? Because it was bad. She pressed against him and turned off her mind. She was through trying to figure this out.

When his hand slid down her chest to the low neckline of her gown she murmured her pleasure and shifted in such a way that left him with no misunderstanding that she welcomed his touch. She wanted his hands on her, ached for his mouth on her.

He laid his mouth against her cleavage and his hands slipped behind her to draw the zipper of her gown down.

He eased the sleeves over her arms to the crook of her elbows and paused. He slipped a few of the pins from her hair and it fell to her shoulders. Becky tossed her head letting more of it come free and tumble around her face. She felt wanton and sexy with the top of her gown falling down and her hair cascading. She could see his eyes behind the mask and they were dark with desire. She looked back at him boldly. She wanted him to see her, wanted what he was offering and she wanted him to know there was no hesitation on her part.

One of his fingers traced a path along the top of her cleavage and she swallowed hard. He pressed his mouth alongside her neck and she closed her eyes and let the pleasure wash over her. The mask didn't feel cold against her skin as she thought it might. It was made of rubber or some type of material that was very much like skin and he made his way along the side of her neck and down to the valley between her breasts. The strong corset, even with the gown unzipped, stayed in place covering most of her.

"You are a goddess," he murmured. He pulled the sleeves of her gown down further and her breasts sprang free. She drew a deep breath as the cold air chilled her and made her nipples pucker tighter.

She'd been told before that her breasts were

beautiful; unique. To her they were nothing spectacular. But for some reason, men reacted to them as if they were works of art. Mr. Mystery was no different. His mouth fell open. She felt a thrill of satisfaction. Behind that suave cool confidence lurked a red blooded male.

"I have traveled the world; seen all seven wonders and yet I am rendered speechless by your beauty." He inclined his head slightly as if to bow to her.

Becky's eyes widened. The man had a way with words.

"It would be sacrilegious for a mere man such as myself to even think about touching such perfection."

He wasn't going to touch her? Becky shifted restlessly. This was new. Most men couldn't wait to get their hands on them. Before that thought could settle, his thumb brushed across her nipple sending a heated bolt through her center. He massaged the aching point, rolling it in his fingers, gently pulling and applying the kind of pressure that bordered just this side of pain. When he lowered his head, she couldn't stop herself from letting her head fall back against the chaise once more.

"So sweet, so beautiful," he murmured. He reached for her other breast and brought it to a tingling ache, stroking and caressing as if memorizing every inch. "The petal of a rose isn't as soft as you."

He rubbed his cheek against the side of her breast, nuzzled it with his nose, and then pressed both together and buried his face in them. Becky wiggled with delight as he stroked and played with each of them in turn. He worshipped them one by one. She'd never had a man spend so much time and attention on them before. She longed for his mouth on her nipple, but it was almost a delightful form of torture the longer he didn't give her what she really wanted. She squirmed as he once more weighted her breast in his hand but didn't seem any closer to taking it in his mouth.

"Ahh my lady, there's no need to race toward satisfaction, we have all the time in the world." He tipped her breast up towards his mouth and Becky could hardly draw a steady breath. The waiting was agonizing and he lapped at her nipple with his tongue sending courses of pleasure zinging through her, but she wanted more, needed more. She whimpered as he applied the same treatment to the other one.

"I've been watching your breasts swell up against the neckline of your gown. The gown I picked out for you."

He traced a pattern around her nipple with his tongue while his other hand fondled her other breast. Finally, he latched his mouth onto her and drew her between his lips. Each pull of his mouth was echoed in the pull between her thighs. She felt the moisture there, and couldn't stop the cries of pleasure that escaped her. Ohhh he was good. He was so good. She groaned as he tongued her other breast, his hand never letting the first one feel bereft.

The music downstairs played out, growing louder as the song changed, but she barely noticed. They were secluded from everyone else. Cocooned in their own little world where nothing else mattered. She writhed under his skillful mouth and hands. Never had she felt so worshipped by someone, so skillfully caressed and adored. This wasn't the fumbling attentions of some men, or the eager, but disappointing lovemaking of others. This man was in a league all his own and she feared that no one else would ever be as good.

Her head spun as if she'd had too many glasses of wine. Need coiled deep inside her belly and she wondered if she was going to climax from his attentions to her breasts. It had never happened before, but she felt like it might now. She lifted her eyelids just far enough to be able to watch him bent over her. The mask disguised him from her. All she could see clearly was his mouth wrapped around her nipple.

She cried out as the tension in her grew tighter. She'd never lost control during sex. She'd always been in charge, calling all the shots, even if she let her lover think he was. This was so incredibly different. She was way out of her league here and not at all in control. Was that what was turning her on? Was that what was making her lose her mind so easily? He lifted his head and looked directly into her eyes. Then he pulled her to him and kissed her hard, his tongue mating with hers. She wrapped her arms around his neck, her bared breasts pressed hard into his crisp starched white shirt.

She felt his hand lift the skirt of her gown and then it was on her knee and her thigh, moving higher. He hesitated at the clasps that held her stockings but then moved past them to the inside of her thighs. She whimpered and arched into him as he found the lace edge of her panties. She was wet and he would know exactly how turned on she was and she didn't care. She wanted him to know. Wanted him to do something about it. He pushed the crotch of her panties aside and slid his fingers into her moisture. Becky shuddered at the first touch and then moaned as he stroked her and slid over her heated center. She struggled to continue kissing him, but found breathing more and more difficult. Finally she tore her mouth from his and buried it in his shoulder as he quickly brought her to a fast hard climax. The room spun out as her climax took her on a wild ride. She cried out as she came but he didn't even pause or try to quiet her. No one could hear them, with the music going on downstairs; someone would have to be right in the room with them to hear her. He murmured against her as she floated back to earth and the quivers in her body slowed down. How the hell had that happened so fast?

He gently eased her back against the chaise and she opened her eyes to look back at him. She felt like a heroine in a historical romance novel. But in the book the heroine would be horrified of what he'd just done to her; for Becky it was just the opposite, she wanted to jump him.

"Now I know why these were called fainting couches."

He didn't respond but stroked the hair back off her face. She still lay half undressed and he leaned forward once more to kiss her breasts. A noise from the other side of the room drew his attention and he whipped his head towards the door.

"Did you lock the door?" he asked.

Becky was still lost in the afterglow and shook her head trying to remember back that far even though it was probably only ten minutes ago or so.

He stood up and she grabbed his hand. "There's no one there." She whispered and dropped her feet to the floor to sit on the side of the lounge. He stopped and looked down at her. Her face was even with his waist and she reached out and slid her hands to his fly. She tipped her head up to look at him as she unbuttoned him and drew his zipper down.

"No, Rebecca." He argued, but she noticed that he didn't stop her. She smiled. No red-blooded male was going to stop a woman with her hands on his zipper.

She took both sides of his pants in her hands and eased them down slowly wanting to draw out the ordeal and make him squirm as he had made her. He sprang up in front of her and she reached for him. She wrapped her fingers around his velvet strength and his hands fell to her shoulders. He shuddered and his hands kneaded her skin. She slid her hand up and down the length of him, watching him stiffen even harder and swell in her palm. She rubbed her thumb across the tip of him. When she shifted, the moon behind her illuminated him and she noticed a large dark birthmark on the juncture where his leg joined his body. She traced her fingertips along it.

"Rebecca," he whispered. It wasn't a plea, not really. Or maybe it was, a plea for mercy or a plea for relief. She wasn't sure which, but he was definitely in her power now and it was a place she was much more comfortable with.

A loud thud against the door made her freeze. "What was that?" she asked harshly, staring up at him. Her hand still held his hard length, but as the sound came again she quickly released him.

The sudden, very vivid image of Louie catching her half naked with her hands around Mr. Mystery shot through her mind. What the hell was she doing? This wasn't good. Not at all. He'd never look at her the same way. He'd be disgusted with her. She couldn't live with that.

She moved so fast she tripped over her gown but she made it to the bathroom and shut the door behind her.

****

Louie couldn't move. What the hell happened? He was in heaven and then he was plunged into hell. With every ounce of strength he possessed he struggled to tuck his rock hard erection back into his tuxedo pants. He moved across the room to the bathroom door. "Rebecca?"

"What?" she whispered.

"I'll go downstairs first. You wait up here about ten

minutes and then come out. I promise no one will know we were in here together. Not even Louie."

She didn't answer.

"Ok?" He urged.

She opened the door a crack.

"I'm sorry. About," she glanced down at him, "well, you know."

Not as sorry as he was. It was wrong. He knew it was wrong, but damn it, right now he couldn't think clearly. All he could see was her dark head bending over him. He forced himself to sound in control even while inside he was ready to hit something. "Rebecca, I never intended for any of this to happen. I'm hoping you'll not hate me for the liberties I took."

She leaned forward and pressed a kiss to his mouth. "I promise next time, it won't be one sided." Then the bathroom door shut again.

Louie bowed his head and drew a deep shaky breath before leaving the room. Out in the hallway, slumped against the wall, was a guy he knew from town. He was obviously already sleeping off whatever he'd drank. Louie shook his head and walked past him.

"Thanks, buddy. I won't forget that," he promised and headed to one of the spare bedrooms at the far end of the hall. He tossed the costume inside the wardrobe and locked the door and pocketed the key. Mr. Mystery was done. From here on out he was Louie. This game was way too dangerous. He enjoyed being with her way too much tonight and that couldn't be. He was only supposed to have a dance with her and look how far things had gone. He closed his eyes as the image of her half naked, reclined in the moonlight, played over and over in his mind.

She was so beautiful. If he thought himself in love with her before it was nothing compared to now. He wanted to kiss her again, but not in disguise, as himself. The chemistry between them was undeniable and he couldn't believe it was only the mask turning her on.

He looked in the mirror and adjusted his pants as well as he could over his hardness.

He opened the door and headed back to the party. A few minutes later he watched as Becky came down the stairs. Her eyes flicked over the crowd. He knew who she was looking for and it made his blood rage with jealousy. It wasn't enough that she'd fooled around with Mr. Mystery, she wanted to find him again.

Her hair was perfectly done up again as was her makeup and only he could see the wild look in her eyes that told him what she'd been up to. He took her a glass of wine, anxious to see what she had to say for herself.

"Thanks," she took the wine from him. "I heard you had to run an errand for Mr. Mystery."

He pretended to be surprised. "What do you know about that?"

She drained half the glass before answering him. "He mentioned it to me." She looked around the room once more.

"If you're looking for Mr. Mystery, he left."

Her head snapped around so fast it was comical. "What do you mean?"

"He's gone. He said he had to catch a plane early tomorrow morning back to Europe. He took the file with him and left."

Her mouth dropped open. Louie reached out and pushed her chin up with his hand to close it.

She jerked from his hand. "Europe? He never mentioned anything to me."

He crossed his arms and tipped his head and stared at her until two spots of color appeared in her cheeks. "I guess he figured I'd tell you. Oh, he did actually tell me to give you a message."

"He did? What did he say?"

She was so pathetic at trying to hide her eagerness. He shrugged. "He said you were fantastic."

Her eyes widened and she seemed incapable of speaking. He bit down hard on his inner cheek to keep from laughing at her.

"He did?"

He nodded. "Yeah, he said the party was the best he's ever attended. You did a fantastic job."

She gave an unnatural laugh. "It was a great party wasn't it? I mean look at everyone that's still here and it's almost what? Three?"

Tom and Callie appeared as if on cue. Callie looked half asleep. "We're heading out. The girls are at my parent's tonight so we're going to head home."

Tom pressed a kiss to Callie's head and she smiled against him.

"If that's the case you two should have left hours ago." Becky hugged Callie.

"I think we still have some energy left or at least I do." Tom said.

Callie blushed but didn't disagree.

"Goodnight." Louie watched them go, wishing he was going to wake up next to Becky.

He groaned and she turned and glanced at him. "What's wrong?"

He touched his stomach. "Too many chicken puffs I think."

She smiled. "You always eat too much of that rich stuff; you'd think you'd learn by now."

Within an hour the house was empty. The band, the catering staff, everyone was gone. Louie walked to the stereo in the corner. The CD he'd played earlier was still there and with a press of a button, 'Lady in Red' played once more. Becky sat in a chair, pulling off her stiletto heels.

He held out his hand. "Could I have the last dance of the night?"

He could tell she didn't want to, but he knew she would, rather than hurt his feelings. "You have to promise not to step on my feet. They hurt so badly." She took his hand and let him lead her into the middle of the room.

He pulled her into his arms and held her close. Her head fell to his chest. "I thought you hated to dance," she murmured against him.

His hips moved against hers as they swayed to the music, hardly moving their feet at all. "I said I didn't like to dance with anyone but you."

He rested his head against hers. The song drifted over them and he sang along softly. She was practically asleep in his arms and he was in heaven. What a night. Tomorrow he'd wake up and think about it and wonder what the hell he was going to do. But right now everything was perfect.

****

Becky rolled over and stretched her arms over her

head. She opened her eyes and it took only a second for everything to come flooding back. The ball, the gazebo, the dancing. She glanced at the settee across the room and grinned. What a night! She shivered in the cool room and shoved her arms back under the thick comforter. At her feet she knew the lump had to be Google and she rubbed her foot up against him. How late was it? She turned to look at the bedside clock. Noon! Oh, oh. Was Louie up? They'd both spent the night at the mansion, but she had no doubt Louie had been up for hours, even though it had to have been four a.m. when he'd said goodnight and headed to the room down the hall.

He was probably extremely relieved that last night was behind them. He'd grumbled about it for weeks. She sat up, pulling the covers with her and leaned forward to run her fingers through the cat's grey fur. Google purred and lifted his head as if to tell her how much he loved her attentions. Leaning over, she planted a kiss on his furry head. "I guess I better get up and see what the Nerdman is up to."

When she came out of the shower a short time later, Louie was sitting in the overstuffed chair. A cup of coffee and some aspirin were on the table next to him. She tucked the towel tighter around her and headed straight for the coffee.

"Thanks." She tossed back the aspirin. "For these too."

"I saw you had a few glasses of champagne. You know that stuff always gives you a headache." His eyes drifted down her body.

Becky sat on the side of the settee, careful to keep her towel tucked properly. She took another sip of her coffee. "You shouldn't have let me sleep so late."

Louie shrugged. "Why?"

He looked rumpled today. The hated glasses were firmly in place, his hair was mussed and his clothes looked like he had pulled them out of the hamper. He didn't resemble the handsome man from last night who had waltzed her around the dance floor to 'Lady in Red'. She sighed and took a sip of coffee.

"What was that sigh for?"

"Nothing. I was remembering last night. It was a

great party wasn't it?"

He shrugged. "I guess. I'm just glad it's done and over with."

Becky shook her head. "You're no fun, you know that? Everyone raved about the house, the food, and the band. Mr. Mystery was so impressed with it all."

Louie nodded, his gaze firmly attached to the top of her towel.

Becky narrowed her eyes. "Are you even listening to me?"

His eyes snapped up. "Yeah, you said impressed by it. He also seemed quite impressed with you." He stood up. "Want something to eat?"

Becky glanced at the clock again. "I better not. We probably have a lot of clean up to do and I have to get home."

"There's no mess."

She frowned. "We went to bed at four and it was in shambles. You took care of everything already?"

"Yes, Princess. Your mother called.

Becky groaned. Her mother would be concerned if she called the house and her cell phone and couldn't find her. "Was she worried?"

"No, she figured you were with me. I told her you had too much to drink and were sleeping it off."

"Nice!" She rolled her eyes. "What else did you tell her?"

A soft look came into his eyes and he leaned down to touch her cheek with his hand. "I told her you were the belle of the ball and that everybody paled in comparison to you."

Warmth flooded her and she lifted her hand to cover his. "Thanks, Nerdman."

Louie pulled back and headed to the door. "I'm cooking omelets, get dressed."

She nodded but even after he left she didn't immediately jump up from the chair. She sipped her coffee and stared off into space thinking about the ball, meeting Mr. Mystery, their interlude. She closed her eyes. Thank God Louie didn't know about that.

****

With Becky finally gone, Louie tried his best to get

back to work. He had to get his mind off last night and what he'd done with Becky. "I'm the biggest heel in the world," he muttered to Google. The cat stretched in the sunlight pouring in the large windows of the dining room. Louie set the ladder up and grabbed the can of ceiling paint. "I can't believe I let things get so far out of hand. If she ever knew what I did." He shook his head and tried to stop dwelling on it. Unfortunately, while his mind insisted that he was the lowest form of life on the planet, his body continued to remember how it had felt to kiss her. Hearing Becky sigh in his arms with pleasure as his hands caressed her body was a dream he never even dared to have while he was asleep. He winced as paint from the roller sprayed him. He couldn't do this today. His mind wasn't on it; he was just going to make a mess.

Luckily Becky wasn't going to be around the rest of the day and since tomorrow was Monday, she'd be at work all day. So he had a good long time to get past this and figure out what to do next. If he came clean and admitted that he was Mr. Mystery, she'd never forgive him. Ever. He knew her too well. She'd feel all kinds of betrayed, and trust was a huge thing with Becky. He'd destroyed that trust the first time he hadn't confessed that he had bought the Ryan House.

He climbed back down the ladder and moved it a few more feet and then climbed back up again. He'd lived with his secret for so long, it was really hard now to think about coming clean. When he made his first million, it was unreal and didn't feel like it really happened. By the time he realized he was worth over five million he wasn't about to tell anyone. Who in Oakdale had that kind of money? And made it so easily? It was hard for him to understand and he didn't feel like he'd done anything more than been at the right place, at the right time. The software improvement he'd made was simply something he toyed around with. Never in his wildest imaginations did he think Bill Gates would have gotten wind of it. Speaking of which, Bill wanted some pictures from the ball. Maybe once he got the ceiling painted he'd go in and download all those from his camera and start sorting through them. Callie wanted some for the newspaper and he promised he'd send her five or six really good ones.

He wanted to see the ones of Becky in her gown. Hopefully, a few of them were so good he could give Margaret one. It was really too bad she hadn't wanted to come out to the mansion. He groaned thinking about Margaret. If Becky found out what he'd done last night, then so would her mother and he wouldn't be able to handle to disappointment that would come with that.

The best thing to do was to make Mr. Mystery disappear; have him never come around again. Better to let Becky think he was a lady's man and to tick her off a bit by not contacting her than have her find out the truth. But he had to keep Mr. Mystery away and somehow when the project here was done...what? What was his plan then? Already he'd become so attached to this place that leaving it behind was going to be tough. He wanted to live here. But did he? Without her? Every room, every color reminded him of Becky. How could he live here? He couldn't. So what was the point in all this? No one else in town wanted this house, or could afford to live here.

What was that old grade school expression, what tangled webs we weave...how true was that? He was in so deep now he had no clue how he was ever going to sort it all out.

Chapter Eight

"He didn't even stay at his own house? Don't you think that's weird?" Callie poured two more cups of coffee and set the pot back on the warming pad.

Becky shrugged. "I don't know. Louie and I are so used to the mess out there that it doesn't bother us to sleep there, but maybe he is one of those neat freaks who needs everything perfect."

"So after what happened, did you see him again? Did he even leave you a note or anything?"

Becky looked away. Maybe she shouldn't have told Callie about what happened, but when she got home and Callie called she couldn't help but tell her everything. She and Callie knew enough of each other's secrets that she knew it wouldn't go any further. "It wasn't as if we had some type of date or anything. It was just a 'moment', something unplanned."

"I think he had it all planned. I think he knew when he kissed you in the greenhouse that he was going to try to get you into bed."

Becky smiled. "I don't think so. You should have seen how surprised he was when I walked into the bedroom. Besides, I can't complain too much since I got the best part of the deal." She smirked and sipped her coffee.

"Look at how calm you take this." Callie shook her head. "I'd be thinking about it and dwelling on it and worrying over it and you're, well, thinking you got one over on him."

Becky nodded. "Well, sort of, I mean I would have reciprocated but we were interrupted and I wasn't about to let anyone see us, you know, like that. That would not be very classy."

"Speaking of classy, you looked beautiful last night. The real lady of the manor and all. That house fits you as if you were born to it."

Sadness washed over her. "Yeah, except its not mine and eventually I'll have to leave. I can't even imagine not ever going in there again."

Callie was unnaturally quiet as she drank her coffee.

Becky stared at her for several minutes. "What are you thinking?"

Callie shrugged. "Nothing, just about the ball and all."

Becky leaned forward. "No, you're not. That's your 'I want to say something but I shouldn't' look. Out with it."

Callie tipped her head and chewed her lip, another sign that Becky wouldn't like what she was going to say.

"What do you think Louie's going to say when he finds out what happened between you two?"

Becky narrowed her eyes, "You make it sound like what I did last night was wrong."

"I didn't say that. It's your life, not mine."

"And you would never have even let him kiss you, would you have, Cal? I didn't do anything more than teenagers do in a parked car. This is no big deal."

Her friend frowned, "I just want you to be careful. You don't know him at all. You have no idea what he's thinking about, what his future plans are for you."

"Future plans? With me? You know better. It doesn't matter who he is, I don't want a man in my life on a permanent basis. Ever." She snorted and stood up and set her cup in the sink. "You've known me all my life; you know that's not what I want. I can't believe you keep pushing that."

"I'm not pushing."

"Yeah, you are. Ever since you and Tom hooked back up, you think everyone needs a man in her life."

Callie was trying to make her feel guilty about last night and she refused to. It had been a wildly erotic encounter, one she could relive over and over in her mind with no problem. It had been hot. With him in the mask and her in her ball gown lying on the settee, it was unbelievable. In everyday life he was probably just as boring as the next guy. Probably kept his socks on when he made love with the lights off. With the mask off, he probably wouldn't even turn her on.

Last night was amazing, but it wasn't something that was going to be repeated. She wasn't going to let Callie or anyone else make her feel guilty about it. They were two consenting adults hurting no one.

Unbidden, Louie crept into her thoughts again. He wouldn't approve. Not that she'd give him the details of what happened, but if she were to see Mr. M. again she knew he'd have a fit. But then it wouldn't be the first time he didn't approve of who she was with. She was so lost in thought she jumped when Callie touched her shoulder.

"I just don't want to see him use you. We don't even know him. I worry, you know?"

Becky nodded, "I'm a big girl, Cal; I know how not to be used. Trust me; last night was no big deal."

Callie pinned her with that annoying mothering look. "What if all he wanted was what he got last night? You ok with that?"

"Why wouldn't I be? He didn't pull me into the shadows and make me," she lowered her voice remembering just in time that the girls were in the next room, 'you know' and then walk away. Come on, you know I don't want the same things out of life you do. I'm not into the whole white picket fence and commitment. I can't imagine being with one man the rest of my life. If we never see each other again or whatever, that's fine. No one was used; no one's complaining. Okay?"

Callie shrugged. "As you said, we're different. As long as you know what you're doing and you're happy, that's all that matters to me."

Becky decided it was time to just drop the whole conversation. "What time do you want to go look at wedding gowns?"

"Any night next week is good for me."

Becky nodded, "Let me talk to Louie and see what the plan is for the house. Maybe Tuesday will work."

Callie looked up as Becky grabbed her coat off the chair. "What's he going to say about last night?"

"Who?"

"Louie," she said.

"Don't start on me about this supposed crush." Becky's stomach clenched thinking about Louie. That day when she'd seen his expression in the mirror hadn't left her mind. "Louie needs to meet someone and he'll get over this supposed crush."

"He did meet someone at Christmas, remember?"

"Yeah, well, he didn't bring her to the ball, did he? Couldn't be too serious."

"So you wouldn't mind if I found him a date for the wedding?"

Becky shrugged. "Knock yourself out. Who knows? Maybe I'll come with Mr. Mystery." Why she tossed that out there she had no idea, except that Callie was starting to get on her nerves.

Callie narrowed her eyes. "Maybe Mr. Mystery keeps his identity a secret because he's got a past. Ever think of that?"

Becky rolled her eyes. "We all have a past Callie, even you."

She regretted the words as soon as she said them. Callie's blue eyes widened first with shock and then pain. Damn. Now she'd hurt her. "You know what I mean; I didn't mean it like it sounded."

For several seconds they stared at one another. Callie shoved her hands in her jeans pocket. "You don't always think before you say things. Sometimes you don't think before you do things either; that's what concerns me."

Becky lifted her chin. "Let me worry about me. You have a wedding to plan and a new life with Tom. I'll call you tomorrow."

She pushed the door open and walked down the porch to her car without looking back. Callie meant well, she knew that, but she already had one mother she didn't need another one. Besides, Callie would never understand that her beliefs weren't the same as Becky's. What happened last night with Mr. Mystery would never happen to Callie. Well, not the Callie today. At one time, Callie Anderson hadn't been above indulging in some hot and heavy scenes herself and maybe that's what Becky should have reminded her of. Actually, if Callie hadn't always done the right thing and for once had let her emotions guide her, she wouldn't have broken Tom's heart all those years ago.

Damn. It wasn't Callie's fault. She cared about her. She was her best friend, practically her sister, and now she'd said nasty things to her. *I'm so nasty to everyone, why do they put up with me? Louie came to mind again. I know how he feels about me, or how he thinks he feels about me and yet I danced with him last night.*

Am I jealous of them? Am I jealous because Callie is finally going to be with the man she has loved all these years and they are going to have a life together? One that I won't be a major part of. They already spent all their time together, time that used to be spent with me. Is that what's bugging me?

The thought of marriage and children had always horrified her, still did, so that couldn't be it. Maybe it was envy that Tom loved Callie and had never stopped loving her. He was solid in his devotion. She knew in her heart that Tom would stand by Callie until they both died.

But men like him are one in a million. She knew far too many men who left when things got rough and it was the woman who had to spend the rest of her life sacrificing and struggling. No thank you. She was much more content in charge of her own life.

A smile teased her lips as she thought of Mr. Mystery looming over her in the semidarkness last night. She'd take a night like that over the white picket fence any day of the week.

****

Becky bounded up the porch steps. She punched in the security code and pushed the heavy door open. "Louie?" She hollered and closed the door.

"Louie!" His car was parked outside; she knew he was here. Was he upstairs or in the den? She looked at the huge clock in the foyer. Almost ten. Good, she had all day to work on the dining room with him. She followed the scent of fresh coffee down the hall, but when he wasn't in the kitchen she kept going to the den.

He was hunched over his laptop typing furiously. His hair was mussed like he'd been raking his hands through it in frustration. His heavy glasses were sliding down his nose and his fingers flew across the keys in that rhythm she recognized as code. She leaned against the door jam and crossed her arms over her chest. "Hey, you look like crap."

He didn't look up or stop typing. "Thanks Princess,

I'll remember that."

"You look like you were up all night." She walked into the den and flopped into the oversized worn leather chair.

"Most of it."

"Why?"

He ignored her and she knew him well enough to know to stop talking when he was in the "zone". After a few minutes he sat back, yanked off his glasses, and rubbed his eyes. He stretched back and his t-shirt pulled tight over his chest. Wow. When did his chest get so broad? Was he working out somewhere? He didn't look as skinny as he did a few months ago. Maybe it was the heavy lifting he'd been doing around here. Either way, he was looking pretty fit. Even tired and rumpled, he looked endearing, almost cute even.

He opened his eyes and met her stare with a frown. "Why are you so perky today?"

"No reason." She shrugged looking away. "I can't wait to see the drapes and get them hung."

"Yeah, well I don't know if that'll happen today." He shifted forward again and stared at his screen. "I can't get the program for the home security system to work. It was doing some really bizarre things last night."

Becky frowned, "Did you figure it out?"

"Somehow I've got those two systems crossed or rigged weird. I don't know what's up. Don't go in the safe room, I can't guarantee I can get the door to open once it's closed."

She raised one eyebrow. "That room is spooky; I don't go in there anyway." She stood up and rubbed her hands down her thigh. "Where're the curtains?"

He pushed away from the desk and stretched again. "I laid them on the dining room table."

Her eyes skimmed down his flat stomach, noting narrow hips and hard thighs beneath his worn jeans. Her gaze drifted to the bulge behind his zipper. Why was she so aware of him all of a sudden? She'd been around Louie's body her whole life and had barely given it a glance; all of a sudden this morning she was wondering things she shouldn't be wondering. How would Louie be in bed? Attentive? Oh, definitely. He was such a perfectionist he'd probably be just as thorough as a lover. Her face warmed at the thought.

Lifting her eyes, she met his and the desire he didn't try to hide was enough to make her breath catch. She couldn't seem to look away either. What the hell was happening? A log crackled in the fireplace and the moment was gone. "I, um, want to see the color of the, uh, material." She spun on her heel and headed to the door.

He didn't follow her. "Did you eat yet?"

She looked back. "Why?" She watched with apprehension while he moved across the room and stopped in front of her.

"I didn't eat any dinner last night and I'm starved."

She nodded and moved out into the hall. That was probably her problem; she was probably lightheaded from not eating breakfast. That's why she was thinking crazy thoughts about Louie and imagining something happening between them. "That sounds good. Did we finally finish all the leftovers from the party?"

"I ended up tossing the rest of them."

"It doesn't seem possible it was a week ago, does it?"

"I'm glad the stupid thing is done and over with so we can focus on the renovations again," he muttered as they walked into the kitchen.

"It wasn't stupid, it was fun."

"It was an enormous waste of time and money."

"You're an old crotchety thing today, aren't you? I think you're under too much stress. Maybe you need to find a way to relieve some of it."

She started to walk past him, but he grabbed her arm. "Are you volunteering to help me with that, Princess?"

She tugged her arm out of his hold and lifted her hand to rest it against his cheek. "Trust me, honey, you couldn't handle it."

His expression clouded over. What was wrong with him? He couldn't even take a joke today. Maybe she shouldn't stay out here. It wasn't like she had nothing else to do on her Saturday. Ok, she didn't, but he didn't need to know that. Since this project started she'd literally set aside every week to be out here and hated the thought of wasting it anywhere else. She walked to the refrigerator and grabbed the creamer. Behind her she heard him leave.

Whatever. She shut the refrigerator and poured herself a cup of coffee. There were some leftover cookies in a container on the counter and she took a handful.

In the dining room, she set her coffee down and picked up the drapes. She stroked the velvety material. The color was absolutely perfect. Holding them up, she moved across the room to the wall. Stunning. Exactly what she wanted them to be. She swung her gaze to the bank of windows, trying to imagine them hanging there. A few seconds later she was out in the hall and bringing the ladder to the dining room. She didn't need Louie to hang them, she could do this. How tough could it be? The rods were already in place. She'd taken them down and cleaned them, but the original rods were so unique she and Louie had decided to keep them.

She carried the ladder to one side of the large window. With the drape over her arm she climbed up. She was too short. By only an inch or so. If she stood up on the top step maybe, but that was really not a smart move. Still, if she was really careful...

"What the hell are you doing?"

She jumped at his voice and lost her balance. Blindly, she reached out trying to grab something to stop her fall, but she knew it was no use. She was going down and it was a long way to the dining room floor.

"Crap!" she cried out, but instead of hitting solid wood floor she landed on Louie with an *oomph*. The impact knocked him to the floor and she ended up in his lap.

Becky took several deep breaths and opened her eyes. She couldn't believe she hadn't hit the ground. She had landed hard on Louie, though. It must have knocked the wind out of him. She twisted in his lap to peer back at him. "Did I hurt you?"

He looked back at her and shook his head, seeming as stunned as she was that neither of them had broken their necks.

"What the hell did you yell at me for?" she asked.

He opened his mouth as if to say something then clamped it shut. Tenderness flooded his eyes and she knew he'd been terrified she was going to hurt herself. Poor guy. His hand came up to cup the back of her head and stroke her hair. She started to smile and tell him she was ok, but then his gaze moved to her mouth. Oh no, what's he thinking? He's not going to, is he? Her heart accelerated, but she couldn't seem to make herself say anything.

Maybe the sudden impact of their fall had scrambled his brains. His gaze lifted to hers. Had his eyes always been that deep of a green? He leaned slowly towards her and she found herself meeting him halfway. His hand skimmed up her back and she tipped her head as their lips hovered Their lips hovered a mere hairsbreadth apart for the most incredibly long moment of her life.

When Louie's mouth met hers, her eyelids fluttered closed. She slid her hand up to wrap around his neck and kissed him back. His lips were warm and sweet and he tasted of coffee. He kissed her as if he was worshipping her lips, paying homage to them with his own. His fingers trailed over her cheek and he cupped her face in his palm. Their tongues touched, and a knot formed in her throat at the dreamy intimacy of the kiss. He tangled his hand into her hair and pulled her closer to deepen the kiss. A sigh of pleasure escaped her, and a really weird feeling washed over her. It was almost as if she'd kissed him before, like this. But that was impossible. She'd never kissed Louie, but it felt natural...not at all new or awkward.

Shifting so her breasts pressed into his chest, she raised both arms and linked them around his neck. Under her bottom she could feel his erection pressing into her and she moaned. Louie slowed the kiss, pulling back slightly and dropping the softest whispers of kisses on her lips, the side of her mouth, her cheek, and her chin. She arched her neck, loving the way tingles raced up her spine as his mouth fell to her throat. She didn't think she'd ever been kissed quite so perfectly. A burning need to roll to the floor and have him cover her roared up inside her. Somehow, she knew Louie was full of passion inside, but was holding it in check. What would it be like to help him unleash the tiger within?

His mouth caressed her ear and down her neck. Then he did what he never should have done.

He spoke.
"Beck?" he whispered.

Chapter Nine

Her eyes flew open. It was like someone had tossed cold water on her. What the hell was she doing? This was Louie, her nerdy best friend. This was wrong in so many ways. She couldn't look him in the eye as she scrambled off his lap and stood up. Smoothing her hair back she laughed and it sounded really unnatural, even to her own ears. "Ok, ok, that's good enough for a 'thanks for saving my life' kiss. I think these drapes can wait until the contractors are back. I'll take a peek at them when you're up—I mean when they're up," she babbled as she picked up the curtains that had fallen. Without looking back she walked over to the table and laid the drapes with the rest of them.

Her heart was racing, her palms were damp, and even knowing how wrong it had been to kiss him, her stomach was a whirl of desire, longing for more of what they'd been doing. She heard Louie leave the room and she closed her eyes and pressed her hands against the wooden table.

What the hell had she done? The one person in the world she'd never want to hurt was Louie. She knew he wanted her; lately, he'd even stopped hiding that fact from her. She never should have let that happen. She wasn't a tease and she wasn't about to let him think there was anything between them, when there definitely wasn't. Was there? What was up with that? She had to admit that kiss had her going from zero to hot pretty quick. There weren't many men who could turn her on that fast.

Unbidden, thoughts of Mr. Mystery crept into her mind. It had been the same with him, as if she'd known him forever. But with Louie, she had known him forever, just not on that level. She and Louie had never kissed, well, not like that. She was sure she'd kissed him before, small pecks on the cheek even a light goodnight kiss on the mouth but never like that.

Two weeks ago it had taken a man in disguise to turn her on; and yet today her nerdy friend Louie was making her want him with a simple kiss?

Something wasn't right. Something was definitely wrong here. They'd been working together for months, side by side, all alone. She had never felt any of this before.

The feel of his mouth on hers crept back to her thoughts and she touched her lips with her fingertips. Who'd have thought the nerd could kiss so well? She frowned. He must have practiced on someone. Probably that rocket scientist geek girl over New Year's. No matter how much he denied it, maybe something did happen in Florida.

She drew a deep, steadying breath. The important thing now was to make sure that Louie was under no false pretenses that the kiss meant anything. The fall had shocked them both and they kissed. That's all. No big deal. They were mature adults; it happened. No need to dwell on it. She'd just get back to work and act like nothing happened.

****

Louie slammed the back door shut with his foot. He set the bucket of wood he'd carried inside down and yanked off his boots. The cold air he had hoped would clear his head, not to mention the rest of him, had sort of worked. At least he wasn't as worked up as he been when he walked out of the dining room. He was an idiot. What was he thinking kissing her like that? Somehow in that split second when he saw her going off that ladder, he'd made the decision that if she didn't break her neck and die right in front of him, he was going to tell her he loved her. It was almost like a deal he made; don't let her get hurt and I promise I'll come clean. Stupid fool. Seeing her in his lap and that she was ok made him kiss her; kissing her once made him forget he had no right to keep on kissing her. In some weird way, once his lips met hers again he forgot that he hadn't kissed Becky before, Mr. Mystery had. Louie had no right to kiss her. Then for her to tell him it had been a kiss out of gratitude; well, he might have deserved it, but it still stung his pride.

The one thing he didn't want from Becky Richardson was pity. He picked up the bucket of wood and carried it to the den. Her coat still hung on the coat tree, so any hope he had that she'd left and he didn't have to face her today was gone. In fact she was sitting on the loveseat in the den. He walked past her to the fire and set the bucket on the hearth. Opening the grate he tossed a few more logs in.

"Have you heard from Mr. M, since the ball?" she asked out of nowhere.

He glanced at her over his shoulder and shook his head. Poking the fire into position, he reset the screen in front of it and turned to face her.

"I would have thought you'd have heard from him before I would."

She narrowed her eyes as he stared down at her. "Why? All we did was dance."

He lifted one eyebrow. Let her wonder how much he knows. "I understood you made quite an impression on him."

She smiled, but it didn't quite meet her eyes. "I make an impression on most men."

"So I've heard." Good. That was more like something he'd normally say to her. Get this friendship back to where it's supposed to be. He struggled not to stare at her breasts, but they were showcased to perfection under her sweater. It was hard enough in the past not to stare, but now that he knew not only what they looked like without that sweater, but also how they felt and how they tasted, it was damn impossible to keep his eyes off her. He darted his gaze back to her face and then away again.

"Did you hear what I just said?"

Oops. Nope, his mind was a long way from what she was saying. "No, I'm sorry, I didn't. I was thinking about that, uh, problem with the wiring."

She tipped her head and studied him as if she didn't believe him, but she didn't comment. "I said I would think he would have contacted you to let you know when he's coming back again to check on the renovations."

Louie walked over to the desk and sat in the leather chair once more. "He told me when he left that he trusted us to handle it. Frankly, I don't get the impression he even cares. He wants the project done so he can dump the place."

Now why had he said that? To get her reaction? He looked up at her without lifting his head. She was staring into the fire. What was she thinking? He looked at her tucked into the corner of the loveseat. Was there anyone in the world more beautiful than her? What would it be like to be with her? Really be with her and hold her in his arms in front of the fire? To turn her towards him and kiss her and slowly peel her clothes off and make love to her while the flames flickered...

She stood up so fast he jumped. "I think I'm going to go the mall. I need some things for spring."

He nodded. "Ok."

She headed to the door and he wondered if he should say anything about what happened earlier. He panicked. What if she wasn't coming back the whole weekend? He might not see her for another week. His chest constricted. "Would you mind picking something up for me?"

She turned to look at him. "What?"

Think, think, think he prodded his brain. "Um, the pet store there has the only brand of food that Google will eat. Could you get me a bag? I'm almost out."

She twisted her lips and her brow furrowed. "That cat eats mice, chipmunks and anything else that moves. You're telling me you only get his cat food at that fancy pet store at the mall?"

"It had the right nutrients he requires."

She rolled her eyes. "Yeah, sure, fine."

He stood up and reached for his wallet and sifted through the bills. "I don't have any change."

She shook her head. "I got it Nerdman, go back to your drawings."

"Will you bring it back out here tonight?"

"You need it tonight?"

"Do you mind?"

"I'll tell you what, if I can't get back out here, I'll leave it at Mom's. You can run by there and get it."

"Why? What are you going to do tonight?"

She pinned him with her gaze and lifted her head. "I don't know yet, but I don't like to be tied down, remember.

If plans come up, I want to be free. So if I'm not coming back and you need it tonight, you'll have to drive over to my mother's and pick it up. See you later. Good luck with that wiring."

****

"Two burgers with the works, basket of fries and a pitcher of beer," Louie gave the waitress the order and she walked away. He looked up at Tom and smirked. "Buddy, I hate to tell you this but you look like you've been through hell."

Tom nodded. "Five females." He held up his hand. "Five; Callie, the three girls, and Becky."

Louie's heart thudded all over the place at the sound of her name. Ever since the 'episode' in the mansion two weeks ago, she'd been avoiding him. No phone calls, no visits. Nothing. The only conversation they'd even had was about the drapes and that had been his attempt to get her back to the project by telling her they were hanging. Her only response had been that she'd get out to see them 'sometime'. He picked up the beer the waitress set in front of him. "Lucky you. How goes the wedding preparations?"

"Don't ask me, I just nod and say 'whatever you want, honey'."

"Well I've heard that's the easiest way to do it."

"To be honest?" Tom lifted his beer. "I never thought I'd have the chance to have Callie as my wife and I'd marry her naked in a blizzard if she wanted me to."

"I know exactly what you're saying," he muttered. "You're a lucky guy. Life works out every once in a while doesn't it?"

"Yeah."

"I'm tired of talking about the wedding. Tell me about the renovations. The place looked awesome the night of the ball, I meant to tell you."

"It's coming along. Slowly, but it's not like there's any big rush."

Tom looked down at his drink and Louie had this weird feeling something was going on. "We've been friends since, what, sixth grade, seventh?"

Oh, oh, the old 'we've been friends a long time conversation' which usually leads to someone thinking they have the right to ask questions. "Yeah, I think so, somewhere in there, but hey, who keeps track right?"

"Right. I was searching through the records out at the town hall looking for some information on my folks' place. "

Louie's stomach twisted into the biggest knot he'd ever had. "I came across something really weird about the Ryan House."

He couldn't breathe. Here it was. His secret was out. How did he ever think in a town this small he was never going to be found out? "I wasn't really being nosy or anything, but well, you know, they are public records and all."

Louie took a long drink of his beer. A sort of calm washed over him.

"It's not my business, I know."

He looked at Tom. He could trust him. He knew if he told Tom the truth and asked him to keep to himself he wouldn't tell Callie. He couldn't tell Callie; as a newspaper reporter she would love to scoop this story. He couldn't blame her; it was a pretty huge story.

"What are you going to do with the information you uncovered?"

Tom shrugged. "I'm not going to do a thing with it, but it sure would be nice to know what's going on."

"If I told you I had my reasons for no one knowing would you respect that?"

His friend nodded. "I just don't know how you hid it all this time. It's been what, six months? Seven? Callie searched all over for information on the owner of the Ryan House."

"I bought it under a company name. Its one I own that no one would associate me with."

Tom pulled the paper out of his coat pocket. "This was really illegal, but I figured if you worked that hard to keep it a secret you had your reasons. This was the only thing in the file with your name on it."

Louie reached for the paper. "You took this from the file?" He glanced around to make sure no one was watching. He scanned it. It wasn't a significant piece of paper, nothing anyone would ever need or miss. Someone in his lawyer's office had screwed up and put his name on it. "Thanks." He shoved it in his pocket.

"Which leads me to my real question...if you are the owner of the Ryan House, then who is the masked man who came to the ball?"

Louie couldn't help the flush that crept over his face at Tom's question. His mind whirled as he tried to conjure something up, but what was the point? "Mr. Mystery at your service." He lifted his mug of beer, finished it and poured another.

Tom sat back against the booth. "That explains so much, and yet so little. You really are in pretty deep aren't you?"

"With lies? Oh yeah. So deep now there's no turning back." He shrugged and leaned back against the booth.

"I heard something else too that was very interesting," Tom looked like the cat that had swallowed the canary.

"What?"

"Callie sort of confided in me that Becky didn't just dance the waltz with Mr. Mystery." Tom did air quotes with his fingers around Mr. Mystery and smirked. "But that she did a little private dirty dancing with him, too, if you get my drift, and now since I know that Mr. Mystery isn't such a mystery after all, my head is conjuring up all sorts of interesting situations."

Louie groaned and raked his hand through his hair. "Yeah, that was another bright move on my part. Originally the idea for the masked ball was just for me to be able to dance with her, have her see me as someone else. It got way out of hand." He pinned Tom with a look. "What did she tell Callie? Exactly."

Tom laughed and poured himself another beer. "Now you want to know if you were any good or not."

"Hell yeah, wouldn't you?"

His friend shook his head. "I wouldn't even dare to dream up the type of situation you're in. But yeah, if I had an inside ear to know what Callie thinks of me in that department, I'd want to know."

Louie leaned forward. "And?"

"All I know is that Becky told Callie it was hot."

Louie smirked and shifted in his seat as his jeans tightened with the memory. "It was hot."

"So now what?"

The smile disappeared from his face as despair settled over him. "Now nothing. I let her think Mr. Mystery went back to Europe and that's it. She'll never find out it was me."

He drained his beer. Working next to her day in and day out was really straining him. It was all he could do most days not to tell her who he really was and reach out for her. The kiss in the dining room two weeks ago still haunted him. She could have found out that day so easily. If things had gone any further, she might have clued in that it was the same guy she was kissing. Somehow he thought that holding her that one time, kissing her, touching her, was going to be enough to satisfy him. How stupid he'd been. He wanted her before; now he craved her like oxygen.

"Hey, where'd you go?" Tom asked.

"I'm in a hell of a mess."

"Yeah." His buddy agreed.

"What would you..." 'Lady In Red' played on his cell phone and he met Tom's knowing eyes. His heart rate hit the roof as he flipped it open. "Hey."

Hopefully he sounded cool and collected, not as eager to talk to her as he was to draw his next breath.

"Nerdman, I need you!" Becky yelled into the phone

He held it away from his ear with a wince. "Be still my heart."

"Stop it, this is serious. I'm out at the house..."

"Why are you out there?" He looked at Tom across the table and shrugged his shoulders. Becky hadn't said she was going out there. She was supposed to be at a bridal show with Callie looking at some fancy wedding favors.

"I wanted to show Callie the drapes. The security system has the doors locked up and we can't seem to get out. Can you come?"

I do every night in my dreams. Louie groaned. "I'll be right there."

He snapped the phone shut. "Damsels in distress. Guess we'll take the burgers to go."

He signaled to their waitress and in a few minutes they were heading to his car. "Want to follow me out there? You can pick up your girls and I'll deal with mine."

Tom shrugged into his coat. "Somehow I think I'll have it easier with four than you will with one."

"You got that right."

****

"Aunt Becky?"

Becky turned from the window to smile at Jenna.

"Do you ever pretend you're a princess living in a castle when you're out here?"

Becky smiled and looked around the newly finished guest room. It was painted in muted yellows and blues with white accents. It was a very feminine room, and she'd done it that way on purpose...wanting a contrast to the rich, almost masculine feel the master suite had. She could easily imagine a little girl in this room, or a teenage girl on the cusp of becoming a young woman. Callie's youngest daughter, Emma, sat in the middle of the huge canopy bed, looking a bit like a princess herself.

Becky climbed up beside her and stretched out. "Sometimes I close my eyes and pretend the house is mine."

Emma giggled and scooted up to lay next to her on the massive pillows. "Do you pretend that your husband is a handsome prince?"

Becky chewed her lip. She never fantasized about a husband, but decided at seven, Emma didn't need to know about that. "I pretend that a handsome prince climbs my balcony over there." She leaned up on one elbow and Emma glanced over to the closed doors. It was pitch black outside, and when she'd looked the last time, it had been snowing hard. She hoped Louie would get here soon so she could get home before it got worse.

"What do you do when he comes in through the balcony?" Emma asked, leaning over and toying with Becky's dark hair.

Becky cupped the little girl's cheek. "We dance." She smiled into her big blue eyes, seeing Callie in them.

"Mama says you and a prince danced the night of the party. She said you looked beautiful."

Becky smiled, remembering the way she'd waltzed with Mr. M. That and her dance with Louie were her two favorite dances of the whole night. "He's not a real prince;

he was dressed up like one."

"He must be rich to own a house like this. Is he rich, Aunt Becky?" Emma asked.

"He'd have to be to catch Aunt Becky's eye."

Becky's gaze flew to the doorway. Warmth washed over her at the sight of Louie lounging there watching her and Emma. In a bizarre flash it felt like he was the dad, and she was the mom and Emma was theirs. He walked into the room, keeping his eyes on her the whole time.

Emma jumped up. Louie caught her as she leapt from the bed into his arms. "Uncle Louie! Did you come to rescue us like real princesses?"

"No, sweetheart only princes can rescue princesses. I'm just an ugly old toad."

"I read that if the princess kisses the toad, he turns into a prince." Emma wrapped her arms around Louie's neck and looked up at him with all the seriousness of a seven year old little girl who still believed in fairy tales.

Becky watched as Louie turned his cheek towards her. "Go ahead try it, but don't say I didn't warn you."

Emma carefully pressed her lips to his cheek and kissed him, then pulled back to watch him. Louie held her tight in his arms and stumbled as if something was happening to him. "Oh, oh. Something weird is going on, Em. Oh no! What's happening to me?"

Emma giggled. Louie grinned at Becky. She couldn't help but smile at his antics. He was such a good guy. He deserved to have kids like this.

The idea of Louie having kids caused her heart to twist. Having kids meant he'd be married to someone else, someone who he'd look at like he'd always looked at her. She dropped her gaze and shifted to sit on the edge of the bed.

"Well, Auntie Becky, did I turn into a handsome prince?" he asked shifting Emma in his arms.

Without looking at him, she slipped off the bed. "Yep, Prince Geek." She stood next to him. "Did you fix the security system?"

"Yeah," he looked down at her and set Emma on her feet. The little girl scampered out of the room. "Sorry about that, but you didn't tell me you were coming out here tonight. You haven't been out here in a couple of weeks."

Warmth flooded her cheeks. "I've been busy."

"I hung the drapes."

He looked like he'd done something wrong and she felt guilty for making him feel that way. It wasn't him. It was her. She was still confused by her reaction to the unexpected kiss and decided it was best to put some distance between them.

"I saw them. They look great."

"Beck?"

Becky shook her head and walked out of the room. She wasn't ready to talk to him about what she was feeling. It was better to just ignore the situation; it would go away eventually.

Tom and Callie stood in the foyer and both looked up as she came down the stairs with Louie behind her.

"We're going to get going, it's getting bad out." Callie said.

Tom nodded and held out Emma's coat for her to put on. When he kneeled and zipped it up for her, Callie smile at the two of them. Becky looked away, suddenly tired of seeing how happy everyone else was.

"Jenna, Amber?" Callie called out to the kitchen. The two older girls came out with their coats already on.

"Drive safe," Becky cautioned as Tom hustled them out the door.

Callie turned back. "Aren't you coming?"

"Yeah, in a minute, go ahead with Tom. I'll drive your car home later."

"Ride home with Louie. My car can stay out here until I can get it." Callie hugged Becky and tucked her head into her chest as she headed out. The wind hit Becky in the face as she watched them climb into the SUV. She waved as they beeped and drove away. She shut the heavy door against the storm.

In the hall, she crossed her arms over her chest and wondered where Louie went. Hearing him on the phone, she wandered into the den. The new furniture they'd bought had arrived and although she'd seen it earlier with Callie, it struck her again how perfect it fit the room. Louie sat behind the new desk talking on the phone. She walked into the room and sank into the new leather chairs. Turning sideways, she draped her legs over the arm and snuggled in. The fire in the fireplace had the room warmed up nice; she closed her eyes and let the soothing sounds of the crackling logs relax her. She realized suddenly that he was talking to her mother.

"Have no fear, Maggie my love; I'll take care of her."

Becky opened her eyes and he winked at her.

"Yes ma'am I will do that. Now you stay inside and take care of that cold of yours. Goodnight."

He set the cordless phone down and linked his hands behind the back of his head and stared at her. "Your mother is worried about you driving in this weather."

Becky shrugged. "Its just snow. No big deal." Inside she was already dreading the drive home, but she was just too comfortable to get up and head out yet.

Louie leaned back further in the chair and propped his feet up on the desk. "I think I like this new furniture."

He looked all the world as if he was made to sit behind that desk, like he'd been sitting in this room for years. It fit him. Odd since she always pictured him with a computer in front of him, but his laptop was closed and off to the corner of the massive desk.

"When are you going to head home?" she asked and picked at her chipped nail.

"I don't know. Nothing much to do at home. I might just stay here for the night. Why go out in that?"

"Yeah."

Several seconds went by and the silence in the room was uncomfortable. Becky wondered if he was drifting off to sleep.

She wet her lips. "So, have you heard from Mr. M.?"

He opened his eyes and pinned her with his gaze. "Nope.

She nodded and picked again at her nail. "Oh."

"What's that mean?"

"Nothing, I was just making conversation."

"Uh, huh." He closed his eyes again.

"Where'd you and Tom go today?"

Louie shrugged. "I set up the wireless Internet he wanted at the house and then we grabbed some late lunch." His eyes opened. "Which reminds me, I think I left the burgers in the car."

"Callie loved the dining room and the guest room."

"That's good. How was the bridal show or whatever it was?"

Becky shrugged and brushed the chipped polish off her jeans. "It was ok, nothing exciting. We found some favors she liked."

"I hope not those candies wrapped in netting." He made a face.

Becky laughed. "No, not those. Do we have wine in the kitchen?" She swung her legs down and stood up.

Louie dropped his feet and stood too. The wind blew hard and the windows shook. "I'll get the wine. Why don't you sit on the couch closer to the fire?"

Becky looked out the window again. She should leave, but then like Louie said, why? There was nothing at home. Her mother didn't feel good; she wasn't going to go over there.

By the time Louie returned she was settled into the deep corner of the leather couch. She'd pulled the light afghan over her lap. He set a tray of cheese and crackers on the side table and handed her a glass of red wine.

He looked at the couch and she swung her legs down. "There's room."

She held her glass out to clink his. "To stormy nights, a warm fire, and good friends."

He tapped her glass and took a drink. He stretched his legs out full length and Becky shifted on the couch. Louie reached out and lifted both her feet into his lap with his free hand.

She smiled. "I pity the fools who aren't us tonight." She took a long drink of her wine and watched the fire. "Do you think Tom and Callie got home ok?"

Louie looked over at her. "Yeah, Tom's a good driver. It wasn't as bad out a half hour ago as it is now."

"Louie?" She leaned her head back against the couch and looked at him from under her lashes.

He turned his head to her. "What?"

"Do you miss your folks?"

He frowned. "I don't miss them like I want them living with me or anything, but I miss being able to pop over for coffee with my Dad or bumping into Mom in the grocery store. Yeah, it's kind of weird that they don't live here anymore."

"I couldn't imagine if Ma moved somewhere."

"Your mother will never move. You and this town are her life."

"True. You'd think she'd want to travel. I can't tell you how many times I've offered to buy her a ticket to anywhere she wants to go."

Louie's hand slipped under the blanket and cupped the arch of her foot. She moaned as he massaged her instep.

"Hmmm, that's nice." She sipped some more wine.

"She doesn't want to go anywhere alone." He leaned forward and set his glass on the floor and then picked up her other foot and treated it to the same massage.

He ran his hand along the bottom of her foot and rubbed the tired muscles. Pleasure washed over her. "That's amazing," she muttered.

He laughed and slid his hand along her calf, kneading the muscles. "You shouldn't wear heels all the time; it's bad for you."

"Hmm. I wish she'd have met someone years ago."

"Who? Margaret?"

"Yeah."

"Why years ago? Why not now? She's not old, you know."

Becky bit her bottom lip as his magical fingers crept along her arch and massaged every place that ached. She curled her toes into his thigh.

"I mean when she was younger. She could have enjoyed her life."

"Maybe she did enjoy her life. You're her life. But she could meet someone now, too."

"And do what?"

Louie laughed, "You think only young people enjoy each other? Physically, I mean?"

Becky was torn between focusing on the pleasure of his foot massage and the fact that she could feel his erection where her ankle rested. The kiss they'd shared sprang to mind and she couldn't help but remember the chemistry that had exploded. Louie certainly knew how to kiss; there was no doubt of that. She swallowed hard and glanced at his mouth while he was looking into the fire.

He did have firm lips didn't he? And that little mole next to his mouth, why hadn't she really noticed that before? It was kind of sexy looking.

"I don't think only the young enjoy sex, if that's what you mean, but she would have had years and years to enjoy someone's company."

"Personally, I think she's still in love with your father and no one else is going to ever measure up to him."

"He left her when she was pregnant. What kind of man does that?"

"I know. I'm not arguing with you about that, but I'm saying what your mother feels. Maybe she loved him so much that no one else will do."

"I never thought of it that way. No matter what I say against him she defends him."

His fingers worked on the base of her toes, kneading and massaging and cradling them in his hand. He slipped off her sock while looking into her eyes. The muscles in her stomach constricted as pleasure filled her. All he was doing was taking off her sock, why was she reacting to him like this? Men had completely undressed her before and she wasn't this affected. She drained the glass of wine and twisted behind her to the small table where Louie had set the rest of the bottle.

Louie held his glass towards her and she refilled it.

"How bad are we for sitting here in Mr. M.'s house enjoying his furniture, his fire, and wine?"

"That's leftover wine from the party. It's not like he was ever going to drink it. He's told me repeatedly to make myself completely at home here for the duration of the project."

Becky watched him over the rim of her glass. The room had warmed up nicely. Or was it the wine making her feel so toasty? Either way, she hadn't been this relaxed and comfortable in a long, long time. Her head lolled back against the sofa. "You know what I could go for?"

"You want me to guess?" His voice was teasing and sexy.

She smiled at him when he wiggled his eyebrows at her. "French toast. I'm just dying for some thick, rich French toast, smothered in confectioners sugar and tons of butter. With bacon, definitely bacon too."

"So fattening, Princess. Don't you worry about your figure?"

She closed her eyes, "Hmm, I try, but sometimes in life you have to just go for it. You have to have what you want and the hell with the consequences."

He was so quiet that she opened her eyes to see what he was doing. His eyes were on her and they were so full of want that her heart skidded to a stop. His hand on her calf that a moment ago had been sensual but friendly, now almost felt as if he was moving in on her. The kiss from a few weeks back popped into her mind, and her mouth slipped open as she found it difficult to catch her breath. All she had to do was inch forward, not even more than a hair. She could see it in his eyes; he was waiting for her to make that first tiny move, offer that unspoken invitation. Was that what she wanted? No. Yes. No. Definitely no. Her relationship with him was sacred. They were friends. He was the only man she trusted and she wasn't about to screw that up.

What she was thinking must have shown in her eyes. His own gaze shifted to the fire and he squeezed her leg once before releasing her. "The way I see it, we have two choices."

"For what?"

"For tonight. That storm is not letting up. I think we should find something to eat in the kitchen, have some more wine, and just spend the night right here in front of the fire."

Becky raised her eyebrow. It wasn't like she hadn't slept out here with him before. She'd been here the night of the ball, but that was different. It wasn't this intimate and they'd both been exhausted. She sipped her wine again, even though her head was already getting woozy. "You said two choices."

"Choice two is we get up right now, and I drive you home and then go to my house. Alone. Cold. Lonely." He pouted and she couldn't help but grin.

Becky looked out the window, or tried to. It was dark and she could hear the wind whipping. She thought of her little house, dark and empty. The long night ahead while the snow came down. Did she really want to go there?

There was no reason for both of them to risk their lives and go out in this weather. They had everything they needed right here. What was the big deal? It wasn't like they were going to sleep together; there were plenty enough beds to choose from.

He leaned forward and she searched his eyes.

"Princess, you are safer here with me in this house all alone than you are with anyone else in your life and you know it. What's the big issue here?"

Chapter Ten

The big issue was all she could think about was what it would be like to kiss him again. Which was crazy. He was Louie, her nerdy friend who she barely even thought of as a guy for most of her life. If she was with any other man, he'd already be trying to get her naked. He'd be talking about warming her up and how much more comfortable she'd be lying on the floor in front of the fire.

"Beck?"

She nodded. "Let's find some food. This wine is making me lightheaded." She tossed the afghan off her lap and stood. The room spun a bit and she swayed. Louie helped her sit back down.

"I shouldn't have let you drink that so fast without some food in your stomach. You sit here. I'll fix us something."

"No, no I'm fine. I just stood up too fast."

He looked skeptical but let her get to her feet again. This time the room didn't spin so much and she focused on getting to the door without weaving. Once in the kitchen, she sank to the chair while he poked around in the refrigerator.

"I think you're out of luck with your French toast and bacon. Could I talk you into a tuna melt, or grilled cheese and soup?"

"Whatever you're in the mood for is fine with me."

He turned and looked at her with an eyebrow raised.

"Don't even think it, Nerdman," she cautioned.

He grinned and shook his head. "A man can dream. Grilled cheese and soup it is."

****

It was so cold. The blizzard roared around him and he couldn't see the house. He couldn't see anything. Where was Becky? He had to find her. She'd been away from him for so long. What if she was lost? He had to find her, had to get to her. He looked down and saw that he was naked except for the mask from the ball. What was going on?

His eyes flew open. What the—. He let his breath out. It was a dream. It was cold, though. That's what woke him up. The room was like ice. It was still dark out and he leaned over to switch on the lamp on the nightstand. Nothing. That's what was going on, no power.

Gritting his teeth, he flipped off the blankets and fumbled to the chair where he remembered tossing his jeans and flannel shirt. The penlight he kept on his keychain gave off enough illumination for him to make his way down the hall to Becky's room. She was curled up in a tiny ball under the blankets. Convinced she was fine, he headed downstairs to get the fireplace going again.

The candles Becky always lit to make the house smell nice sat on a table in the foyer and he found the matches and lit several. He had the fire roaring and was sitting on the couch staring into it when he looked up to see her.

She had a blanket wrapped around her shoulders, her hair was mussed, and her gorgeous green eyes were sleepy.

"Its cold upstairs."

He held out his hand and she sank to the couch and tucked her bare feet up. She leaned sleepily against him and he sat back and put his arm around her, holding her close. "The power went out. You'll be warm here, go back to sleep."

She yawned. "What time is it?"

"A little past four. Shhh," He stroked her head and she settled it against his chest. "Go back to sleep."

"Is it still snowing outside?"

He hadn't looked out, but he could tell by the wind it more than likely still was. He nodded and rested his chin on top of her head. He could stay like this forever. Let it snow all it wanted. He had Becky in his arms; they were warm, and the rest of the world didn't exist.

When her even breathing told him she was back to sleep, he eased out from her arms, slid the throw pillow under her head, and put another blanket over her. He stoked up the fire and made his way to the kitchen for some tea and to check out the weather.

Luckily, the stove was gas and he was able to light it with a match. He knew there was no instant coffee; both of them would have to make do with tea this morning. While the water heated, he gingerly opened the back door to the small mud room. The snow was coming down at a steady clip. It was impossible to see very far into the yard, but it looked like at least a foot or more was on the ground already. The trees he could see were bending over with the weight of the storm. How long had the power been out? He'd better head to the basement and check the pipes. If they burst, there'd be a real issue.

Everything in the basement appeared fine, but as a precaution, when he was upstairs, he turned the faucet in the powder room on to a slow trickle. There was no way of knowing how long the power would stay out.

Back in the den, he sank into one of the big leather chairs and watched Becky sleep as the glow of the fire danced off her face.

An hour might have passed, maybe longer, before she yawned and blinked her eyes open. He was still staring at her. She squinted into the fire and sat up.

The blanket fell to her waist and he thought he'd never seen anything so beautiful as the sight of her in one of his older flannel shirts as a nightgown, and her hair tumbling around her shoulders. He would give just about anything in the world to be able to wrap her in his arms and make love to her in front of the fire while the storm roared on.

He stood up before he acted on impulse. "There's still no power, but I can boil water for tea."

"How long do you think the power will be out?"

Louie walked to the door. "I have no idea, but I'll tell you this. Before next winter I'm going to buy a generator so this doesn't happen again."

She was quiet for a minute and he realized what he'd said. "We won't be here next winter."

"Yeah, I know, but if this happened to us, it will happen to Mr. Mystery or anyone else who winds up here. It makes sense. I thought of it before, but with everything else going on..." He shrugged, hoping she wouldn't even think about his slip up. He had no idea what his plan was for next winter, but he'd already made up his mind that he'd be living here. With or without her. He'd put his blood, sweat, and soul into this place; he couldn't walk away. The truth would come out. No one was going to buy that he was a caretaker or something. He lit the burner again and pushed the thoughts away. There was still a good six months of renovations ahead.

She walked into the powder room and he cautioned. "Leave that sink dripping." He heard her mutter a response.

When she returned, he set a steaming mug of tea in front of her.

"Is the phone out?"

"I haven't checked."

She stood up again and picked up the phone on the wall. "It's out. I wanted to check on Mom."

He never thought about the rest of the town. What if the power outage was widespread? Was Margaret ok? What about his parents and Becky's house? His mind raced while he speed dialed Margaret from his cell phone. If her phone didn't answer, he'd have to call Tom and have him go check on her. He impatiently waited and then she answered.

"Maggie? You ok, darlin'?"

"I'm fine and I'm hoping my daughter was smart enough to stay out there with you. Callie said she was with you when the storm started."

"Yeah we're here together. You have power?"

"Yes, why? Is it out there?"

"Yeah, it went out sometime in the middle of the night. Do you know if Callie has it or Tom?"

"I spoke with Callie this morning; that's how I knew Becky was with you. She didn't mention anything about the power, so I'm guessing it's fine. Do you want me to go over to your house? Are you worried about it?"

"No. I definitely don't want you going out in this. I'll call Tom later and have him check on it, but if you and Callie both have power, chances are it's fine. Must be just out this way."

"So, stuck in that beautiful house, a storm outside and no power. What are you and my darling daughter going to do to entertain yourselves?"

Louie smirked at the suggestion in her tone. Becky appeared in the doorway to the den and he let his gaze take in her entire length. She'd left the blanket behind and even in slouchy sweatpants and his shirt she looked as sexy as a swimsuit model. "Margaret, I will do everything I can to keep your baby girl warm." He paused pretending that she said something. "Yes, I know we really should conserve our body heat. I'll let her know that."

Margaret laughed at the other end. "Good luck, Louie. This could be your big chance. Have Becky call me later, and let me know when your power comes back."

"Will do, Maggie. Bye."

"My mother didn't want to talk to me?" She padded inside and sat on the edge of the couch.

"She said to call her later. She has power and so does Callie."

Becky nodded. "That's good. If I was home alone I wouldn't have known what to do without power."

"Sure you would. You've lived here all your life. This isn't the first time you've lost power in a storm."

She shrugged. "I've never lost power at the house, and I really don't remember us losing it at my mother's. Maybe once or twice, but it seems like it was only for a short period of time. I don't remember worrying about the pipes freezing."

Louie leaned back in the chair and propped his feet on the footstool. He grinned. "That's because I was always right there to check on them for you. I've never let my two best girls worry about things like that."

"You do take good care of my mother and me."

"That's what us white knights do, we rescue damsels."

"A white knight? Is that how you see yourself?"

He sobered instantly and watched her. "No. Not at all."

Before she could respond, he jumped up again and moved to the windows at the far end of the room.

"How long do you think we'll be stuck out here?" she asked.

He shrugged. "I don't know. I don't even dare try to get the snow blower going until this lets up."

The long driveway to the mansion wasn't something the town plowed. He would have to call to have it done by a private company. He knew they would be busy today and really, there wasn't any rush. The longer he was out here with Becky alone, the happier he was.

"Well, what are we going to do today then?"

Without turning back to look at her, he pictured them in bed in the master suite, a fire in that fireplace keeping the room warm but not too warm. Their body heat would be more than enough.

He cleared his throat and the image from his mind. "I don't really know. Any ideas?"

"I was kind of thinking we could take some candles up to the attic and look through some of those boxes we've talked about before."

He turned back around and looked at her. "The attic? Do you know how cold it'll be up there?"

She shrugged. "I know, but we could put on some warm clothes and we could even bring some of the boxes down if we wanted. Aren't you curious as to what's in them?"

He'd only been in the attic to run wires and have it insulated. There were a lot of boxes up there. He figured eventually they'd have to go through them and get rid of the stuff, but today? "Beck, those boxes are just full of old junk. Why do you want to poke around in them so bad?"

"Curious, I guess. Who knows what's in there? There might be something valuable."

"Princess, I'm sure the Ryan family didn't leave any family heirlooms in boxes in the attic. That's just old papers and junk no one wanted to take the time to toss out."

"You don't have to then, but I'm going up there and start looking. There's nothing else to do. I'm not going to sit here and do nothing all day."

He looked at her and again, could think of a million things he would like to do trapped in the house with her all day. Dusty boxes in the attic were not on that list. "What about the mice that are probably up there?"

She shrugged. "We'll chase them out."

He narrowed his gaze. "We'll chase them out?"

"Ok, you will, but I'm not afraid of mice if that's what

you're implying."

"Ok, we'll see who screams first when they race across your foot."

She stood up. "I'm going to get more tea and put on a heavy sweatshirt, and then I'm going up there."

Resigned to the project, he joined her at the door. "There're a couple kerosene lamps in the basement. I don't know if I can get them to work, but I know I saw kerosene down there with them. I'll see if I can rig up two of those."

She grinned like a kid who'd been given a huge stick of candy. "It'll be an adventure, Nerdman."

Louie rolled his eyes. How on earth she could be this enthused about poking through someone else's old junk was beyond him.

He was surprised by how good the condition of the lanterns were when he carried them out of the basement. Obviously, power outages weren't a rare thing at the Ryan house.

The second floor was noticeably cooler than the first and by the time they got to the attic, it was definitely cold. "I told you it was going to be too cold up here."

Becky shivered but headed right to the first pile of boxes. "So we stay up here for a while and then go warm up and come back again. Stop complaining."

Louie set one of the lanterns on the floor by her and then handed her a flashlight. "Here, you'll need this; these lanterns aren't all that bright."

She brushed the dust off one box and lifted the cover. Louie leaned over her shoulder as she gently unwrapped a china tea cup. Becky gasped and looked at him as if to say 'told you so'. "This is gorgeous! These must have been in those built in china cabinets in the dining room. Oh, we have to put these in there."

Knowing that box was going downstairs, he picked it up and set it by the head of the stairs. "Anything you want to go downstairs, I'll put here and then we'll take them down when we're finished."

She nodded but was already moving on to the next box. More china and crystal. More boxes were added to the pile by the stairs. "I can't believe they stored all this up here. I wonder if Mr. M. knows about this?"

Louie shrugged. "All he told me was that he bought the house and all the contents, no matter what was found."

"I think we should set aside anything we decide should be thrown out. The next time he's in town, he can go through it."

Louie looked away. "I don't think he cares, Beck. We should just toss it."

She shook her head. "No, we might be wrong; it might be stuff he wants. They're not our things. He should go through it."

"Maybe that's just your excuse to get him back here again."

She looked up at him and narrowed her eyes, but he caught the telltale flush on her cheeks. She wanted to see him again. Tom was right; Becky had thought that night was hot. He wondered what she'd tell him about it. Him, Louie. How much should he push?

"Why would you think that?"

He shrugged. "I don't know, just a feeling I'm getting. You constantly ask when he's coming back to town."

"I do not! I haven't asked you at all. All I said was he should be coming back; this is, after all, his million dollar project."

"I don't think the guy cares, Beck. He bought the place as a tax investment. He told you that."

Oops.

"How do you know that's what he told me? Did you and he talk about me?" Becky stood up and walked over to him, staring intently into his eyes. "Did you and Mr. M. discuss me?"

"Get over yourself. No, we didn't discuss you. Well, not about anything personal anyway. He told me that he got the impression you weren't pleased that the mansion was sold to someone for a tax investment."

She seemed to accept that and walked back over to her boxes. "I don't. I think it's horrible. This house needs a family in it."

"It's too big these days for a family. What's he going to do? He's not married."

She shrugged. "Then he should finish the renovations and put it back on the market as a one family home."

"Get serious, Princess. Families today can't afford this type of place and those that do don't want to live in Oakdale, NY."

But she wasn't listening to him. She was sorting through yet another box and this time, she sat back on her heels with some papers. They looked like letters and he knew she was going to be reading through each one.

"I'm going to take some of these downstairs and get some tea. I'll be back. Want anything?"

She shook her head and listened to his footsteps as he headed back downstairs. That china was going to beautiful in the cabinets. Maybe this afternoon she'd wash it all up and put it away. What were these letters? Spying an old wooden stool, she brought it over to the box and perched on it.

The box in front of her looked like a ladies hat box. It was covered with a flower pattern and dust. Inside were a pair of white gloves and the very faintest, tiniest scent of perfume. Under the gloves were envelopes, notes, letters. This must have been someone's keepsake box where she stashed away items to save. The notepaper was old, but not ancient. These weren't from some other century, just a few decades ago. She unfolded the note and saw beautiful feminine penmanship.

"My darling Micky,"

Micky? That had to be Michael. Michael Ryan. From what she'd gathered over the years on the history of the house, Michael Ryan was the youngest son. She couldn't remember what the older brother's name had been, but she knew for certain there had been a Michael Ryan. This was obviously a note written to him by a girlfriend or something. Should she read it? Why not? Michael Ryan had been dead for over twenty years. Killed in some type of race boat accident if she remembered correctly.

"To every time there is a season and ours is done."

Oh, oh. This was a 'Dear John' letter or rather a 'Dear Micky' letter. Becky chewed her lip, feeling bad for the dead guy.

"In a place in my heart, you will always reside, but the time has come for both of us to stop living this fantasy. You have to do what you have to do. I could never live with myself if you lost everything because of me. It's not right,

Micky, and we have to accept it. I already have. Time has a way of healing everything, and I know that in a few years, we'll look back on this as what it was, puppy love. Or a case of two people falling in love at the wrong time and place. Please don't try to change my mind. I'm doing everything I can to be strong and let go. I have to. You have to."

Becky flipped to the second page of pink stationery, fascinated by the break up of this long ago relationship.

Tonight when I told you that I'd found someone else, my heart was screaming for the pain I was causing you. But you know I am not the woman you are meant to be with. The disapproval from parents would be huge and it's enough to wake me up. They expect better from you. You were born to marry someone like Suzanne. You are a Ryan. It's what has already been set in place. Suzanne knows the role she has to play, she knows all about the life you both lead. I don't and I can't. I'm not leaving you just because I think it's for the best for you, I'm doing it for me as well. I need a simple life, Mick, and we would never have that together.

Michael, you and I are going to be in the same town most of the time. I hope that we can handle this as adults. The fact that very few know what went on will at least spare us the gossip. Our own children could end up in school together, Mick, we have to be able to put this behind us and move on. What we had was beautiful, and I will never forget you, but it's time to grow up. We had a fling; a teenage romance, it was never meant to be more than that. You have responsibilities in life and so do I. Its time we both got on with it.

Please don't make this harder on me than it is. I love you, Mick, I'll always love you, but it's not right. I'm marrying someone else and so are you. We owe it to them to walk away from what we had and accept that it's over.

Be happy and always remember what we had as what it was, a beautiful love affair that had its time. Goodbye, Micky.

Your Irish Lassie

Becky's eyes filled with tears at the raw emotion in the letter. It was very clear that this woman loved Michael Ryan and was only giving him up because of some displeasure, real or imagined, on the part of his parents. Who was she? Did she still live around here? Her mind raced trying to think of who it might be. She had to be old. Michael Ryan died when he was only twenty-two. So if the woman was the same age as he was...her mind drifted as she picked up an entire pile of letters on pink paper.

She flipped through, noting the dates, almost a year of letters. The next letter she picked up was dated only a few days before the breakup. This one was on white paper with the name Michael P. Ryan embossed at the top. The handwriting was definitely masculine and flowed across the page in large letters.

"My Lassie,"

"I ache already for you and it's only been ten minutes since you left my bed. Your scent lingers on my pillowcase and I continuously bury my face in it remembering how I buried my face in your breasts and made you giggle."

Becky wiggled on the stool. Now this was getting good. Seems they didn't just have an affair of the heart, these two.

"I hate that you have to leave me before dawn or I you. I desperately want to wake up to the sun shining on your beautiful face and kiss you good morning. I want to linger in bed until noon and feed you breakfast. The things I imagine we could do with jam! I need you, Lassie, I swear I'll figure this out. I'll find a way for us to be together forever, no matter what. I can't live without you. I don't want to live without you. The times during the day when I can't reach out and touch you and let everyone know you are mine are pure torture. I love you, Lassie, God help me, but I love you. Don't worry about this Suzanne business, you know who I love and want. I will sort this all out. I will do whatever it takes to make you my bride and love you forever."

This guy had it bad! Knowing that he was going to get his heart broken made his words all the more poignant. Poor guy.

"I don't care that you work for my family. That doesn't matter to me and it shouldn't matter to you. No one can help who they fall in love with. Yes, I should have fallen for Suzanne, she's the woman who is perfect for me. But

she isn't you, my Lass, never could be. She's so cold and uptight and you are so warm and loving and giving. When you hold me in your arms and take me into your body it's as if you are sharing everything you have with me, as I am with you. I adore you! I miss you so much. Perhaps, even now, with dawn approaching, I should come to your room and kiss you awake. Let them find us. Who cares? Maybe we should let the world know that you belong to me. Then what could Suzanne do? Nothing. She'd be forced to say she won't marry me and I'd be free."

So Michael was being forced by his family to marry this Suzanne. Then she remembered that Michael Ryan and his fiancée, Suzanne, had been killed in the boating accident. Hmm, where did that leave the mystery woman? There weren't any letters after the break up letter. That was the last one according to the dates. Maybe her mother would know. Margaret knew the family, sort of. It couldn't be that hard to find someone in town who might know who she was. There might even be records here in the house that said who worked for the Ryans during that time period.

Maybe Louie even knew. She grabbed the hat box and put the lid back on. Carefully picking up the lantern, she headed down to the first floor. Wow, the temperature difference was amazing. The warm air hit her and she realized her hands were like ice.

"Louie!"

Louie came running out of the kitchen, his eyes wide with fear. She collided with him and laughed

"What? What's wrong? Something happen? You ok?" He grabbed her shoulders. "What's the matter?"

She frowned at his fear. "Nothing's wrong. I wanted to show you what I found. Jeez, Nerdman, what did you think, I saw a ghost or something?"

Louie stepped back and she could see he was embarrassed. She tipped her head and patted his arm. "I'm sorry. I didn't mean to scare you. I was just excited. Look what I found."

Louie looked down at the dusty box and she lifted the lid.

"Love letters. Michael Ryan was having a hot and heavy love affair with one of the servant girls, but from what I can tell, his mother broke them up."

"You read them?" He looked shocked.

"Yeah, what's the difference? He's long dead and I don't even know this woman. Besides, they were left behind and that means they are the property of Mr. M. and he asked us to sort through everything. He won't care if I'm reading them."

He lifted one eyebrow. "No doubt Mr. M. is like every other man in your life and has no problem with you doing whatever you want to do."

"I'm going to take these in by the fire and read through them."

"Now?"

She glanced back over her shoulder. "Yeah, why? Did you have something else you needed me to do?"

He shook his head. "It stopped snowing. I was going to see if I could shovel my way to the snow blower and get it started."

"Did you want me to help you shovel?"

"No, but I don't think you should read through those letters."

"Ok, pretend I'm not. I won't even tell you what they say. That way you won't feel like you've invaded their privacy."

In the den she noticed he'd cut up cheese and crackers. "Ohh cool, I'm starving. Thanks. You really need to go outside right now? Why don't you sit here with me and have some?"

"All right. You want more tea or a diet cola?"

Becky settled on the couch and crossed her legs under her and set the box on her lap. "Whatever you're having is fine."

She picked up the letters and decided the best thing to do would be to start at the beginning and read them to the end rather than the other way. She lifted them all out and set them on the couch. Underneath were a few pressed flowers, and a black velvet box. She picked it up and opened it and her mouth fell open.

"Wow!"

In the box lay the most breathtaking emerald and diamond necklace she'd ever seen. She knew, without any doubt, it was the real thing. Next to it was one matching earring.

She fingered the jewels and wondered about the missing earring. A quick look through the rest of the hat box revealed nothing more.

She was still staring at her find when Louie returned. "Look at this." She commanded and turned the box to face him.

Louie set their glasses on the side table and took the velvet box from her. "This was in the attic?" He whistled softly. "If these are real, they're worth a fortune."

She nodded. "They must be real. I mean, why wouldn't they be? With all the money they had, of course they're real. But I wonder where the other earring is. Do you think it's in another box?"

"I don't know, but we're not going back up there right now to look."

She took the box from him again and picked up the earring. "We'll have to turn these over to Mr. M. He should have them appraised and sell them or whatever."

The necklace sparkled and she couldn't resist lifting it out of the case. She looked at Louie, who rolled his eyes, but he took the heavy jewels from her hand and unhooked the clasp.

Becky scraped her hair off her neck and turned around. When the necklace settled against her throat, she reached up and fingered it.

"Let's see," he said.

She turned and waited for his reaction.

He nodded. "Nice."

"That's it? Just nice? I have thousands of dollars of diamonds and emeralds around my neck and all you can say is nice?"

She stood up and walked out to the hallway to look in the full length mirror. "Amazing," she whispered looking at the stones. Even wearing the old flannel shirt, the jewels looked fabulous on her. She sighed. "Gorgeous, just gorgeous."

Louie came up behind her and stared at her. "You are definitely a woman made to wear expensive jewelry."

She looked at him in the mirror. "Hmm, how do I take that?"

He shrugged and looked at her once more before

heading back to the den. She followed and sank back to the couch, pulling the box of letters onto her lap.

The first letter was dated a year before the break up letter in July.

"You're going to read all of those?"

"Uh, huh." She lifted the letter out of the envelope.

"Dearest Sweet Lassie,"

She looked up at Louie who shook his head. "Stop trying to make me feel bad for reading these, I'm not hurting anyone."

"Do what you want, you will anyway."

She stuck her tongue out at him, and went back to the letter.

"I should apologize for the kiss I stole in the gazebo a short time ago, but to apologize would indicate regret and that I do not have. Kissing you was like every fantasy come to life. You are so sweet and your lips tasted like ripe plump raspberries fresh from the garden. Your eyes are like the finest emerald jewels."

"This guy is so full of it!" she muttered, but couldn't help fingering the necklace at his comment on emeralds.

"To discover that you feel the same way about me is nothing short of a miracle. I find myself staring off into space thinking of you all the time and wondering when I can be alone with you again. Say that you want that too, my angel. Please. I'll be in the greenhouse tomorrow evening just past nine. I feel I must warn you, though, if you come, I shall kiss you again. I can't stop myself. I am addicted to the sweet nectar that is your mouth."

"You really should hear this guy. He's so corny. I don't know whether he's full of it or truly head over heels in love. Should we take bets on whether she went to the greenhouse or not?"

"Don't involve me in this. You're the one reading the personal letters between two strangers."

Becky tucked the letter back into the envelope and picked up the next. "Yep, she went to the greenhouse!"

"I'm going to see if there's any cookies."

Becky picked up the next letter. For several more notes the words exchanged were all about kisses and meeting in the greenhouse. "Ok, ok, so you kissed. How long before you did it?" she muttered, flipping anxiously through the pink papers.

Louie came back in with a package of oreos. He set it on the table and sat down next to her, picking up the notes she'd set aside.

"Ok, now we're talking. Listen to this, Nerdman."

"My precious Lassie,

How I ache with missing you. I can still feel your soft skin against mine. Your breasts are so beautiful with the moonlight falling on them. When I enter you and your eyes darken with passion, it's all I can take to control myself long enough to please you. The sound haunts me still. The way it feels when you open your thighs and allow me entrance to your most precious secrets is beyond words. To know that I was your first is an honor that I do not deserve and one I do not take lightly. I pray only that I will be your lover forever."

Becky paused and looked up at Louie. He was as mesmerized as she was and she tucked her hair behind her ear and went on.

"My deepest desire is to make love to you the way you deserve, on the finest of silk sheets, but to know that you would lay with me anywhere humbles me. You truly do love me as much as I love you. So many want me for who I am, and what I can do for them, but you, you only want my heart. It's yours. Have I told you enough? It's yours. Do not worry about anyone finding out about us. In time, when it's right, I will stand before this entire town and declare you as my own. I promise that to you. Someday we won't sneak around and hide. Someday we'll be together forever."

Becky picked up her can of Coke. "Is it hot in here or is it me? This was some love affair." She looked at Louie. He was looking at her with this weird expression. "You ok?"

"Huh?" He blinked as if he'd been a million miles away.

"I asked if you were all right. You've got this weird look on your face."

He shifted next to her. "I was thinking about how I'd feel if I was dead and knew someone was reading something that personal."

Becky uncrossed her legs and stood up. "If you were

dead, you wouldn't know about it anymore than he does."
She picked up the next letter. "People publish old love
letters of dead people all the time. Would it matter less if
it was a hundred years ago instead of what, twenty five or
so?"

"These just seem so private, or maybe it's because of
where we are. I don't know, it doesn't feel right."

She grinned. "Do you think old Micky is going to
haunt us for reading them? Hmm, or maybe you don't
want me to read them because they're turning you on and
you're embarrassed."

He scowled at her but she couldn't help but notice the
bulge in his khaki's. He was definitely aroused. "You
think that's all it takes to excite me? A few old love
letters?" He shook his head in disgust.

"Ok, then let's keep reading." Becky stood up and
walked to the fireplace, leaning one hand against the
mantle.

"My lover,"

She looked up to make sure she had his attention. He
stuck his legs out and crossed them at the ankle.

"You look like you want more. I thought you said I
shouldn't read them?"

He shrugged. "You're going to anyway. We have
nothing else to do. You might as well entertain me."

Becky scanned the letter and bit back a smile. This
should be good. She walked back across the room and
settled on the arm of the couch next to him. She stretched
her arm along the back behind his head and leaned in
towards him as she read.

"My lover,"

*"Do I ever express what you make me feel? When you
hold me in your arms, it's as if we're the only two people in
the world. You make me feel beautiful and desired and so
incredibly alive. When I remember how I snuck into the
den this morning, knowing the rest of the house still slept,
and found you there waiting for me, I still grow warm all
over. When you locked the door and closed the drapes so no
one would disturb us, I thought I would surely melt with
desire. I can still see your eyes darkened when you slowly
unbuttoned my blouse and slid it from my shoulders."*

Becky's nipples tightened at the image of what had to

have happened, right in this den. She could easily picture the couple being careful to be quiet, even as they slowly drove each other crazy. Her fingers toyed with the button on her flannel shirt and her insides fluttered as she went on.

"When you gaze at my breasts, you make me feel as if you've never seen anything so beautiful in all your life. It's a look of almost worship and it makes me so incredibly excited. Even now, hours later, I can still feel your hands as they touch me, caressing my nipples and making me want you so bad I can deny you nothing."

Becky glanced up and locked eyes with Louie. Her plan to get him all hot and bothered didn't seem to be working, but she sure was getting turned on. She wet her lips and went on.

"With you, I am never afraid of what the future holds. I find myself giggling as I think of all the places we've shared our love, the greenhouse, of course most often, but your bedroom, the library, the den, even the laundry room where we almost were caught, but you were quick and so very good, my love, that you were easily able to cover for us. What on earth would we do if we were caught? But when I'm with you and you are touching me, kissing me in places I never even knew two people could kiss one another, it's the last thing on my mind. I have no shame where you are concerned and at the very touch of your hand will make love with you. I never knew this was what desire was, what love was like. You've taught me so much and I can't believe how naïve I was before. When you left me tonight it was as if my heart walked away and only you can bring it back. I count the hours until I hold you close again. Good night my lover. Dream of me."

Becky swallowed and slowly folded the letter back up. Sensing Louie's gaze on her, she looked up and time seemed to stand still. Reading the other woman's words out loud somehow made them even more sensual. Louie wet his lips and she immediately remembered the kiss they'd shared. He was thinking about the same thing, she could see it in his eyes, and the way he gazed at her mouth. Somehow she had to break this tension or there could be a real problem here. Was there a problem? They were all alone with nothing to do, what would be so wrong with fooling around with one another? Maybe recreate a few scenes from the letters.

Oh no, not good to be thinking that way. She shook her head as if to break the tension. She started to move away, but he settled his hand over her knee and stopped her.

"Let me see a letter," he said.

As if in a trance, she reached into the box and picked up one on the formal Michael Ryan stationery as opposed to the pink stationery that she now knew the other woman used.

"My love goddess,"

He looked up at Becky and she shrugged. He went back to the note.

"Tonight on my boat will stay in my memory forever. Having you all to myself for hours on end alone out on the lake was paradise. Watching you walk around my cabin naked and free of worries of anyone catching us was something we should have done a long time ago. I don't know why I didn't think of it before. Where else could we be so alone? Forgive me for not doing this sooner! When I slid my arms around your waist from behind and you leaned forward, inviting me to take you...ahh my Lassie, what can I say? I'm hard as a rock for you just remembering it. Thank goodness the table held us both, can you imagine if it hadn't? Oh, my Lassie, the very sounds of you crying out as I thrust deeper and deeper, there is no one in this world who can get me as worked up as you can. I can't even imagine what life was like before we were together. How boring and stagnant it must have been. Then later, when we made love again and you were sprawled on my chest with your hair falling around your naked body, it was as if we were the only two people in the world."

Louie's hand caressed her knee. She had no idea if it was on purpose or just an automatic reaction but his fingers began to knead the muscles of her leg.

"Your body was made for pleasure, and I thank God every day that it's me you choose to share it with. I can't wait until the day you carry my baby and your body grows lush and full with motherhood."

Louie looked up and Becky stared back at him.

Reality blended with fantasy and she didn't know if it was Michael Ryan speaking or Louie or a mixture of both but she was caught up in the moment. It was tough to breathe normally and she'd long ago given up wondering why it was so hot in the room. Her internal temperature had risen several degrees and her pulse quickened. Her breasts felt full and aching and she wondered what he'd do if she leaned forward and toppled into his lap. Would he kiss her again? Touch her? Would he dare or would he be embarrassed? He read on.

"I love knowing I've brought you to the very peak of pleasure when you scream my name and dig your nails into me. I pray that you never want to be like that with anyone else. No, not pray. You won't. I can't let you. I have to have you in my bed forever. Promise me, Lassie, promise me I will be the only man you ever take to your bed. I worry the longer our affair remains a secret, that someone else will steal you from me. I would fight an army of men with my bare hands if anyone tried to take you from me. I would die if I had to know someone else shared your treasures. You are mine. Forever and ever!"

Louie lifted his eyes from the letter. "It sounds to me like our Mr. Ryan had a bit of a premonition that something wasn't perfect in paradise."

She cleared her throat, hoping her voice would come out natural sounding. "I think he sounds like most men do. Wanting to keep her all to himself, and yet, he never stood up to his mother and fought for her."

"How do you know? All we know from her letter is that she left. Maybe he went after her."

Becky shook her head. "No, he died in some boating accident, I remember that. He was with his fiancée and her name was Suzanne, not Lassie."

"Well we don't know for sure that he wasn't still doing Lassie, even while he was planning on marrying Suzanne, do we? Just because she sent him that letter doesn't mean it really ended."

Becky frowned. "I don't think she would have stood for that."

Louie laughed. "How do you know that? She's having this hot fling with this guy, doing it everywhere with him from the gazebo to his boat and you don't think she's the type of woman to keep coming back for more? Besides, he's the wealthiest man in town; you don't think she's benefiting from that?" He picked up the necklace at her throat, his fingers brushing her skin. "Isn't it you that's always telling me a woman should take whatever she can get from a man since they only want one thing?"

She jerked away from him and stood up, needing to get away. "I never said that."

"No? So you think maybe this necklace was just a birthday present?" He shook his head and gave a harsh laugh. "You know darn well she took him for whatever she could, especially knowing he was that hot for her."

Never in a million years did Becky think she'd be the one defending a love affair to Louie. She was always the cynical one not believing in any of it, but something of Lassie's tone in her letters, and in Michael's reply, touched her. Somehow she knew this was the real thing. This was a real love affair, not just hot sex. "What difference does it make if he was rich or not? It sounds to me like they are both mutually enjoying this, what's the harm there? Besides, so what if they didn't spend forever together?"

Louie shrugged and walked away from her to the other side of the room. He looked like he was laughing at the letters and she had no idea why she was defending these long dead lovers.

"You know, just because you don't believe in sex doesn't mean the rest of the world doesn't."

His head snapped up. "What are you talking about?"

"You. You think only two people who are going to be together forever should indulge in sex. You can't understand why two people can be hot and heavy and not have it mean forever. That's not bad, Nerdman. What is bad is to live a sexless life because you are waiting for that perfect person."

Louie narrowed his eyes at her. "You think I'm celibate because I'm waiting for the right woman?"

Becky wasn't sure how far this argument was going to go, but she was done with him making her feel guilty for her sexual relationships. This wasn't about Lassie and Michael and she knew it and so did he. This was about every man she'd ever slept with. He'd never approved and he was saying it loud and clear. "That's exactly what I think. Hell, you couldn't even get laid by the rocket scientist you met at Christmas and I bet she was more than willing."

He crossed his arms over his chest. "How would you know that? Hmm? How would you know what I've done and haven't done? Just because I don't tell you every little detail of my sexual life the way you tell me? Maybe we did it all weekend, maybe we did it in the car, and in the bedroom and on the roof. Maybe we went at it like dogs. How would you know my business?"

Becky stepped back as images played through her head. The she narrowed her eyes. "I know damn well you didn't. Which leads me to the same question. What's wrong with you, Nerdman? Why can't you get it up?"

His eyes flared and for half a second she knew she'd gone too far. He came across the room steadily, his words low but lethal. "You want to know what's wrong with me? Really? Ok, maybe its time that we had this out. We got nothing else to do today right? It's you, Princess." He said 'Princess' in such a way that made it sound cutting and insulting and she frowned. He'd never talked to her like that before. Her eyes widened with shock as he went on as if it was pouring out of him.

"You are the reason I can't, as you so eloquently put it, 'get it up' for any other woman. I don't want any other woman. I want you, my Princess. Only you. Since about the seventh grade, when I figured out that girls were different than boys in a really, really good way, I looked around and there you were. I want you. There, I said it. I want you, and you're so damn clueless you don't even know it. No, I don't have mindless sex because that's not what I want. I want sex with meaning. Sex between two people who truly love one another. Whether or not Lassie and Michael loved each other or just loved what they did to each other, who knows, who cares. All I know is when I have sex it has to mean something. I have no interest in sex just so two people can get one another off!"

His words were fired at her like bullets and she cringed as some of them hit their mark and hurt, but she ignored most of them. All but one sentence.

"You want me?"

Chapter Eleven

It wasn't really anything new. She knew he did, but hearing him admit it, out loud, when they were all alone like this, was something else all together. It took everything up several notches.

He raked his hands through his hair and his shoulders drooped as if a huge burden had been lifted, but he didn't look relieved. He looked dejected and beaten.

"Yeah, Beck. I do. No more secrets, no more pretending. I said it. You can laugh at me or whatever, but quit teasing me and stop playing your stupid little games and trying to turn me on." He laughed harshly. "Hell, I don't even know if you can stop. You don't have to do anything but breathe and you turn me on. Your bare feet excite me, your voice, your hair, your smell. There's really nothing you can do that doesn't get me hot. Do you have any idea the hell I go through every time I'm around you?" He shook his head and turned away from her.

She stared at his back for a long time and her eyes filled up. "Why didn't you say something? I thought we were friends, I mean, we've talked about everything."

He turned back around, but didn't look at her. He walked to the door. "Not about this we can't."

She'd be damned if he was going to walk away from this conversation. He brought it up, now it was time to have it out. She followed him down the hall to the kitchen. He glanced at her in disgust from the sink as he rinsed the plate.

"That day in the living room, when you kissed me, there was something there. I felt it."

"So?"

"So." She took a deep breath and moved to stand next to him at the sink. She bit her bottom lip but pressed on. "Maybe we should explore it."

He turned his head to look at her as if she'd grown horns. He shut off the water. "What the hell are you talking about?"

She smiled, hoping to lighten the mood a bit. She reached out her hand and rested it against his forearm. "We've got nothing else to do today, why not see where it might lead?"

"No."

She pulled back, feeling as if he'd thrown cold water on her. "What do you mean 'no'? You just said you want me, I just told you I enjoyed that kiss. You don't want to see if anything else could be as good?"

He dried his hands on a towel and moved away from the sink. "No."

She slammed her hands on her hips, feeling incredibly insulted and annoyed. What was that whole speech about if he didn't really mean it? "Why not? We're both mature..."

He put his hands up. "I swear, if you give me that whole consenting adult speech I'm going to throw you outside in the snow."

She raised one eyebrow. "Maybe that would cool me off, because I have to tell you, Nerdman, hearing you admit how much you want me and how I turn you on has me pretty excited." She reached out a hand and stroked it over his shoulder.

He stepped out of her reach and her hand fell to her side. "I'm not interested in being another notch on your stiletto heels, Princess." He strode to the door. "I'm gonna shovel."

The door shut behind him with a bang. Becky stared at it in shock. What the hell was that about? Her cheeks burned from his insult and she refused to let herself feel bad. She'd never made it a secret that she had a full sex life. So what? Men did it all the time. She'd just stood here and all but invited him to an afternoon of something far more exciting than shoveling and he'd rejected her? He'd rejected HER. Who did he think he was? He was nuts. That's what he was, nuts. And a jerk. He was...ohhh, she was so mad she couldn't even think up something bad enough. He was a geek and a nerd and why the hell she'd ever thought she might want to kiss him again was crazy.

She yanked open the refrigerator door, purposely ignoring the fact that he suggested keeping it closed while the power was off, and pulled out a Diet Coke. She slammed it shut and popped the top on the can. He was an idiot. She smirked. Tomorrow he was going to wake up and realize he'd had the opportunity of a lifetime and he'd blown it. Well, that ship sailed on by. You blew it, Nerdman, opportunity will not knock again.

She must have been crazy to even think about it. She padded back down the hall to the warm den and curled up on the couch with the letters. Reject me, will you? Any other guy would be on his knees begging for the chance to be with me and you choose shoveling. She glanced out the window, but couldn't see him. He must be in the back. She shrugged and set her diet Coke on the table. Your loss, Nerdman.

She opened up one of the letters but her mind kept drifting back to Louie reading them. It wasn't as much fun without him. She stared into the fire. Michael Ryan was dead, but was the woman he loved? Did he love her or was it the excitement of not being caught that had him turned on?

Her eyes felt heavy and she slid further down into the corner of the couch and closed her eyes. Images of Louie flashed through her mind. The kiss they'd shared had shocked her. She never imagined kissing Louie and if she had, she'd always assumed it would be almost brotherly, certainly not the toe curling passion that had flared to life. It was the same with Mr. Mystery. She frowned. A flash of desire had flared between them from the moment he took her in his arms on the dance floor. She smiled, remembering the kiss in the greenhouse and then later. Never in her life had she been that into someone so fast. What was wrong with her?

It had to be because she hadn't been dating much this year. Once she and Louie started work on the project, she'd put off all dates. Even Roger had stopped calling after she'd turned him down one too many times. That had to be what it was. With Mr. Mystery it was still the whole mask thing, that 'sex with a stranger' fantasy that turned her on. Combine that with her lack of a love life in recent months, and of course she was excited.

And with Louie? What was her excuse there? There was never a time when she didn't remember him pretending to be madly in love with her and offering to take her to his bed. It was a game they'd always played. Wasn't it? When did it change? When did he stop pretending and become serious about his feelings for her? She flopped her hand over her head and struggled against the sense of disappointment that settled over her. Was the friendship they'd always shared nothing but a sham? Did he just pretend to be her friend to be near her? Was he no better than any other man she'd ever been with? Wanting only one thing from her? She thought she knew him, how could it be that she never really did?

The back door opened, but she didn't move. When she heard him come in the den she dropped her hand from her eyes and turned on her side on the couch to watch him. He stood in front of the fireplace, warming his hands. His hair was matted down from the stupid hat he always had to wear, his jeans bagged at the rear like always. This was what she found irresistible a little while ago? Then he turned his head and looked at her and the pain in his eyes made her heart clench.

His cheeks were red from the cold and he sniffled. "I got enough shoveled that we can get out as soon as the plow comes up."

"You think they'll be out today?"

"I'll call later and see what I can find out. Why? Are you in a hurry to leave?"

She sat up and brushed her hair back, ignoring the pointed look he gave her. An hour ago she'd all but planned on staying through another night with no problem but now she had this sudden urge to put some distance between them. "I should check on Mom and my house."

He snorted. "That's what I figured you'd do."

"What?"

He turned around and faced her. "Run. You always run when things don't go your way."

She stood up. "Quit analyzing me. I hate it when you do that."

He raised one eyebrow, but didn't comment. Instead,

he glanced at the box of letters. "Did you read any more?"

She shook her head and walked away to the windows. "I wasn't in the mood."

Silence descended on the room. Behind her she could hear him adding logs to the fire and settling the screen grate back in place. For several long minutes she just stared out at the snow filled yard.

"Maybe we should talk about this," he said.

She whirled around. "Oh, I see, now you want to talk about it. Well, you know what?" She raised her hands in the air and then dropped them back to her side. "There's nothing to talk about. Seriously. NOTHING."

The muffled, but still loud, sound of a truck startled her and she looked out the window to see the familiar pickup truck with the big plow on the front. Brownie Johnson waved to her from the cab, his ever-present cigar wedged between his teeth as he drove, then backed down the winding road of the property.

"I'm going to get my stuff and head out." She walked out of the den without looking at him and went upstairs. Several minutes later, she'd changed into the clothes she wore yesterday. The guest room looked the same way it did when she'd woken up this morning, but everything else had changed. An idea occurred to her all of a sudden and she sank to the bed. She'd once told Louie that if she ever turned the tables on him and took him up on all he'd been promising over the years, he'd run scared. And he had. Was that it? Did she scare him? Did the thought of being with her scare him? She frowned. Or, was he serious when he said he wouldn't be, well, whatever he'd meant by the notch comment. Now what did that mean to the two of them? Where did they stand now? Were they friends? Not like they were yesterday, or even before they'd kissed. Things were awkward and tense between them, that's why she'd stayed away. Maybe the time had come for the friendship to end. Her stomach was sick at the thought.

****

While Becky was upstairs, Louie tried to get himself under control. When she'd suggested spending the afternoon, the way she'd suggested, he'd been shocked speechless. He wanted nothing more, but he couldn't. He knew it wasn't going to be enough. If he slept with her today, or even tomorrow, when it ended, as he knew it would, everything would end. He'd lose her. He always believed in his heart that if she ever looked at him the way she had when he'd been reading the letters, that he would do everything in his power to show her that love wasn't what she thought it was and that he loved her and would never let her down. But Becky wasn't offering love, she was offering a way to pass the time. As much as that appealed to a certain part of him, he knew it was never going to be enough.

She came down the stairs with her purse on her shoulder and grabbed her parka off the coat tree.

"I'll drive you home."

"No, thank you. I'm a big girl, I can take care of myself. Been doing it for years." She didn't look at him as she walked to the front door.

He slid his palm against the door to stop her from opening it. She looked up at him with annoyance. He swallowed hard. "I'm sorry."

She tossed her hair. She always did when she was really ticked off. She put her hand around the doorknob but he didn't let go.

"Come on, I gotta go."

"I'm not letting you leave with this between us."

She lifted one eyebrow and he tried not to flinch. He knew damn well if Becky wanted to leave, he couldn't stop her.

She sighed. "Look, its no big deal. We both got caught up in the moment. You know, a roaring fire, the storm trapping us here, some old mushy letters. It was an idea, a way to pass the time. Frankly, I'm glad you were thinking clearly. I mean, imagine it: you and me?" She laughed, but her eyes were still icy cold. "It's creepy or something, you know?"

Creepy? She thought being with him would be creepy? He let go of the door and captured her face in his hands. Her eyes widened as his mouth swooped down and captured her parted lips. He slipped his tongue inside without letting her protest and kissed her as if he had every right to. He closed his eyes and pretended he wasn't Louie the geek, he was Mr. Mystery, full of confidence. He could make this woman want him, he'd done it before. Her hands came up to rest against his forearms and she stroked her tongue against his. Spurred on by her response, he tilted her head and cupped the back of her head in his palms. She kissed him back and arched into him. Louie shifted until the door was at his back and took all her weight against him. Her hips settled against his and he slipped one knee between her legs. Her hands went around his waist and he lifted the hair off her neck and wound it around his fingers. Slowly he began to break the kiss, easing his lips from hers, not convinced she wasn't going to hit him. She opened her eyes and searched his. What was she looking for?

He swallowed hard. "I want you, I've always wanted you, and I never won't want you. You make me crazy," he whispered. He kissed her again, harder this time, trying to show her how much he meant everything he'd said. He loved her desperately and there was nothing in the world harder than walking away from her.

Her breasts pressed into his chest and he grabbed her slender rear end in his hands and lifted her against him. She whimpered and her need caused his own arousal to escalate. In a few more minutes he was going to say the hell with tomorrow and carry her into the den and do what they both wanted to do.

The only thing stopping him was knowing that when it was over, she'd soon grow bored and then she'd move on. He'd be left in far worse shape. He doubted he would live through losing her once he'd truly had her.

The sobering thought gave him the strength to gently pull her arms from around his neck and break the kiss. He somehow managed to get them both back on their feet. By the look in her eyes, he could tell she fully expected him to lead her upstairs. Instead, he shoved his hands in his pockets and turned away.

"Drive safe," he croaked and walked into the den and shut the door firmly behind him.

If he expected her to slam the front door and cuss him out, he was mistaken. He listened from inside the den as she left the house. He moved across the room and watched as she climbed into her car and drove away. He leaned his forehead against the cool window and drew a deep breath. What an idiot. You could be with her right now, here in the den or upstairs in that enormous bed; either way you could be doing what you've longed to do for over half your life and instead you send her out into the cold.

It didn't matter. He'd done the right thing. Becky Richardson might indulge herself with him for a short time, but he wasn't someone she was going to stay with. Not for long anyway. He'd be fun to while away the afternoon with, maybe even all night, but when reality set in, she'd regret it. He couldn't live with that.

Chapter 12

"Good night, Becky."

Becky looked up from her typing, surprised to see Stan Peterson leaving. He was always the last one at the law firm to leave, most said because he dreaded going home to his empty house now that his wife was gone. She leaned back in her chair. "Good night, Stan."

The elderly lawyer paused by her desk. "You've been here late every night this week. I told you before, we'll bring in temps if the workload gets too much."

She shook her head. "No, it's fine. Its just one project, I'm almost finished, but thank you."

She stood up and followed him to the door and locked it behind him. Looking back at the clock in the reception area, she was shocked to see it was after seven. What difference did it make? There was nothing to do at home. In the week since the storm and the subsequent 'scene' at the mansion with Louie, she'd avoided both him and the Ryan house. The distinct chime from her instant message program had her slipping back into her chair.

"Why are you still at work?"

Louie. She wet her lips, thinking about what she wanted to say. She had nothing to say to him...yet *a lot* to say to him. All week, all she could think about was that kiss and how hot it was and then how humiliated she'd felt when he left her. She was mad at him, but at the same time, she missed him and the mansion.

"I'm busy." She typed back.

Lightning fast came his response. "Did you eat dinner? Or even lunch?"

"None of your concern." She answered just as fast.

It had been a long standing game with them; that she could type just as fast he could. She wasn't about to let him win.

"I'm going to come by and take you out to eat."

"NO. I'm not done here."

"Really? Or is it just that you don't want to see me?"

"Whichever."

"Are you mad at me?"

"For what?"

"You know."

"No, I don't know. Remind me."

When his response didn't come through immediately, she leaned back in her chair with a smirk. Crossing her arms over her chest, she waited. *Wiggle out of that one, you worm.*

"Never mind. Have a good night."

Becky frowned. That was it? He wasn't going to talk about it? That rat. She leaned forward again and quickly typed before he closed his program. "Wait a minute."

"What?"

"I need Mr. Mystery's email. I want to tell him about the necklace and earring. Unless you already did."

Again, a pause, and she waited impatiently. Was he so annoyed he wasn't going to give it to her? Finally, the screen moved. "I didn't say anything to him about them. Did you read the rest of the letters?"

"Yes."

"And?"

She shook her head. "It's too much to go into in IM."

"I offered to take you to dinner."

"I can't do that with you right now."

"Cause...you're mad?"

"I'm not mad."

"Ok, then have dinner with me."

"Fine. But bring the necklace and the earring and send me his email. I want to tell him I have them."

"I locked them in the safe room."

"All right, that's probably a good idea."

"I'll be right over."

"I want to go change; I'm in my work clothes."

"Tight skirt, high heels, silk blouse...no need to change on my account, that's my favorite look."

She couldn't stop the grin that split her face. This was the Louie she was used to. The one who teased her and made her feel sexy, but safe. Maybe she'd built everything up in her mind to be more than it was. Maybe it was ok after all. She could at least try to meet him halfway, right?

"All right, but you had your chance, remember that. That ship sailed, so no touchy-feely or trying to put those big old nerd lips on me again."

"Promise, Princess."

"Let me shut things off and I'll be ready when you get here. Bye."

"Bye."

When he pulled up in front of the law firm and climbed out of his car, she was shocked at how happy she was to see him. It felt like years, not just days since they'd last been together. He smiled and she smiled back.

"How about that Italian place off the expressway? I'm in the mood for Italian tonight."

"Callie and Tom went there the other night. They said it was pretty good."

"How are they? I haven't seen them since last weekend."

Becky settled into the bucket seat of Louie's old car. "They're good, you know, busy with wedding plans. What a fiasco. So glad I'm never going through that."

Louie didn't comment and she didn't look at him as they rode through town. His eyes strayed from time to time across the seat to her legs, the way they always did when they were together. In the past, she would have slapped him or made some comment about his perverted ways, but this time, she found a special delight in shifting so that her skirt rode up even higher. The quick glance he gave her was all the satisfaction she needed to know she was affecting him. It didn't hurt to remind him of exactly what he'd passed up.

She looked at his profile, happy to see he'd left his glasses home. His hair was freshly cut too, not flopping in his eyes like usual. His clothes were even neat, for Louie. The jeans were crisp and the shirt was one she'd never seen before. Had he cleaned up for her? For dinner? She looked back out the windshield and felt butterflies stirring inside.

"So tell me all about the hot affair."

At her sharp glance, he grinned. "Michael and the mysterious Lassie?"

"I knew what you meant. Well, it appears that the affair lasted just over a year and like you heard before, it was pretty intense. But you know, I really think that the two of them weren't just in lust. I think they really loved each other."

"I'm surprised. You, who thinks love doesn't exist."

"I don't think it doesn't exist, I just think it doesn't exist for everyone."

He pulled the car into the crowded parking lot and climbed out from behind the wheel. While he was walking around the car, Becky slipped two more buttons open on her blouse. When he opened her door, she shrugged off the blazer. "It might be hot in there," she explained as she left the jacket in the car.

His eyes clung to her cleavage, as she'd anticipated. Whirling from him on her high heels, she walked ahead, knowing darn well he'd watch her hips sway with every step. *Eat your heart out, Nerdman.*

When he joined her at the door, she flashed him a brilliant smile and tucked her hand through his arm. "This was such a good idea, I'm glad you talked me into it."

He narrowed his eyes and she knew he was wondering what she was up.

They each ordered wine and settled back against the red leather seats. "Did you say anything to your mother yet about what we found?" Louie asked. "I wonder if she knows anything about the tragic lovers."

Becky sipped her wine before answering. "She was sick this week, so I didn't get a chance to talk to her about it."

"Sick? Is she ok?" Louie leaned forward.

Becky studied him, noting the concern on his face, the way his eyes were full of worry. "The doctor says it's a bad cold, but she just can't seem to shake it."

He nodded. "I'll call her tomorrow. She's not still trying to work is she?"

"She actually had to cancel a couple of appointments."

Louie raised one eyebrow. The waitress brought their salads and Becky removed all the garbanzo beans and cucumbers and shifted them to Louie's salad. Then she took all the tomatoes off his and put them on her own plate.

"When you eat out with other people, who do you dump the stuff you don't like on?" he asked

She smiled. "No one, I just shove them to the side." She picked up her fork. "What about you? Who eats your tomatoes when I'm not around?"

Louie picked up a tomato she'd missed and reached across the table towards her. Instead of setting it on her plate, he held it to her mouth. Becky tossed her hair and leaned forward, knowing her blouse would gape. She wrapped her lips around the tomato and delicately licked the dressing from his fingers as he released it. She watched him from under her lashes as she eased back against the seat.

The waitress whisked away their salad plates and brought their pasta dishes.

Louie shifted in his seat and picked up his fork. For several seconds, he didn't say anything, just ate as if he hadn't eaten in months. Becky bit her bottom lip to keep from grinning.

"Why don't you come over for dinner on Sunday and we'll talk to my mother about the letters and the jewelry? Maybe she can shed some light on this mystery woman."

He nodded, and wiped his mouth before answering her. "Do you really think she might know? The way she sounded, she barely knew the Ryans."

Becky shrugged. "It's the only place I know to start. If she doesn't know anything, we'll ask Callie next. I haven't talked to her about it either, before you ask. She's all tied up with the wedding stuff."

"Did you hear they want to take pictures in the gazebo?"

Becky nodded. "Yep, I'm going to email Mr. Mystery and ask his permission. As soon as you get me that email address," she hinted.

Louie's face reddened and she narrowed her eyes. "I'll get it for you tomorrow."

"Tonight."

"What's the rush?"

"The wedding is only a few weeks away and I want him to know about the jewelry."

He narrowed his eyes. "Why don't we wait and find out what we can from Margaret about it, first?"

What was his problem with her having Mr. Mystery's email address? "Either way, they're his emeralds, so what difference does it make what we find out about them?"

"You're going to be like a dog with a bone on this thing, aren't you?"

Becky raised one eyebrow at his reference to a bone, but decided not to tease him. "Nerdman, I will hurt you, really bad, if you don't get me that email address."

He grinned and a light came into his eyes as he eased forward. "I'm beginning to think that all these years of you threatening to hurt me are just a bunch of bluff."

Becky leaned across the table. "I'd say try me, but you're chicken."

A red flush started at his neck and crept into his face as she watched. "I told you why. It's a bad idea."

She shrugged and sat back again. "So says you, but we'll never know."

The waitress appeared at their table. "Can I get you anything else? Coffee? Dessert?"

Becky set her napkin down next to her plate and shook her head at Louie's look of inquiry.

"No, we'll just take the check, please. Thank you." The waitress took their plates and walked away. Louie looked over at her, but she pretended an interest in the painting on the wall across the room. "What's wrong now?"

She really had no idea. All she knew was she was annoyed with him, again. "Nothing."

He snorted and she narrowed her eyes, but didn't comment. The waitress returned with the check and Louie fished out his card to pay. Becky reached for her purse and pulled out some cash. "How much is mine?"

"Don't worry about it." He set his card on top of the bill.

"No, seriously, I want to know how much I owe you." She reached for the bill but Louie picked it up, along with his card.

The waitress was nearby and he held it out for her. "I invited you to dinner."

"I don't want you buying me dinner." Even to her own

ears that sounded childish and whiny, but she wasn't about to let him pay her way.

"You can buy next time." He signed the statement and put his card away.

Becky doubted very much that there'd be any more dinners out with Louie. Somehow, something had changed, shifted in their relationship. Ever since the kiss, make that *kisses*, she'd discovered she wanted something from this friendship that he wasn't about to give her. The easygoing way things had been was over.

Completely depressed at that thought, all she wanted to do was get home and be alone with her brooding. She picked up her purse and Louie stood up. When he placed his hand at the small of her back, she jerked away. It was raining hard as they reached the front door.

"Stay here, I'll bring the car around." He ran out without waiting for her reply.

****

Louie was soaked to the skin by the time he reached the car. He knew Becky was ticked off at him, again. Maybe dinner had been a bad idea. It had started off well enough, more like they used to be, teasing and talking, even laughing. Then IT had come up again. How was he supposed to convince her that the two of them having sex was the worst possible idea in the world when right now that was all he could think of? When he'd picked her up at the office and she was wearing that tight straight black skirt with her stiletto heels, he'd just about come undone. All he could think about was those hot movie sex scenes where the guy takes the secretary right there on his desk. When she'd deliberately, and he knew she did it on purpose, taken off her jacket before going into the restaurant, it was all he could do keep control. Her nipples had puckered behind the thin silk blouse and tormented him all through dinner and she was fully aware of it. It was bad before when he didn't know what they felt like, but now having experienced those treasures, he wanted more.

He pulled the car up as close to the front door as he could and she ran outside and climbed in.

"Thanks," she muttered, fluffing out her hair. She glanced at him as she buckled her seatbelt. "You look like a drowned rat."

"I can't believe how hard it's raining." He squinted, trying to see through the windshield. The wipers couldn't keep up and he turned on the defrost to clear the inside of the window. He pretended to focus on his driving to avoid saying anything stupid, but she didn't seem to want to talk, anyway. Several minutes later, they pulled in her driveway. The security lights came on.

"I want you to come in," she said and unhooked her seatbelt.

Louie shook his head. "No. I'll watch you from here until you're inside, but I'm going to head home."

"I want you to give me that email address tonight so I can send him an email."

"I'll do it when I get home."

Becky shook her head. "No, I want you to come in and give it to me."

He looked at her quickly to see if she was aware of what she'd said, but she didn't seem like she was in a teasing mood. She was just plain irked. Guilt settled over him and he sighed and unbuckled his seat belt. He cut the engine. "Fine, maybe it'll let up before I come back out."

Becky ran from the car to the house, but in the fifteen seconds it took them both to get to the porch, they were completely drenched. Lighting cracked and thunder boomed as he waited for her to punch in the security code. Her blouse clung to her skin like plastic wrap and the flimsy bra she wore did nothing to hide her breasts from view. Like a wet t-shirt contest, her nipples poked rosy red against the white material.

He stood dripping on the floor mat as she shut the heavy door. He didn't want to turn around and look at her; he was already as hard as a rock and it wouldn't escape her notice. He also knew that his self-control was gone. They were both soaked, it was warm in her house, and he wasn't going anywhere for a while. To think that nothing was going to happen tonight was pointless. He turned to face her.

She'd raised her arms to lift her wet hair off her back and it made her breasts rise up high and proud. The brown circle around her nipples caught his gaze and he couldn't stop staring.

"You've been staring at my boobs since high school, how can they still be so fascinating to you?"

He swallowed and lifted his gaze to hers. "Seventh grade."

She raised one eyebrow, "Really? Seventh grade?" At his nod, she shrugged. "One would think that after all those years, you'd be used to them."

Not in a million lifetimes would he be used to seeing her breasts. Not in a million lifetimes would he ever stop wanting her or needing her. But it wasn't the same for her, and he knew it. She wanted to 'explore'; that's the term she'd used before. Explore. Check it out, try it on, whatever other term that meant it was a temporary thing. Only problem was, he couldn't handle temporary. Not with her. She'd kicked off her high heels and her stockings were molded to her legs. Her fingers were at the buttons on her blouse and as he watched, she slid first one, then the second one free.

"You know how sometimes when you want candy, you obsess over it and obsess over it and then you eat so much you could burst, and the craving is gone?"

He had no idea what she was talking about, but he nodded anyway as another button came open.

She laughed and eased her blouse from the waistband of her skirt and shoved it off her shoulders until it slid to the floor. Her bra was a lacy scrap of nothing. What was the point in even wearing it? His hand twitched and he fisted it closed, forcing himself not to reach out for her.

"Beck..." He began to argue, but he already knew he was too far gone. Becky was going to seduce him, here and now, and there wasn't anything he could do to stop her. Her fingers rested on the front clasp between her breasts.

"I really don't know why you are so obsessed with these, every woman has them. I bet even that geek girl in Florida had boobs, of some sort." She flicked the clasp and it sprang open. Her breasts popped free and he had this irrational image of the fake peanut cans he played with as a kid, the kind with the cloth snake in it that sprang out when the top was opened.

Think with your head, he ordered himself. *You know that if this happens tonight, the friendship as it's been for years will be changed, maybe even finished.* Then again, based on dinner tonight, it already was. So if the friendship was already on its way out because things have gotten stirred up with her, what was the point in not doing this? He had no clue.

"You need to get out of those wet clothes," she said softly and bunched the hem of his t-shirt in her hands and lifted it upward.

He took over and ripped it over his head and flung it to the floor. Becky moved closer and took his hand, bringing it to her breast. "Touch me."

And he did. Her fullness filled his hand once more and he molded it in his palm, growing hard as a rock as memories washed over him of the last time he'd touched her like this.

"How do they feel?" she murmured as he explored each one completely with his fingertips.

He grazed her extended nipple with his thumb and she whispered words of encouragement as he repeated it with the other before rolling them in his fingers.

"Breasts are the most amazing works of art God ever thought to create."

He weighted both of them in his hands and looked into her face as he caressed her. It was more than obvious she enjoyed what he was doing.

"They were intended to nourish babies, but they were also designed for sexual reasons. If touching them didn't bring the woman pleasure, would the man still want them as desperately? Would they still hold the wonder that they do if he didn't know how much the woman liked them to be caressed?"

Becky shivered and he knew they should both get changed or at least out of the wet clothes, but she'd started this and she needed to know she wasn't the only one who could tease and torment. She moaned when he leaned forward and lifted one full mound to his mouth. He kissed the side of her breast, nuzzled it with his face and breathed in deeply the scent that was all Becky.

"Your nipples are like cherries on top of a sundae, the best part, the part you save for the very end."

She trembled in his arms and he took the red peak into his mouth and suckled. Her hands skidded across his shoulders as he bent over in front of her. Her fingers sifted through his hair as he kissed her.

When he lifted his head, he was satisfied he'd made her as crazy as he was for her. Becky's eyes were hooded and dark with desire as he looked into her face. "Your plan isn't working, Princess," he said and straightened up.

"I think it's working just fine." She reached for him but he stepped back.

"No, it isn't. I'm not getting over my obsession with your breasts. I want more." His hands fell to his belt buckle and her eyes widened as he unhooked it, unbuttoned his fly and drew down his zipper. Her eyes followed his hands and she gave a slow smile when his boxers appeared complete with his tented erection.

A sudden roar of thunder exploded and lightning lit up the front hall windows. The lights flickered and went out.

Chapter Thirteen

Louie couldn't see a thing, but he could feel her and smell her as she came even closer. Her hands were on the open waistband of his pants and she shoved them down. He spanned her waist and held her tight as she kissed his neck. Awkwardly, he stepped out of his pants.

"I love a good hard…rain, don't you?" She nibbled on his earlobe and sparks coursed up his spine.

He throbbed painfully behind his boxers. He found the zipper of her skirt and slid it down. The material slipped to the floor in a wisp. He filled his hands with her compact rear end.

Becky pulled back and for a moment he wondered if she was having second thoughts, but she took his hand and led him through the doorway to the living room. A second later, she pushed him down to the couch and landed in his lap. He'd give anything if he could see her half naked in his arms. She kissed him and he responded with an urgency he couldn't help. There was no hesitation in his hands on her skin, no tentative touches. Maybe it was the dark that gave him confidence or maybe it was knowing she wanted him as much as he wanted her. He was confident and touched her as if he knew exactly what she wanted and how she wanted it.

His hand settled on her leg and he discovered that somewhere between the hall and here, she'd ditched her pantyhose. How she did that with one hand while walking with him into the living room made his head spin. He traced a pattern up her bare thigh to the edge of her panties. Becky shifted in his arms and he slipped his hand between her legs and found her moist and warm.

She moaned and sucked his tongue into her mouth. He rubbed the lace between her legs. She wiggled against his hand and he slipped his finger beneath the elastic and into her wetness. Her murmurs of pleasure spurred him on and he continued to stroke her. He kissed her neck, the top of her chest and moved her off his lap to the couch. Still kissing her, he removed her panties and settled his hand between her thighs. She cried out hoarsely.

He kissed one breast and then the other, licking the extended peaks, rolling his tongue across each one. His fingers dived and dipped beneath the silken curls. Becky squirmed in his arms and cried out as he let her breast pop free of his lips and kissed his way down her belly. He slid to the floor in front of her. He ducked his head to the bountiful feast between her legs and reached for one plump breast. Lightning lit up the room and gave him a moment's glimpse of the short dark hair between her beautiful legs as they lay open for him.

He nibbled the tender skin of her inner thigh, hard enough to leave a mark, and then soothed it with his tongue. He'd given her a stamp of possession where only he could see it.

"Ohhh, Louie," she cried out as he covered her with his mouth and kissed the very essence of her. He suckled gently, only increasing the pressure when she purred and whimpered his name. Her hands were restless, flittering across his shoulders, sifting into his hair, but not pushing him away. She lifted her hips higher, encouraging his attentions. He held her firm even when she cried out and pleaded with him. He continued to caress her. He slid one finger inside as her body convulsed. His ego soared as she screamed his name on a long strangled cry. The thunder roared outside and a storm raged inside him. Her body stilled and she moaned softly. His erection unbelievably grew even harder.

Once again, the night of the ball came to mind when he'd satisfied her the first time, but this was different. This time she knew who he was. "Your skin is like the petal of a rose, soft and sweet." He trailed open-mouthed kisses along her thighs.

Her fingers sifted through his hair and he nibbled at the crook of her leg, kissing the back of her knee.

"I had no idea you could talk so sweet, Nerdman. I thought if it wasn't in html code, you couldn't speak it."

He stood up and loomed over her, resting his hand along the back of the couch. He couldn't see her, but he could hear her move her head to look up. He lowered his mouth and kissed her. She clung to him and pulled him down on top of her. Her thighs spread open and he nestled his hardness against her moist heat. Her fingers slid into the back of his boxers and squeezed his rear end. He pressed into her, wanting her so bad he knew he was going to explode.

"You don't even know what html code is." He smiled against her neck and nibbled on the soft skin of her collarbone.

Becky arched her back and pressed her hips up towards him. "Does it have anything to do with this?"

"Not a thing, Princess." He kissed her again and she pulled his shorts down.

"Then I don't give a damn what it means." She kissed him hard and he jerked when she filled her hand with the soft sacks beneath his erection. When she took his hardness in her palm and held him, he ripped his mouth from hers to gasp for a steadying breath.

He shed his boxers as Becky lifted her hips towards him and with her guiding, he slid inside her. He groaned as she enfolded him in softness and heat. His head swam and her hands clasped his bare rear and squeezed. She bucked her hips up and urged him to go deeper. He drove into her.

"Yes!" she cried out. "Oh yeah, Louie, that's it, that's it."

He certainly didn't need to be asked twice; harder and harder he pumped, pushing them both to the heights they craved. Becky's muscles clenched him tight and he lowered his head, searching for her breasts. The world began to tilt and turn and his head roared as loud as the wind outside.

"Come on, Louie, let go for me, come on, ohhh Louie now, now!" she called out and he obliged, shaking and trembling as his body jerked and pulsed and then exploded inside her. He felt her shaking under him and knew he'd brought her with him. For a second he rested, careful to keep his full weight off her body. His head nestled against her breasts he listened to her harsh breathing that matched his own.

The rain beat against the window and lightning

continued to flash, but the thunder sounded farther in the distance.

Becky slid her arms around him and he lifted his head, wishing he could see into her eyes, but the room was too dark.

"You ok?" she asked.

"I'm fine, you?"

"Hmmmm," she murmured. "That was good for a first course."

He chuckled. "Oh yeah? First course, huh? Does that mean you don't think I should go back out into this storm?"

She shoved at him and he moved off her, thinking she wanted to lie next to him, but she got up. He could just make out her shadow in the room. "Where you going?"

"Don't worry, Nerdman."

She came back with the light of a tiny flashlight. She moved to the table on the other side of the room and lit a few candles, then stretched up on tiptoe to reach some on the shelf. Louie stared at her back, the curve of her spine and her perfectly formed round rear end. He couldn't stop himself from moving across the room and wrapping her in his arms from behind. His hand splayed across her bare belly and he nuzzled her neck. Becky arched her head and raised her arm to caress his hair.

Holding her in his arms, having the right to touch her and kiss her was like every dream he'd ever had come true. If it was only going to be for one night, then he was going to make the most of it. He turned her to face him and kissed her with all the hunger he had inside. Her head fell back and he lifted her in his arms and carried her back to the couch. This time when he sat down, she straddled his lap. Her fingers sank into his hair and massaged his scalp. His hands splayed across her back and held her pressed against him. Her breasts were like soft cushions against his chest. Becky lifted her hips and then settled over him. Pleasure exploded inside him.

She rubbed her hands on his chest. In the low light he saw her look up at him from under her lashes. "How's that feel?"

Louie closed his eyes as she clenched her muscles

around him and then lifted her hips and brought them down again. He'd never felt anything like this in the world. "Amazing," he whispered.

He lifted one of her breasts and kissed it reverently. She rose and fell on him and her murmurs of pleasure echoed his own. He felt himself begin to tense, to pulse and grow harder and harder as he tried to hold himself back and not let go.

"It's ok," she whispered.

"No, not yet."

He wanted this moment to last longer, wanted to be inside her as long as he could.

"I can't wait," she moaned.

He bucked his hips up as she came down and together they shot to the sky again.

"Beck, God, Beck!" he growled. She jerked in his arms and cried out in a long moan of pleasure. Her mouth fell to his shoulder and she bit him as she climaxed.

Fireworks went off, and lights of color flashed behind his eyes. She collapsed against him and he wrapped his arms around her and rubbed her back. He kissed her neck and murmured to her as their breathing returned to normal.

It was several minutes before he shifted and grabbed the afghan and covered them both. Her narrow couch wasn't made for two, but it suited him just fine. He could lay here forever holding her naked against him. She snuggled into him and he closed his eyes, completely content and satisfied.

When he opened his eyes again, it was still dark in the room. The candles were still burning so he must not have been asleep very long. The soft glow allowed him to see her beautiful face. He stared at her. What the hell had he done? There was no way this was going to turn out good. She might decide that being lovers was good for a while, but he knew her too well. Becky tired of men the way most people tired of new cars. It was all very new and exciting in the beginning, but once the first payment was due, it was nothing but a noose around your neck. He never wanted to be that noose.

Somehow, he had to play this cool, get out of this without hurting her before she was sitting around figuring out how to do the same thing.

Her hand wrapped around his already stiffened erection and he realized she wasn't asleep after all. She snuggled up against him and kissed his chest. "Nerdman?" she whispered.

"Hmm," he grunted as if sound asleep.

"I was wondering," she started.

"What?"

"After all these years, was I worth it?"

He opened his eyes to find her staring at him. He brushed the hair back from her face and cupped her cheek. "Princess, you rock my world, and not just that way." He almost told her he loved her, but he held back. It wasn't the time and knowing her, it would make her run even faster.

Her lips twitched in a short smile. "How long do you think this rain is going to keep up?"

He shifted on the couch until she was under him again. "Who cares," he whispered and covered her mouth with his. *How am I ever going to live without having her like this?* He made love to her slowly, worshipping her with his mouth, his hands, and finally his body. He didn't leave one inch of her unkissed or unloved. It didn't matter how many other men had been in her arms before, none of it mattered except that she was with him now. Tonight. When tomorrow came, he'd have to deal with it.

****

Becky woke up alone on the couch. The blanket was tucked around her and sun streamed in the window. The scent of coffee wafted from down the hall and she stretched and smiled like the well-satisfied woman she was. Who'd have ever thought that her nerdy buddy was such an accomplished lover? Hmm, was it true as her mother always said, still waters run deep? All these years, that nerdy act was really hiding a man who knew exactly what to do and how to do it.

She wrapped the afghan around her shoulders and padded to the kitchen, eager to find him and see if he had any plans for the day. If he did, she was about to change them. He wasn't in the kitchen. A half empty coffee cup and the newspaper told her he'd been there and had been up for a while. Looking at the clock, she realized it was

191

almost eight. From upstairs she could hear water start up and realized he was in the shower. She headed to the second floor, already thinking of him wet and soapy.

His clothes from last night were on her bed. She dropped the blanket and slipped into the bathroom. It was already steamy and she quietly pulled back the shower curtain to surprise him. Louie smiled and held out his hand. The shower was hot, exactly how she liked it, and she stepped into the tub and closed the curtain. She turned her back and tucked her rear end up against him as the water washed over her. Her hair clung to her back and he lifted it up and pushed it aside to kiss her neck.

Shivers raced down her spine as he nuzzled and nibbled and her body woke up and wanted him again. His hands slid across her skin, soaping down her breasts and then slid lower. He knew exactly what she liked and how she liked it and she reveled at how fast he could bring her to the brink of a climax. She reached behind to find him rock hard and bulging. Before he could make her completely lose her mind, she turned around and sank to her knees in front of him. Her hands stroked up and down as she drew out the moment when she'd taste him. His hands fell to her head and the water cascaded over them both. His body was so firm and taut and his thighs were muscular. When had he become so fit? She ran her hands up the inside of his thighs and focused on making him crazy.

Suddenly, she froze.

A wine colored birthmark marked his skin where his thigh connected to his body. She jerked back and stared at it again. Memories flooded through her; the night of the ball in the bedroom, Mr. Mystery, the same birthmark. No. It wasn't possible. What was going on? Her heart and body screamed denial, but her mind was working around reality. Was the masked man really Louie? In disguise? It wasn't Mr. Mystery? What the hell was he up to? Why had he lied to her? Memories of him kissing her, touching her during the ball, lying to her about everything.

"What's wrong?"

She shook her head, not quite understanding, but knowing she had to get away from him. She stood up and tore out of the shower, almost falling in her haste to escape.

"Hey, what's wrong? What's going on? Beck?"

She grabbed her robe off the hook on the door and ran into the bedroom. Her hair dripped and she wrapped her arms around her body as she began to shiver. Louie raced into the bedroom, one of her pink towels wrapped around his waist haphazardly. She stared at him again, hoping she was wrong. Wanting so bad to be wrong.

He stepped towards her. "Beck, what's going on? You're white as a ghost. Sit down. What's the matter?"

"Don't touch me!" She backed away.

His face twisted in shock and he stopped in his tracks. "Tell me what's wrong. Are you ok? Are you having some type of attack or something?"

"Take off the towel," she ordered.

He furrowed his brow. "What's going on?"

"TAKE OFF THE DAMN TOWEL, LOUIE!"

He narrowed his eyes at her screech. "I had the towel off in the shower and you left."

She moved across the room and reached for the pink material, but he grabbed her hand. "Stop it, Becky. Tell me what the hell is going on."

She yanked her hand out of his grasp and pushed the wet hair out of her face again. The hate she felt for him right now was more than she ever thought she'd feel for another human being. "You have a birthmark."

He nodded. "I've had it all my life. What's the matter? Does it bother you? I never really think much about it anymore. Does it repulse you?"

"It was you," she said through clenched teeth.

"Uhm, what was me? What are you talking about?" He tried to reach out to her again, but she stepped back.

"You touch me and I swear to God, I'll rip your eyeballs out and throw them at you." She put her hands out as if to ward him off.

"You're nuts."

"Oh am I? Am I nuts, Mr. Mystery?"

He froze and she knew right then that she was right. He had guilt all over his face. "What did you say?"

"The night of the ball, in the bedroom, I was about to give you the hand job of your fantasies and the moon lit up the room and I saw it. I remember thinking it was unusual, but that was all I thought. Until now." She blinked to keep the tears that were forming from spilling over. "You are some kind of slime. My God, I thought we were friends and all this time, all these years, you were just waiting for an opportunity to get me in bed, no matter how you had to go about it. All your supposed joking about my body, it was all true wasn't it? You went so far as to disguise yourself as someone else just to get your hands on me. You son of a bitch!"

"Princess, I..."

"Don't you ever call me that again! Ever." Her body shook harder and she took several deep breaths, trying to calm down. Her teeth chattered and she wrapped her arms around herself again, the now wet robe no longer providing any warmth. Images, conversations, all flooded her brain and made her head ache. "I have half a mind to tell Mr. Mystery what you did and let him deal with you, too. There must be some kind of law against pretending to be someone you aren't."

Louie's face turned red. "There is no Mr. Mystery."

"What?"

He moved across the room and she backed up, but he was only reaching for his clothes. He took off the towel and again she stared at the stain on his upper leg. He put his boxers on and reached for his pants. Why hadn't she noticed it last night? It had been dark, but still. She closed her eyes. What the hell had she done? Had they done?

"Mr. Mystery doesn't exist, or rather he does exist, but it's me. I'm Mr. Mystery. I own the Ryan House. There's no one else."

She snorted. "Oh, is that supposed to make me feel better somehow? Get real. Like you own a million dollar mansion. What do you really think? I'm that stupid? Get the hell out of here. Just shut up and get the hell out of my house."

He zipped up his pants and pulled his shirt on. Calmly, he stepped into the bathroom with his towel and came out again. "I'm going, but I'm not lying to you about this. I bought it last fall and I'm renovating it and paying for the renovations."

What was he talking about? How was that possible?

She stared back at him, so angry and so confused she could barely think straight.

"And Becky, just for the record, I hadn't wanted last night to happen. Remember? I'm the one who said it wasn't a good idea and I'm the one who said I wasn't coming inside last night. But as always, you had to have everything your way."

At the door, he stopped and turned back. Hurt filled his eyes but she ignored him. The bastard.

"Since I have nothing left to lose, I'll tell you this too. I love you. I love you more than any other person on this planet. I've loved you since we were kids and now after last night, I love you even more. When you stepped into the shower a few minutes ago, my heart exploded so hard it hurt. It's not just your body I want, it's all of you. If it was only your body, what I feel would have burned out a long time ago. The night of the ball, nothing was ever supposed to happen. All I wanted was the chance to dance with you as someone you might show some interest in. I knew you'd never see me as anyone but Nerdman." He half smiled at the nickname, but Becky didn't say a word. "I never intended to hurt you, and I'm sorry. As I said, it went much farther than I intended. But I'm not sorry about last night. Maybe when you've had time to calm down and think this through, you'll find that what we did last night was something that comes around once in a lifetime. It was good, Becky. We're good together."

"Last night was no big deal. Who do you think I am? Some innocent? It was good." She shrugged and looked away. "But it was far from great."

He walked out. She heard him leave a short time later and she sank to the carpet on her bedroom floor, dropping her head into her hands. What the hell was going on? In the past ten minutes, everything in her world she believed to be true was gone. Last night she'd slept with the one man she thought she could trust above anyone else and it turned out he was worse than any man she'd ever been with. He was a liar. He'd used her and deceived her. Had he been planning this? He had to have been. He brought up the whole idea of the Ball, he came home at Christmas with that idea.

And the Ryan House? It was his? All this time he'd

let her believe there was a mysterious owner and it was him? What an idiot he was. If he bought that house, he must be in debt so deep he'd never get out. What a fool.

Nothing made sense. He'd lied about so much. The night of the ball, claiming he couldn't dance as Louie and then waltzing her around as if he was Fred Astaire as Mr. Mystery. The costume, the mask, the kiss in the gazebo. Would he ever have told her? What if she'd never seen the birthmark? How long would he have let her believe that there was another owner?

What an idiot she was. These past few weeks trying to convince him they should be lovers, and him pretending it wasn't a good idea. That was probably part of his plan, too. Let her think he was reluctant, that he was worried about what would happen to their friendship. Oh God, she was a fool. She had to make some sense out of this, had to get a grip.

She needed Callie. Needed her calm words of wisdom to make sense out of all of this. She pushed to her feet and grabbed her phone, then sank to the side of her bed. When Tom answered, she almost hung up, but instead forced her voice to sound normal.

"Hey Tom, is Callie there?"

"Sure, you ok? You sound strange."

"Oh, no, I'm fine. Maybe spring allergies or something."

"Hmm, ok, let me get her for you. She's doing some laundry."

Becky waited and in the background, she could hear giggling and muffled talking and then Callie came on the phone, sounding out of breath. "Hey, what are you doing up this early on a Saturday morning?"

"Cal, do you have any time this morning that you could come over here? I mean, I know you're busy and all but..."

"What's wrong?"

"I don't want to talk about it on the phone." Her voice cracked and she chewed her bottom lip.

"Sure, honey, I'll be right there. Give me ten minutes to get dressed."

"Thanks."

She hung up the phone and stared at the wall across

the room. She should get dressed. No, she should take a shower, she still had soap residue in her hair.

Over an hour went by before Callie showed up at her back door. Becky glared at her. "Good thing I wasn't lying in a pool of blood."

"I'm sorry. I know. It's just that Tom..." Her voice trailed off and a blush stained her cheeks. "The girls were at an overnight," she explained.

"I'm sorry, I didn't know or I wouldn't have called." She wasn't really sorry. Tom and Callie had the rest of their lives to make love, the rest of their lives to be together.

Callie poured herself a cup of coffee and sank to the chair at the kitchen table. "What's wrong?"

"You aren't going to believe this when I tell you."

Several minutes later, after she'd shared all the details, including the shower scene, with her best friend, Becky had tears running down her face and she sniffled into a tissue.

"I still can't figure out how he came to buy the mansion. There's no record anywhere. I searched and searched. There's nothing around that says who the owner is." Callie sipped her coffee.

Becky nodded. "Maybe he's lying about that, too, although what he has to gain, I don't know. Maybe he's covering something else up. If he did buy it, he's got to be in debt over his head. His parents will have a cow if they find out." Louie's parents were notorious for being extremely frugal people. Knowing their son was buying a million dollar mansion wasn't going to set well.

"Maybe he told them when he went there for the holidays."

Becky shrugged. "I don't know, I don't care. He's an ass and I never want to see him or talk to him again."

Callie set her coffee cup down. "How could none of us know any of this? I mean, I'm telling you, I talked to Mr. Mystery—er—Louie as Mr. Mystery and I would never in a million years have known it was him."

"How do you think I feel? I kissed him. Made out with him, for crying out loud, all the while thinking how bad I was being and that if Louie found out he'd despise me. God!" She swore again, so disgusted with herself she couldn't stand it.

"I think I might have an idea about why he bought that house," Callie said, looking into her coffee cup.

"I don't care why he bought it."

"Beck, think about it. That house has always been your dream house. Everyone around knows how much you love it."

Becky pushed back her chair and shook her head. "Don't even try that with me. He didn't buy the mansion because of me. That whole 'he loves me' was just a game to him all these years, just as I said it was. Only I thought we were playing the game together, but in reality, he was playing it, thinking that someday I'd go to bed with him."

"And you did."

She hung her head to her chest and rested her hands on the kitchen sink. Images from last night raced through her mind, but it wasn't the images that bothered her. It was how she'd felt. For the first time ever, she'd felt a real connection with a man. She'd felt as if they had made love and were maybe even on the road to something more. She lifted her head, wiped at her eyes and drew a deep breath. "I feel like such a fool. I feel like one of those girls who really believes the football player when he says he loves only her as they climb into the back seat."

The phone rang and Becky ignored it. She knew it was him and she wasn't about to talk to him. Shortly after her cell phone chimed, she glanced at the caller ID and then turned it off. When Callie's phone rang, she lifted her eyes in question to Becky.

She shrugged and listened as Callie answered. "Hey, Louie."

"Yes, I'm with her. No, she's not going to talk to you, not right now."

From across the room, Becky could hear Louie and could hear from his tone he was agitated. "Give it some time. I don't know what's going on, but talking to her now isn't going to help. Leave her alone for a while."

Becky rolled her eyes. What side was Callie on here? It didn't sound like she was chewing out the jerk too much.

"Yes, why don't you do that? I'll see you then." Callie closed her phone.

"You'll see him? *SEE* him? What are you doing?"

Callie moved to the counter and loaded her coffee mug in the dishwasher. "I can't help but believe there has to be some logical reason behind all this. If I were you, I'd want me to find out what I could."

"Or are you trying to scoop a story?"

Callie half smiled. "I won't pretend the reporter in me isn't chomping at the bit to get to the bottom of this story, but that's not the real reason I want to talk to him tonight. My two best friends are in the middle of a major drama. I want to help. My only way to help right now is to find out what's in his head. Right?"

She had a point and at least she was honest about wanting the details of the mansion for a story. Becky nodded.

Callie folded her in her arms and for a minute, Becky let her comfort her. She rested her head on her friend's shoulder and more tears flowed. Callie rubbed her back as if she was one of the kids.

"It's all going to work out, somehow. I know it is. There has to be a reason behind all this and I'm going to find it, I promise."

Becky pulled back and again swiped at her eyes. "It doesn't matter. This isn't something I can ever forgive him for. He lied to me, for months and months and then to top it all off, he used me. In the worst possible way he used me and I let him."

Callie picked up her keys and her purse. "Have a shower. Try not to think about it. I know that's asking a lot, but try. He's coming over at seven and I'll call you right after he leaves."

"Fine. I have to go over to my mother's and work on the books later today."

"It'll be good to get your mind off this."

"Kiss the girls for me and say hi to Tom."

"I will."

Callie left out the back door and Becky ran her hands through her hair and climbed upstairs. If she sat down again, she was just going to start dwelling and feeling sorry for herself. So what if they had sex? He didn't know how much it meant to her and he never would. If she played this cool, he'd come out looking like the idiot, not her. He *was* the idiot anyway. What kind of stupid fool lies and pretends to be something he isn't? If he bought the Ryan House, he was in over his head. The cost to renovate that place was more than the sale price of the house. She couldn't even fathom it. How did he secure the loan? His business wasn't worth that, not even close, and she knew his parents didn't have that kind of collateral.

Maybe he had a rich uncle. Who knows? Who cares? She stepped into the shower, purposely blocking out the memory of being with him a few hours ago. What was he doing now? Thinking of her? Knowing he'd ruined their friendship forever? Did it matter to him? Did he care? Did she? Tears streamed down her face and sobs racked her body. She leaned against the wall and let the water pour over her as she cried like she'd never cried in her life.

****

Louie stared out the window of the den. He wore the same clothes he'd had on since yesterday, but couldn't be bothered to change. Making love with Becky had been the most amazing event of his life. When she'd stepped into the shower this morning and he'd wrapped her naked body in his arms, he'd had this thought that maybe, somehow, she'd realized they had something special. He'd at least hoped they were starting something that was going somewhere other than just to bed.

He closed his eyes as he leaned back in his chair. He never knew she'd seen the birthmark the night of the ball. It had always been a part of him and he never gave it a second thought. When he was a baby, his mother had made a fuss over it and taken him to doctors to make sure there was nothing wrong, but once they'd assured her it was perfectly normal, it was never really mentioned again. Even the few women he'd been with over the years hadn't commented on it. It was such a damn minor thing.

Why hadn't he come clean after the ball? Why hadn't he sat her down and said, "Look Beck, I have something really kind of funny to tell you."

Because she would have been just as mad at his deceit then as she was now. Well, maybe not quite as mad. But now, after last night, she felt used and deceived. All her life, Becky had insisted men weren't to be trusted. Her father had abandoned her mother while she was pregnant and Becky had never forgiven him or all of mankind for it. He rubbed his temples as he thought about the years of their friendship, the laughter, the teasing, and the love. He loved her and he knew she loved him, even if only as a friend. Last night he'd tried his best to show her that there was real love there, not just buddy love.

And what about his other secret? The money and the house. He opened his eyes and looked around. What difference did it make if people knew he was loaded? If they treated him different because of it, so be it. He shouldn't be ashamed to have money any more than folks should be ashamed who didn't have it. He set his jaw. He'd done a lot of good with his money since he'd acquired it a few years ago. Unknown to Miss Rebecca Richardson, he'd completely paid off the mortgage on her mother's beauty shop and apartment. Margaret still made a payment every month, thinking it was a mortgage payment, but it went straight into solid investments and she had more than enough money to retire any time she wanted. He was going to wait until the time came when Margaret wanted to slow down and then have her lawyer tell her the good news. He also carried the mortgage on Becky's house and had done the same thing. He didn't have a wife and kids, but he took care of those he loved.

He didn't need the money, what was he supposed to do with it? He'd donated huge chunks to worthy charities. He was the anonymous donor of the new hospital wing, he was the anonymous donor for a lot of improvements in Oakdale, and when the one thing Becky loved more than anything on earth was going to be sold and leveled, what else was he supposed to do?

And he didn't regret it. He stood up and shoved his hands in his pockets. He loved this house as much as she did. Unable to sit still any longer, he took a quick shower and changed clothes. Today was a perfect day to finally get rid of his old car and buy one he'd always wanted. He also had some folks to talk to. His parents first and foremost, and then when he saw Callie and Tom tonight, he'd give Callie an exclusive story about the hometown boy who'd made a fortune literally overnight.

It felt good to have the weight of the secret life off his

shoulders and if he kept his mind off Becky, he was even looking forward to this new chapter.

An hour later, he opened the front door, his conversation with his shocked parents still ringing in his ears. As he stepped onto the porch, a man emerged from a car in the driveway. He was tall with dark hair that showed a hint of gray. Louie guessed him to be in his late forties. The man looked up at the house for a moment, then approached Louie where he waited on the top step.

"Can I help you?" Louie asked, crossing his arms.

The older man looked at him through narrowed eyes as if trying to see if he recognized him, then said, "Who are you?"

Louie lifted one eyebrow and felt his chest swell. "I'm the owner of this property." Wow. That was some rush. His lips twitched into a grin, but the other man didn't seem impressed. He nodded slowly and looked around.

"When did you buy it?"

"Last fall. Is there something I can do for you?" Louie uncrossed his arms and slowly came down the porch steps.

When Louie was face to face with him, he saw that the man's skin was leathered like he lived somewhere in the sunshine year round. He wore shorts and sandals; not exactly the proper attire for this time of year.

The man nodded as if taking in something and Louie wondered how long he should be patient. "Look, buddy, I don't mean to be rude, but I was on my way out. If there's something I can do for you, let me know. Otherwise, I'll have to ask you to move on."

The other man turned his head to look him directly in the eye. "It wouldn't be the first time I've been asked to leave this property."

Louie frowned.

The man sighed. "This was once my family home."

Louie blinked. "Excuse me?"

The stranger stuck out his hand and Louie shook it automatically.

"I grew up here," the older man said, his eyes taking on a faraway look. "I'm Michael Ryan."

Chapter Fourteen

Louie released the handshake. "Michael Ryan, the son who died in the boating crash?"

"That's what folks believe, yep." He rocked back on his heels and grinned.

Louie stared and all thoughts of car shopping fled.

"Mind if we walk in the back? I always loved the yard."

Was he a wacko? He couldn't be Ryan. Ryan was dead. Obviously, he was playing some sort of game. Louie touched his pocket, feeling for his cell phone, knowing the police could get out there pretty quick.

"Don't worry, I'm not a nutso. I can prove who I am." He looked up at the house once more and then headed towards the back.

Louie shrugged. The guy seemed harmless. Maybe he was a distant relative or something. He followed him through the side gate.

"It's been twenty-six years since I've been home. That's a long time." He turned and looked at Louie once more. "I didn't catch your name."

"Louie. Louie Hanson."

"And you say you bought the house last fall?"

They'd reached the back door by now and the man stood and stared out over the freshly mowed lawn. Louie watched him for a second and swore he saw tears glisten in his eyes, but the man gave his head a brusque shake and walked on.

"When I was a boy, this lawn looked like it went on for miles. I'd run out here with my brothers and I'd be out of breath before we reached the back barns."

Louie wasn't sure how to respond so he just let the other man ramble. It seemed he was talking more to himself than anyone else, anyway. As they reached the gazebo, Louie remembered the letters. He glanced at the other man. If he really was Michael Ryan, and Louie didn't believe for a second he was, then he'd know about the letters and he'd know exactly who the woman was.

"So listen," Louie started. The man looked at him but continued to walk.

"Yeah?"

"It doesn't escape me that Michael Ryan was blown to smithereens in a yachting accident."

"Yep. It was a bad scene all right. It took months to recover from it."

"Yeah, well, not that I don't believe you, but maybe I could ask you a couple of questions."

The other man stopped and looked at Louie through narrowed eyes. "I told you I could prove it. We'll go inside in a minute and I'll tell you all about it."

Louie shook his head. It was one thing to be outside in the yard with this lunatic, but he wasn't about to let him into the house. "I found a box in the attic with some items in it that belonged to Michael Ryan."

"I didn't really have time to pack before I died," the other guy smirked.

"In the box was a stack of letters and some other personal items that belonged to someone Mr. Ryan seemed to have cared about."

His jaw tightened. "You read those? They were pretty personal letters, boy."

"Yeah, well, dead men usually don't come back to complain."

"You want me to tell you what was in those letters?"

Louie shook his head. "Nope, I know what was in the letters. Just tell me who the woman was and describe the jewelry that was in the box."

The older man shut his eyes for a second and Louie thought he saw pain in his them when they opened again. "My Lassie, God, she was a beauty." He looked off into the distance. "She had hair the color of the leaves on that oak tree in the fall, and eyes as green as the lawn. She was the most beautiful woman, only a girl really, I'd ever seen. The jewelry you speak of was a necklace, emerald and diamonds and matching earrings, but there would have only been one earring in that box. The other one was lost the night she walked out of my life."

Louie stared at him as if seeing a ghost and the other man looked at him once more and chuckled.

"I told you, everyone thought I was dead, but I'm not. I'm alive and well."

"How? What?" Louie didn't even know where to begin.

"All in time, my friend, all in time. Right now, humor me. Let me wander my childhood home once more and then let's go inside and find something to drink so I can tell you all about it."

What else could he do? He fell into step and listened as the other man described the mansion the way it was twenty-five years ago. They talked about what Louie had done to the yard and what his plans were and when they reached the outbuildings, they stopped.

"I didn't bring the keys with me. They're on a hook inside."

Michael Ryan nodded. "The one in the mud room right inside the door. That's ok, let's go have that drink and we'll chat inside."

After giving the other man a full tour of the house, Louie poured them both a generous drink and settled in the leather chair next to him in the den.

"I assume you're dying to know how it all happened."

"You might say so. Your family thought you were dead. Your parents, your brothers, all of them." Louie took a sip of the scotch and grimaced. Why had he poured such a drink?

"Good. That's what I wanted them to think." He took a generous drink of his own and closed his eyes as if savoring it. "I'd forgotten what good liquor tastes like. My God, nothing like it."

"Why you do it? What did you possibly have to gain by not coming back here?"

"My freedom." Michael took another long drink and leaned his head back against the leather chair.

"You were engaged. Suzanne Crosby right?"

"Yes, one of THE Crosby's. It was my parents' plan that the two oldest families in Oakdale combine their money and their bloodlines. My brothers were already married and had done well for themselves and I was expected to follow suit."

"Is she just *supposedly* dead, too?"

"Suzanne? No. Poor girl really is fish food. The boat that picked me up said they saw, well, bits of her floating on the water when they hauled me in. They thought I was dead until I opened my eyes. I don't remember anything about the explosion or them finding me, nothing. The first I remember was several days later, and for some reason, at the time it seemed like a good idea to pretend to be someone other than a rich kid. I gave them a phony name and said I'd been working on the yacht that blew up. When we arrived in port, I refused to see a doctor and disappeared into the crowd."

"Your family was devastated. My parents told me they never got over it."

Michael looked down into his drink and Louie could see remorse creep into his eyes when he looked up. "I didn't really plan on being dead for twenty-six years. At first I thought, I'll just take a break, you know, for a lark, have some fun, and be someone else for a while." He drew a deep breath and finished his drink and then shrugged. "Time flies, don't it?"

Louie understood. As bizarre as it seemed, he sort of got it. This guy was just going to have a little break from his real life, have fun slumming it for a while, and it soon turned into too long. Too long to go back home, too long to say, 'Oops I'm really alive.'

"After a while, well, it just seemed better."

"So why now? Why are you back now? Do your brothers know yet?"

"No one knows but you and me."

For a long time the other man stared off into space and Louie wondered what memories were haunting him. "You still didn't say why now."

Michael stood up and walked to the liquor cabinet, but he didn't pour another drink. Instead, he poured a glass of club soda and added some lime. "I was searching on-line. Curiosity, I guess, a need to maybe reconnect with my past, I don't know. I saw that my parents had died and then I saw that the house was sold."

He turned around and faced Louie. "I didn't come back for my share if that's what you're thinking. I've lived without the Ryan money for over half my life, and to be honest, I don't miss it."

"How've you been living?"

Michael walked to the large picture window overlooking the gardens and Louie waited, knowing the other man had to have a fascinating story to tell. He was also waiting for him to clear up the mystery of the woman in the letters.

"I bummed around in the beginning. You don't need much on the island to get by, but soon I ended up in business with some locals." He turned around and grinned. "Seems some of my father's business sense rubbed off after all. We made a fortune!"

"Doing what?"

"Fishing excursions, then a resort and soon the whole package. We cater to people who were just like my father. They come to the island to get away from it all, but they don't want to rough it."

"I still don't know how you kept your identity a secret."

"It's surprising how little people question you once they've accepted you. I gave them a tale of my former employer's yacht blowing up and they bought it. Gave them a fake name and I was all set."

"So why are you back? Why now? The house?"

"Not really. This place stood for everything I didn't want in my life."

"What then?"

"Louie, right?"

Louie nodded.

"This will sound really strange coming from a tough old guy like me, but I have a few regrets and one of them was that gal you know about from the letters."

"The one you called Lassie?"

The older man's features softened and his eyes once more took on a far away look. "Yes, my Lassie." He turned back and grinned. "I saw a tiny blurb in the Oakdale gazette on-line and realized it was her. She's still here in Oakdale and she's widowed. I stopped thinking and caught a plane. I've come back to see her."

****

"Ma?" Becky walked through the apartment, but it

was obvious in a few seconds Margaret wasn't home. A note stuck to the fridge with an old magnet said she'd gone to lunch with Callie's parents and would be back around three. It was past two already; she might as well wait for her.

She pulled out a container of yogurt from the refrigerator, grabbed a spoon and headed to the living room. It was way too quiet and her mind raced, thinking back to last night, this morning, even her conversation with Callie. No matter which way she looked at it, Louie was wrong. She'd been so careful all these years to never let a man close enough to hurt her. And now she'd gone and fallen in love with her best friend, just to learn that he was a snake.

Disgusted with her thoughts, she paced the small living room. Men were only good for one thing, she'd told herself that for enough years. Why had she let Louie be the exception? She looked around at her mother's apartment.

This was where she'd grown up. Because of a man. This was what her mother could afford because her father had deserted her and then died, and there'd never been any money. She'd always pretended it didn't matter that she had to go to the park to swing, instead of in her back yard like Callie could. The apartment above the beauty shop had been the perfect solution for a working mom. Margaret had been close by all the time. Close by but busy. Always busy working and trying to stay a step ahead of things. She remembered her mother saying they'd buy a little house someday, but it never happened, and after a while, it seemed unnecessary.

Men were only concerned with themselves. They weren't to be counted on. First her father proved it to her and then Louie reinforced it.

Becky tossed the yogurt into the kitchen garbage and set her spoon in the sink. After a visit to the bathroom, she wandered into her mother's room. It smelled like Margaret. Her mother had always worn the same light fragrance. Her room was neat as a pin, as always, with nothing out of place. A picture of Becky and Callie rested on the tall dresser and on her nightstand was the latest gossip magazine she loved to read before bed.

With a sigh, she flopped down and flipped through it. An ad for Mother's Day caught her eye and she realized it wasn't that far off. Last year, she'd decided that this year she was going to do something really special for her mother. She sat cross-legged in the middle of the bed and stared at her mother's small jewelry box. Margaret had very little good jewelry, but the box that held it was an absolute mess. It probably came from the five and dime when she was about sixteen and she still used it. *That's what I was going to do. I was going to have one made for her with her initials on it.*

Excited, she slid off the bed, snatched it off the vanity and carried it back. When she was a little girl, her mother would let her play in her jewelry and try on her necklaces and large pins. Her mother would put her hair up in a twist and they'd have a tea party.

Becky pulled out the little drawers, remembering those days. Maybe she'd even buy her mother a new pin or a mother's ring. The contents of the drawers hadn't changed since she was little. The same dime store jewelry was tangled with the few good pieces her mother owned. Becky began to sort through it all, remembering some, not others. She slid her grandmother's large opal on her finger and grinned when it spun around. Her grandmother had been a very large woman with big fingers.

The third little drawer came out easily enough but when she went to put it back in, it wouldn't go. She pushed harder but something was blocking it. She lifted the box up and looked in the slot. There was a wadded up tissue in the back corner. She pulled it out and realized there was something wrapped inside.

When the emerald and diamond earring fell into her hand, she looked at it for a second before she realized what it was. How on earth had the earring gotten here? Her mind raced. Louie said it was in the safe room. Why would it be in her mother's jewelry box?

Wait a minute. Oh, my God. Oh, my God! Becky fingered the prongs that held the precious gems in place. One of the diamonds was missing. It wasn't missing before, she would have noticed. This wasn't the same earring. This had to be the match to the earring. How did it get here? Why did her mother have it?

She turned it over in her palm and it hit her. Along with it, a wash of chills raced through her.

Lassie, from the letters. No. It wasn't possible. Was her mother, was Margaret, the woman in the letters? Her mother and Michael Ryan were the lusty couple in those letters. Her chest constricted and her stomach clenched. This was too much. Hearing the front door, she quickly wadded the earring up in the paper again, but instead of shoving it back in the jewelry box, she stuffed it in her pocket. She had to be sure and she wouldn't be sure until she saw both earrings together. She had to talk to Louie.

Louie. It all hit her again. She hated him. Damn him, just when she needed to run this past him. Damn him!

"Becky?"

Becky put the jewelry box back on the dresser and walked out of the room. "I'm in here."

Margaret was in the kitchen unpacking a bag of groceries and Becky automatically started putting the things away. She glanced at her mother. She'd always been a beautiful woman, everyone said it was where Becky got her looks. But whereas Maggie had the red hair and pale skin of the Irish, Becky had inherited her father's darker hair and eyes. She had her mother's curvy figure, and they still both wore the same size.

"Ma?"

"Hmm?" Margaret fixed the coffee pot and set it to brew.

"Remember a while ago we were talking about the mansion and you said you weren't there very often when you were a kid?"

"Yeah?"

"I wondered why, I mean, didn't you know Michael Ryan or his brothers? They would have been in the same year as you school."

She watched her mother's face and she could have sworn her smile slipped just a bit, but she covered it up. "Honey, I went to the Catholic High School, the Ryan boys were at Oakdale High."

"Oh yeah, I forgot."

"You know who I saw at the grocery today?" Her mother picked up the brick of cheddar cheese and began to slice it and put it on a plate.

Becky half listened as Margaret went on about all the people she saw and what they said and what they were doing. She pulled out the box of crackers and added several of them to the plate with the cheese. The earring felt like it bulged in her pocket and she hoped her mother wasn't going to ask what it was. Maybe she should just pull it out and confront her with it, see what she said, watch her face for a reaction. Anything.

"Rebecca? Honey? Are you ok?"

Becky looked up at her and stared into her sage green eyes. "I'm fine, um, I didn't sleep much last night."

Then she cringed, remembering why she hadn't slept. She and Louie. It felt like a lifetime ago that all that had happened. So much had happened in twenty-four hours. She started yesterday annoyed with him, ended it making love with him, then this morning to discover he was Mr. Mystery, and then this afternoon, the earring.

Her mother's hand on her forehead startled her. "Rebecca, honey, what is it?"

She stepped away and swiped at her tears. "I'm fine, I'm fine. I'm just, I don't know, I'm just emotional today, I had a huge fight with Louie and..."

"You're this upset over a fight with Louie? You know its nothing, he'll come over in a day or two with your favorite candy and tease you until you laugh and forgive him."

"Not this time, Ma."

"Oh now, you sit down here and have something to eat and you can tell me what happened. I'm sure its all a misunderstanding. Louie would never hurt you, he loves you."

There were some things in life Becky wasn't about to talk with her mother about and the fact that Louie had deceived her and used her and slept with her under false pretenses was one of those subjects. The fact that she'd figured it out when she was about to...well it just wasn't something you discussed with your mother.

What she really wanted to do was bring up the earring. Her cell phone rang and she recognized the ringtone. She ignored it.

"Aren't you going to answer that?"

Becky shook her head. "It's not important." Her mother watched her steadily so she picked up a cheese and cracker and shoved them in her mouth.

The phone on the kitchen wall rang and Margaret picked it up. Becky knew who it was.

"Yes, she is. Of course you can, she's right here. Becky, its Louie, he needs to talk to you and he says it's urgent."

Becky rolled her eyes, but obediently crossed the room. She wasn't going to talk to him, but she wasn't going to get her mother in the middle of this either.

"What?" she answered.

"Don't hang up on me. I have something you are really going to want to hear."

"I don't want to hear anything. Not your excuses or your apologies or anything. I don't..."

"Would you shut up for two seconds and just listen? I know you're mad at me and we'll deal with all that later but this is huge. You will never guess who is sitting in the den right now drinking whiskey."

Becky's eyes narrowed and her stomach clenched. "So help me God, if you tell me it's Mr. Mystery and he wants me to talk to him and clear everything up."

"I told you there was no Mr. Mystery. I own the mansion, Beck, I need you to come over here right away. You are not going to believe who is here."

"I'm not coming out there, not now, not ever."

"I know you're pissed, and you have every right in the world to be but this isn't about us. It's something else. I can't tell you over the phone. Please, Beck come out here. Trust me"

"Trust you? Trust you? I'll never trust you again in my life, I'll never—"

"Ok, Ok. At least do this for me. Go into the bathroom and call me from your cell. I can't do tell you when you're right there with your mother."

"But—"

"Becky!"

"Fine." She hung up the phone and faced her mother. "I have to go, um, help Louie with something."

Margaret smiled. "I told you everything would be ok. That's fine, dear, why don't you both come back over later and I'll put some supper on?"

Becky picked up her purse and jacket, the earring still burning a hole in her pocket. As much as she didn't want to see Louie, she was anxious to show him the earring and see what he thought. She kissed her mother's cheek. "I'll give you a call in a bit."

In the car, she dialed Louie's cell phone. "I'm on my way out there." She hung up before he could reply. Tears filled her eyes again and she blinked rapidly before they fell. He was a son of a bitch and after this one time, this last trip out to the house, she was done with him. She would show him the earring, and keep the conversation strictly about the letters and the mystery and nothing about the two of them. Last night never happened as far as she was concerned, except for the fact that it was the end of their friendship. She wanted nothing to do with Louie Hanson ever again.

The drive seemed to take forever, but she finally pulled into the horseshoe driveway and parked. As soon as soon as she stepped from the car, Louie came out and grabbed her arm.

"Don't touch me." She jerked away from him and he held up his hands in surrender.

"I need to talk to you before you come inside."

She glared at him, making certain he knew how furious she was, but she followed him around the side of the house. She crossed her arms over her chest as they stopped.

"I know this is going to sound weird, but hear me out."

She rolled her eyes.

"You know how everyone believes that Michael Ryan died in that boat crash?"

She stared at him.

"He didn't. Die, that is. He was in the crash, but he survived."

Becky narrowed her eyes. "What are you talking about?"

"They never recovered his body, only that of his fiancée Suzanne. That's what Callie said when she researched the old records."

"It was a huge explosion. Everyone was blown to

bits."

"Not Michael Ryan. He lived and he's here in the den drinking whiskey."

She stared at him and her mouth fell open. What an absolute idiot he must think she is. She spun around to head back to her car.

Louie grabbed her arm and she gouged his hand with her fingernail. "Hey!" he jerked away.

"Don't you ever, *ever* put your hands on me again. What do you think? I'm stupid? Some guy in there says he's Michael Ryan and you want me to believe it? Or are you that gullible? Ryan's dead. Has been dead for over twenty-five years. He has a grave in the cemetery. I've seen it when I've gone with my mother to put flowers on her parents' grave. He's dead, you moron."

"I can prove he's not. Come inside. There's more to tell you about this, anyway."

She hesitated, but she still had the earring to show him. Then she could walk away. He swept his arm to indicate she should lead the way and with a flounce of her hair she walked ahead of him. She stepped up to the newly renovated porch and couldn't help the feeling of disappointment that settled in the pit of her stomach. She loved this house and loved the months she'd felt a part of it. Now it was over. It represented lies and betrayal to her. She waited for him to open the front door and followed him inside. She kept her eyes straight ahead, determined not to look at all the things she loved so much.

Louie led the way to the den. The two huge oak doors were open and she couldn't help but be a little curious about this guy who was claiming to be Michael Ryan. She stared as the man rose from the chair and looked directly at her.

Louie introduced them. "Rebecca Richardson, I'd like you to meet Michael Ryan."

Becky stared at the other man. She'd seen pictures of him, of course. When she and Louie had cleaned out the attic, there'd been tons of family photographs. The other man held out his hand and she shook it.

"It's a pleasure to meet you."

"I don't know what to say." She stared at him,

realizing he looked just like the pictures she'd seen.

"It's hard to accept, I know, but I've already proven it to your friend and I have no problem proving it to you, too."

The earring weighed heavily in her pocket and she thought for a second about pulling it out dramatically and asking him to explain why it was in her mother's jewelry box, but something held her back. There could be a very good explanation why Margaret had it and then again, there might be an explanation she didn't want to know about. Had her mother stolen it when she was a young girl? Was that why she didn't talk about the Ryans or the house or want anything to do with any of them? Had she found it and never returned it?

Louie handed her a glass of diet Coke.

"Will you sit down so we can talk?" Michael Ryan looked at her intently. She moved to the leather sofa and sat down, taking a long drink before placing the glass on the table.

"I'm listening. I'm not believing, but I'm listening."

He told her the story and her eyes grew wide. When he mentioned the letters and the woman, her heart beat wildly.

"So, as I told Louie, I've finally decided I've lived in exile long enough and I have this crazy idea to come back."

"And you think that this woman who you loved years ago is going to be happy to know you're alive?"

Michael Ryan smiled ruefully. "I can't begin to hope she'd be happy to see me. I'm taking my chances."

"You know we read the letters so don't think I'm rude, but didn't she end the affair because you were going to be married to Suzanne?"

He nodded. "Yep. The kicker is, that morning on the yacht I had made up my mind that I was coming home and telling my parents that I loved someone else and I wasn't marrying Suzanne."

"So when the yacht blew up and you recovered, why didn't you come right home or get in touch with her or whatever? Suzanne was dead. There was nothing standing in your way."

He gave her a funny look. "My brother Patrick called

the ship a few hours before the accident. He told me he'd run into her and that she'd just married someone else." He stared down at his hands. "I was beyond devastated and furious. I wanted to come back here and beat the other guy to a pulp. Thoughts of him with her tormented the hell out of me." He shrugged. "What would that have served? She was married. I loved her enough to not want to ruin her life. The explosion was a convenient way for me to not have to come back here and see her with him and not have to live the life my parents wanted."

Becky couldn't believe the tale he'd just told her. It had to be true. He knew too many important facts for it not to be.

Louie sat down next to her and she glared at him. "Becky, there's another piece to the story that Michael hasn't told you yet."

She looked into the brown eyes she knew so well and memories of last night when he'd made love to her surfaced. His eyes had been so full of love and, for the first time, she'd felt as if she was with someone who truly loved her, not just wanted a night of hot sex. She swallowed hard and forced herself to look away. She still had to deal with everything between them, but she knew what Michael was about to tell her, and she had to deal with this discovery first. She reached into her pocket, careful to keep the wrapped earring in her fist.

"I have something to show you," she said, looking at Michael but knowing Louie was watching. "I was at my mother's today and I found this."

She opened the tissue and held up the earring.

"Shit!" Louie swore but she ignored him, it was Michael's reaction she wanted.

He held out a shaking hand and she handed him the earring. He smiled. "She kept it. All these years she still had it." He closed his eyes and Becky glanced at Louie.

He nodded. "It's Margaret. Michael's Lassie is your mother."

Michael opened his eyes and stared at her. "Yes, Becky. It's a bit awkward that you read those letters, but I assure you I loved your mother with everything inside me. I would have given her the very moon if she'd wanted it."

Becky walked across the room and Michael stood up. He reached out his hands and she squeezed them. "I believe you would have. I wish things had been different."

"So do I. But I was young and by the time I'd worked up the courage to stand up to my family, she was married to another man."

"You want to see her?"

Michael's face split into a huge smile. "I do, but I have no idea how she'll react. I'm just a memory to her; I'm sure, but the fact that she kept this all these years..." He looked at the earring, then back up at Becky, "maybe a small part of her heart is still mine."

"You should have come back. My father didn't even stick around long enough to see me born."

Michael Ryan cursed and paced across the floor. "I don't know who he was. She and I—." He waved his hands. "Well, you two are adults, you read the letters. I didn't know she was even seeing anyone else. I never thought we had secrets, but I must have been wrong."

Becky shrugged. "I know very little. She rarely ever talked about him, but she must have loved him. She's never let anyone say anything bad about him. If I so much as uttered anything negative, she'd cut me right off. I always got the idea that she loved him, but he didn't feel the same. He died before I was born."

****

Louie stared at Becky and Michael Ryan. They were completely clueless. It was obvious exactly who Becky's father was and he was sitting right there. The same intense eyes, the same way they twisted their mouths. Michael's hair was salt and pepper but the dark hair was definitely the same shade as Becky's. How many times had Margaret said Becky had her father's dark looks? He swallowed hard. The real clincher was Becky's middle name; Rebecca Michelle. He smirked. Margaret was certainly clever if nothing else. Still, it wasn't up to him to tell these two the truth. There was only one person to break that news.

He cleared his throat. "What's the best way to do this? Should we talk to Maggie alone first or just surprise her?"

Two sets of blue eyes turned and looked at him.

Michael spoke first. "Tell me about her. It's been a lifetime ago since I've seen her."

Becky smiled and Louie's heart clenched. Last night she'd smiled like that at him, the way he'd always dreamed she would. Last night had been the beginning of all his dreams coming true and he'd really screwed it up. She was so angry at him; she'd probably never forgive him. He had to make her understand; make her realize how much he loved her.

"My mother is probably the sweetest person on this planet. She raised me alone. She worked long hours at the beauty shop and when the owner retired, she managed to buy it and she's been there ever since. We lived in an apartment over the shop."

Becky went on describing Margaret to Michael, who laughed at times and other times, shook his head in disbelief.

He still held the earring and looked at it once more. "I tried to give her gifts like this all the time but she'd never take them. Said it made her feel like we were doing something wrong. The only gifts she ever accepted were these. I pleaded with her to keep them and she did, until the day she left me." He shook his head. "The day she gave me that last letter, she'd put these in there with them, but then realized she'd forgotten one of the earrings. I left the next day on the cruise."

Louie paced the floor as the two talked. What was the best way to break this news to Margaret?

"What if we told her that I needed a ride? Do you think she'd come out?" Becky asked.

Louie turned around. "She might, but it would really shake her up." He turned to Michael. "Ever since I bought this place, we've been trying to get her to come out and see it and she refuses. Now, obviously, we know why."

"So let's go to her. I'm sorry kids, but I can't wait another minute to see her. I've waited twenty-five years."

Louie walked over to Becky and started to take her arm, then thought better. "I'd like to have a word or two with Becky before we do that, if you'll excuse us a minute."

He jerked his head and surprisingly, Becky didn't argue as she followed him from the room. Louie pulled the double doors shut and then led the way down the hall to the kitchen.

The minute the swinging door to the kitchen was shut, she turned on him.

"My head is spinning." She yanked open the refrigerator and pulled out another can of diet pop. "I can't believe this. I just can't, yet it makes perfect sense. Why didn't we even suspect? I mean, my mother not wanting to come here, the letters calling her Lassie."

"We had no reason to suspect anything."

"And to fake your own death." She took a long drink of her cola. "For twenty-five years, I mean, who does that?"

"What do you think your mother is going to say?"

Becky let her breath out on a long sigh. "I have no idea. Maybe she was kind of glad he was gone, you know. She married my father and Michael left her to marry that woman. If it were me, and I was in love with someone, I would..."

She stopped. Louie met her gaze before she tore it away.

"Never mind."

He reached out his hand but she stepped away and ignored him. Ok, so she was still furious with him. They'd deal with all that later; right now his main concern was Margaret. Margaret was like a favorite aunt or a second mother to him and the last thing he wanted to do was see her upset. He desperately tried to think of an easy way to break the news to her.

"I suppose if we refuse to take him to her, he'll just show up at the beauty shop. That would be worse wouldn't it?" Becky asked

He nodded. "Yeah, he's back; he's not going away until he sees her."

"Then I think we should be there when he does. She might want our support. Besides, we don't know this guy. Just because he's Michael Ryan, doesn't mean he's a good guy."

Louie nodded. "True."

She rinsed her pop can and tucked it underneath the sink in the recycling bin. "I suppose there's no time like now."

Becky reached the door and Louie watched her. If he let her walk out the door, they'd never have this conversation. Once she figured out exactly who Michael Ryan was, there was no telling her reaction. "Becky?"

She paused and flipped her head around to stare at him.

"I know you think what happened, what I did, was unforgivable..."

"I'm not discussing this with you."

"I love you."

"No, you don't."

"Yes, I do."

She shook her head. "No, you don't. That's not love. You took what I thought was a friendship, a real trusting relationship, and you blew it to pieces all because you wanted to play a game of make believe."

"And what about you? You didn't play make believe? Fooling around with a masked stranger?"

"This isn't about what I did, it's about you."

"Ok, ok, go ahead; put all the blame on me. That way you come out of it looking like the victim."

She narrowed her eyes and stared at him. "Are you trying to twist this around to be my fault? I didn't lie to you. I didn't lead you on or do anything to make you lose trust in me. You did that." She pointed her finger at him. "You used me. You used our friendship to your own benefit. Friends don't do that to each other. Ever."

She pushed through the door and was in the den by the time he caught up with her.

Louie looked from father to daughter and wondered again why neither of them seemed to notice. The way their mannerisms mimicked each other was eerie. Becky laughed at something Michael said and Louie's heart nosedived to his stomach. She'd never laugh at him that way again. She was right. He'd used the friendship they shared to his own advantage, whether intentional or not.

"Well, are you two going to take me to her, or do I call a cab and go myself?" Michael Ryan rocked back on his heels. The look of determination in his eyes was one Louie was all too familiar with. He'd seen the same look in Becky's eyes time and time again.

The short ride to Main Street was a quiet one. Louie

drove Becky's car and Michael rode in the back seat. The older man seemed unconcerned about returning to his hometown. From the way his eyes were focused straight ahead, it seemed all he was thinking about was seeing his Lassie again.

Becky stared out the side window, not trying to make conversation either. He suspected she was nervous. There was simply no way to know what Margaret's reaction would be. When they pulled up in front of the shop, Becky took out her cell phone.

"I'm going to let her know I'm back and I have company with me."

Louie couldn't hear the other side of the conversation, but Becky's face reddened and her gaze bounced off him before she opened the car door. He suspected that her mother knew about the fight between the two of them and typical Margaret was probably trying to play mediator.

"She's got dinner waiting."

Louie watched Michael pause and look at the beauty shop before he followed Becky through the door that led to the stairs. In front of the apartment door, Becky glanced at Louie and, for the first time, he felt as if she was asking for his help.

"If I tell you two to leave, you leave, no questions asked," she commanded and while Louie nodded right away, Michael Ryan didn't commit. Becky glared at him and the other man gave a quick nod.

A million thoughts raced through his mind as they stepped through the door. Margaret had married someone else shortly after breaking things off with Ryan. Was it because he was engaged to be married, or was it because she wasn't in love with him? No matter how lustful those letters were, the truth was, hot passionate affairs burn out and maybe Margaret didn't have any deep feelings for her lover when it was all done. Louie glanced at Becky. Last night, they'd made love for hours. They couldn't stop touching each other, and yet today, if she had a knife, Louie was certain she'd have plunged it through his heart.

"Maybe we shouldn't do this," he muttered as Becky turned the knob.

Two identical sets of blue eyes, with the same look of disgust, turned on him. If he'd ever doubted these two were related, he didn't now. He only wondered what Margaret was going to do about it.

He shrugged and walked through the door. "Maggie, my love, I sure hope that's your Shepard's Pie I'm smelling."

"Oh Louis, I'm so glad you talked some sense into that daughter of mine, she does have that stubborn streak of her father's."

Margaret came out of the kitchen. Her smile was bright and warm as always. She looked from him to Becky and then beyond. Her brows pulled together. Her eyes registered confusion and then shock. Her face went white and Louie quickly crossed the room to her side in case she passed out.

She dropped the bowl in her hands. Fortunately, it was a plastic storage container and was empty. It simply bounced on the wood floor. "Holy Mother of God," she whispered.

Chapter Fifteen

Louie walked over to Maggie and slipped his arm around her shoulder. "Come on Maggie, let's get you a chair."

Maggie stiffened her back. "What in all that is holy is going on?"

Michael Ryan walked slowly across the room. "I'm sorry to shock you like this."

Maggie put her hand to her chest and closed her eyes. "This is obviously a dream. This isn't happening. You're dead. You've been dead for twenty-five years."

Louie dropped his arm as Maggie brushed him off and he stepped away from the couple, feeling a bit like he'd just tuned into a soap opera.

Michael reached out his hand. "Touch me, Lassie. I'm real. I'm not a dream. I'm not dead."

Maggie stared at his hand for a moment and then at his face. "There were no survivors. They had a funeral. There's even a grave, although there's no body in it."

Michael looked chagrined. "I was rescued by a fishing boat. I didn't die, I just chose to disappear."

"Why? Why would you do something like that? To your family, your friends. To me?" Margaret sounded as if she was getting hysterical.

"Ma, why don't you let me help you sit down and I'll get you a cup of tea. There's a good explanation for all this."

Margaret shook her head and waved towards the kitchen. "There's a bottle on the top shelf of the cupboard. Will you get that down for me, please Rebecca?"

Becky didn't argue and Louie watched her walk into the kitchen. He had no idea if he should follow her or stay here. It was very awkward.

Becky returned with the Irish whiskey, something he'd only seen Margaret drink during times of crisis. Well, if this wasn't a time of crisis, or at least high drama, he didn't know what was. He took the bottle from Becky and the two glasses she carried with her. He poured two fingers of whiskey in both and handed one to Michael. The second one he handed to Margaret. When she reached for it, he cupped her hand in his around the glass.

"Maggie, look at me." He waited until her eyes lifted to his and she focused on him. "You ok?"

She nodded and then tossed back the liquid.

Louie cringed at the face she made.

"Lassie, you have no idea how very sorry I am about all this."

Maggie's green eyes turned to emerald ice. Louie had never seen her look so angry.

"You're sorry? You pretend to be dead, cause everyone who..." she stumbled and then finally said, "...loved you, complete and utter heartache and you say I'm sorry?" She gave a harsh laugh and tipped her glass up a second time, but the whiskey was all gone. Wisely, she simply set the glass down without refilling it.

"For twenty-five years, I've grieved for you. I've cared for your grave and the graves of your parents. Your mother died of a broken heart. They say she never got over losing her youngest son. How incredibly selfish can one human being be?"

Margaret's Irish brogue was thick, and Louie's eyebrows rose. He'd never seen her so out of control. Beside him, Becky looked more and more uncomfortable and he wished he could reach out to her, but he knew she wouldn't accept his comfort.

"You don't understand, Lassie."

"My name is Margaret. Lassie was a girl, a young foolish and stupid girl. I'm neither young, stupid, nor foolish. Why did you come back here? Your family is all gone. You have nothing to gain by showing up here."

"I didn't come to gain anything. I came to see you. It was time to put things right."

"You're about twenty-five years too late. You were engaged to Suzanne, you don't have anything here to put right. You made your decision before you ever took that cruise."

"Becky told me your husband walked out and left you

pregnant." Michael blurted.

Louie cringed as Margaret lifted her chin. "My daughter is wrong. My husband never left me, because he never existed."

Becky gasped. Louie blinked. Oh boy. This should be good. Guess Margaret wasn't going to waste any time straightening things out. He edged closer to Becky, this was going to really shock her and like it or not, he was going to be there to help her through it.

Michael's brow furrowed. "Patrick saw you. He saw your wedding ring. The news in town was that you were married and expecting a baby."

"You listen to gossip? You who used to tell me it didn't matter what folks said? My parents were very strict Catholic. There was no way their only daughter was going to be pregnant and not married. We let it out that I had eloped with a soldier who was shipping out, a whirlwind romance. When he 'died' no one questioned it."

"Wait a minute." Becky spoke up for the first time.

Margaret's pale face seemed to go even paler as her gaze fell to her daughter. "Rebecca..." she began.

Becky frowned. "If there was no husband, who was my father?" Her eyes widened as things fell into place. Louie glanced from her to Michael and he saw the same light come on in his eyes, but it was Becky he was concerned about. Her entire life history had just changed.

"I have a daughter? Becky's my daughter?" Michael looked from Becky to Margaret and Louie didn't know who was going to need him to catch them when they collapsed.

Becky glared at her mother. "All these years, I was a Ryan and you never told me? You let me believe that I was some unknown man's kid and he didn't want me?"

Louie thought about the house and how connected Becky had always felt to it. Maybe it wasn't so bizarre that she'd always had this obsession with it.

"Rebecca, I know you're hurt and you don't understand, but you have to believe me when I tell you it had to be that way. I couldn't walk around carrying his baby. He was engaged to someone else, and then he was dead. His mother was so devastated, can you imagine how she would have felt knowing he'd been..." she seemed to struggle for the right word but then narrowed her eyes and glared at Michael, "Diddling with the maid."

Michael let out a low moan and stared at Becky and then back at Margaret. "If I had known, I would have come back. If I had known, I wouldn't have taken the cruise."

"You'd made your decision. You chose Suzanne and you went on your little love boat trip with her. I found out I was pregnant before you left, but I wasn't about to use that to change your mind. I wanted your love not your obligation."

"You worked for the Ryans?" Becky's face was white and Louie slid his arm around her waist. The fact that she didn't push him away told him loud and clear that she was in shock. "Ma, you always let on that you barely knew them."

"I knew them. I knew them all too well," Margaret said with a look of disgust.

Michael crossed the room and reached his hand out to touch Margaret's face. Louie thought with the fire in Maggie's eyes, she would have slapped him away. Instead, he was shocked to see tears well up in her eyes and then slide down her cheeks.

"Maggie, my love, I'm so sorry. I don't know what to say except that if I had known you were carrying our baby, I would have never let you do that alone."

"I didn't need your charity or your family's wrath. I knew they'd try to buy me off with money and I wanted none of it. I raised our daughter by myself, bought my own business, and am quite comfortable, and I did it without the Ryan money or name."

Michael brushed at Maggie's tears, but she pushed his hands away and took several steps back from him.

"Lassie, you won't believe me, I know you won't, but the morning the ship blew up, I was going to tell Suzanne I couldn't marry her. I was devastated that you had married someone else and I knew I couldn't hurt another woman by marrying her when I didn't love her the way I should. I was going to come back, get my things, and move on. I thought maybe my father's company could settle me somewhere else and I could be the hard working executive he always wanted. I couldn't stay in Oakdale knowing you were with another man. The accident gave me the perfect opportunity to reinvent myself. Not once did I suspect that the baby you were carrying was mine." He shook his head.

After a brief moment of tension, Margaret was in Michael's arms and the cries of anguish from her were like nothing Louie had ever heard before. He gently led Becky away down the hall towards her room to give the couple some privacy. It was apparent that what had begun as an affair twenty five years ago had never ended and while he was thrilled for them both, he was worried about the daughter they both seemed to have forgotten.

He pressed her to sit on the side of the bed and stepped back to look at her. "You ok?"

"My entire life was a lie. I don't even know if my name is really Richardson. There was never a man named Richardson, so how can I be Rebecca Richardson?"

"I'm sure once they both calm down and the shock wears off, she'll explain it more clearly."

"Did you see my mother? I've never seen her that furious."

"Passion. He sparks strong feelings from her. We read the letters; you know what they were like."

Becky shuddered. "I can't think of those letters. It was different when they were two strangers."

"How are you feeling about all this?" He shoved his hands in his pockets and stared down at her.

Becky shrugged. "I don't know. My head is whirling. You don't know what it's like to believe something your whole life. I always thought my father was a loser who didn't want me or my mother."

"It sounds to me like if he had known about you, he would have taken care of you both."

Becky looked up at him. "Taken care of us? With money, maybe. I don't know that he would have really stood up to his family and married her. Do you?"

"It sounds lame, but yeah, I think he would have. I believe him. I think he would definitely have married her and the hell with what his family thought. You have to realize he was a young guy, younger than we are now. I know how hard it is to stand up to my own parents."

Becky narrowed her eyes. "Did you tell them about

your little secret?"

"I called them this morning and told them everything."

"And?"

"They were shocked, and I'm sure they'll have a lot more questions later."

Becky shifted and reached into her pocket. She pulled out the earring. "I should tell my mother I found this."

"Its pretty quiet out there, do you think we should go back out?"

Becky stood up and brushed back her hair. "Yeah. If they want to be alone, I'll drive you back out to the house."

"Actually, I was kind of thinking of shopping for a car today. You wouldn't want to help me, would you?"

She glared at him. "Don't think just because I'm in shock right now and talking to you, that this is done. Our friendship is over. So, no, I'm not going car shopping with you or anything else. Once I drop you off today, frankly, I'd like not to see you at all."

As if someone had landed a sucker punch to his gut, Louie felt all his air leave his body. So much for hoping she'd ever forgive him. He didn't bother to answer as she walked out of the room and down the hall.

****

Becky stood for a moment just watching her parents. Her parents! How weird was that thought? They sat side by side on the couch, her mother's hand clasped firmly in Michael's. Maggie looked up when Becky walked in. She held out her free hand.

"Rebecca, come here."

Becky obediently moved across the room and sat down in the wing chair opposite the couple. The earring was still in her hand. "Ma, I found this earlier today."

She held it out to Margaret who took it with trembling fingers.

"I wasn't snooping. I was going to have a jewelry box made for you for Mother's Day and I was looking through your things to get a feel for what I wanted it to hold. The drawer wouldn't go back in and I found that in the back corner."

Margaret fingered the precious gems and smiled. "This was all I had of you." She looked at Michael. "I thought of mailing it to your family but I was terrified somehow they'd find out about us and put two and two together, so I kept it."

Michael took the earring from her. "I wish you had sold it, maybe it would have helped support you both when I couldn't."

"Actually, it did support us. When I wanted to buy the shop, I didn't have any type of collateral. I took it with me to the bank and the manager was nice enough to use it as a down payment. He tucked it into a safe deposit box and when I'd paid off enough of the loan, he gave it back to me. I never could have bought my own shop if I hadn't had this. I've only got about five more years left on the mortgage and it will be completely mine."

Michael grinned. "I wish you'd kept the whole set. Just think what you could have done with it. You could have sold it and..."

Margaret shook her head. "It wasn't right, Micky, you know it wasn't. I didn't want what you could buy me. I wanted you." She lifted her chin and looked at Becky. "I raised our daughter without the Ryan money or name."

"You did a fine job, Lassie. She is a beautiful girl."

"She looks like you." Margaret smiled.

Becky glanced at Michael, not seeing whatever it was her mother saw. Her mother's words over the years slipped through her memory. *'She has her father's eyes. She has her father's stubbornness.'* Becky looked at Michael. She'd never had a father. She had no idea how to feel about this stranger sitting across from her whose genes were responsible for half of her DNA.

"Becky, I'd like to get to know you. I may have missed out on your entire childhood, but I'm hoping that I'll be able to be involved in the rest of your life. Maybe have some grandkids someday."

Margaret gave a brief laugh and stood up. "That you might be waiting on for some time. Our Becky has no interest in marriage or babies, or so she says. Now my casserole was done some time ago, I suggest we sit down and have some supper."

"I should go." Louie stood at the door.

"Nonsense, Louis. You can't leave now, it's your favorite." Margaret stood up.

Becky caught Louie's gaze but she refused to second the invitation. He knew how she felt and he knew she wouldn't welcome him staying.

He looked away, then kissed Margaret's cheek. "I'll take a rain check, Maggie. To be honest, my car is on its last legs and I was going down to the dealership and see what they have on the lot."

Becky felt her mother's gaze on her but she stood up and walked out of the room. Michael followed her to the kitchen. She opened the refrigerator and took out the water pitcher. Michael looked around and Becky wondered what he was thinking. The apartment was small, but it had been their home her whole life and she hated thinking he was comparing it to the kitchen at the mansion.

"You ok?" he asked, leaning against the counter.

Becky shrugged. "I have no idea."

He laughed. "Actually, me either. Pretty wild, huh?"

Margaret came into the room and glanced at the two of them and her eyes filled again.

Becky sighed. "Stop it."

Margaret wiped at her eyes and moved to the oven to remove the pie. "It's going to be a while before I really believe this isn't all some bizarre dream." She glanced at Michael again and blushed. Becky rolled her eyes and sighed, but inside she was thrilled. All these years Maggie had waited for a man she never thought she'd see again here on earth and now he was there. Unbelievable.

Over dinner, mother and daughter did their best to catch Michael up on all the local happenings over the years and sat spellbound listening to his tales of life in the small village.

"And you never married anyone or..." Margaret asked pointedly.

Michael leaned back in his chair and winked at Becky. "I can't tell you, my Lassie, that I was a complete celibate for the past twenty-five years." He leaned across the table and grabbed her hands. "But I will tell you that I never fell in love, my heart was here with you, always."

Becky stood up. "This is getting way too mushy for

me." She set the plates in the sink and began to rinse them off. "The next question is, what are you going to do about the rest of your life? It's not like you can waltz into the bank and declare yourself alive is it?"

Michael sat back again but Becky noticed he kept her mother's hand tight in his and his eyes on her face. "I think the first thing I need to do is contact my brothers. They have a right to know before I go public. Then, yes, I would very much like to be back in Oakdale and all that implies."

"Oh, Michael, the house. What about the house? I mean, Louie bought it thinking you were dead." Maggie said.

"Louie bought the house from Michael's brothers," Becky pointed out. "They were the heirs of his parents. I don't think it will be an issue, but I can check with the lawyers at work."

"Don't bother, Becky. I don't want the house. Louie is welcome to it."

"Her whole life, she's had this obsession with that house. As a little girl, she would go on and on about it until my teeth ached from clenching them." Margaret laughed.

Michael shook his head. "That had to kill you, to talk about it and all."

Becky turned off the water. "She didn't talk about it much, occasionally a few things here and there, but she let me believe she didn't have any connections to the family."

Margaret turned red. "Maybe I was wrong. I shouldn't have let my parents dictate to me. Maybe it would have given your mother some comfort to have a grandchild." Her voice broke and tears filled her eyes. "I was scared. I thought, what if they tried to take my baby from me? What if they decided I wasn't fit to raise her, not having their kind of money?"

Becky stepped behind her mother's chair and hugged her. "You did the right thing, Ma. I know that. Don't worry about it."

But inside she couldn't help but think, 'what if'. The money wasn't important, that wasn't what she wondered about. But she'd had grandparents and uncles and all those family members that everyone else always had. Her mother's parents had died when she was a toddler. She barely remembered them. Callie's family was the only 'family' she'd ever known.

Then a thought occurred to her. "I think I have an idea of how you can come back to Oakdale."

Michael looked up and she went on.

"My best friend, Callie, is a reporter for the Oakdale Gazette. I can ask her to come over first thing in the morning and you could give her an exclusive. That way, the story would come out and you could walk through town and everyone would know what was happening. You'll still have to explain it a million times, but it might help if people knew the story first."

Maggie nodded. "Callie is terrific, Micky. She'd tell the story exactly how you'd want it told, no media spin on things to make it look bad and sell papers."

Michael nodded. "Ok, but first I need to get in touch with my brothers. I hate to do this by phone, but I'm not willing to leave here again right away." He lifted Margaret's hand to his mouth. "But first..."

He stood up and with a little bit of effort, dropped to one knee at the side of the table.

Becky's eyes widened. "Oh no."

Margaret gasped.

"First, I'm going to make you my bride, if you'll still have me, Maggie, my love."

Becky wanted to tell her mother to stop and think. Just because they were wildly in love before, and just because this was all very romantic and amazing that he'd come back, didn't mean they could make it work. They were different people, they were strangers. But none of it mattered because Margaret had already said yes and the couple wasn't wasting any more time. Their lips were locked on each other and Becky quickly slipped out of the room and out the door.

****

Louie pulled the unfamiliar car into the driveway and grinned as Tom looked up from his yard work. His buddy's eyes widened at the sight of the expensive vehicle.

Louie climbed out of the black Jaguar and shoved his

hands in his pocket. "What do you think?"

Tom gave a low whistle as he walked around the front of the car and ran his hand across it. "That's quite the ride, my friend."

Louie lifted the hood and the two men looked at the sparkling clean engine. "I'm test driving it this week."

Tom glanced at him. "The week? They let you take this out for a whole week?"

Louie shrugged. "I'm learning real quick what all the extra zeros at the end of my balance in the bank really mean."

His friend laughed. "I can imagine."

"It's no big deal." Louie shut the hood.

Tom opened the passenger door and looked inside. "Yeah, I can see it's no big deal."

But it wasn't. Louie couldn't care less about the money. He couldn't buy the one thing he wanted most in the world, Becky's forgiveness. He missed her so much it was like someone had physically cut out his heart.

"Wanna a beer?" Tom asked as he shut the door.

Louie pushed the remote to lock the car and followed Tom to the backyard. The garage door was open and the contents were strewn around the back patio. "Getting ready for the new family?"

Tom came out the kitchen door with two bottles of beer and handed one to Louie. "Yeah, now that the weather is improving, I figured I should get rid of some stuff. Callie's house goes on the market this week, so we'll start moving things over here."

"Let me know when and I'll give you a hand."

Tom sat down on the worn patio furniture and Louie watched him glance around. "You know my parents, pack rats to the end. It's going to take me a month just to clean out the garage."

"I know the feeling."

"So what are you going to do about your folks' place? I mean, now that the cat's out of the bag and everyone knows you're the owner of the Ryan place, are you going to sell it?"

Louie shrugged. "I don't know, not right away. I don't know what I'm doing about anything yet. Even buying that car seems like more than I want to do."

Tom nodded. "Have you talked to her at all? Seen her?"

Louie shook his head. "Not really. If I show up, she disappears. So I stopped showing up."

"Everything ready for Margaret's wedding this weekend?"

He nodded. "Yep, Michael's brothers are here and staying out at the house with him. I moved to my folks place to give them some privacy."

Tom set his beer down. "Does it feel weird? I mean, to have them back there and yet you own it?"

Louie peeled at the label of his bottle and looked out over the neatly mowed lawn. The new wooden swing set they'd built for Callie s youngest daughter caught his eye as did the new glider. This was a home, not that enormous monstrosity of a mansion that felt cold and lifeless without Becky's laughter. "There was a time when I thought it really was mine, but it's not." He drained his beer and turned back to look at Tom.

"If you hadn't told me last winter to stop living in the past and worry only about the here and now, I might have let my pride get in the way of a life with Callie."

"She's never going to forgive me for what I did. She's made it more than clear."

Tom shrugged. "Think of everything she's been through this month. Not just you and all that, but Michael coming back, and what all that meant and now her mother is getting married. Give her some time, let things settle down a bit and then try to talk to her."

But Louie knew it didn't matter how much time he gave her. Becky wasn't ever going to get past the fact that he lied to her and she thought he'd used her. To her, it was unforgivable, and he agreed.

He stood up. "Thanks for the beer."

"Hey, where you going? Come on, I could use a hand with this junk. It'll take your mind off everything."

Louie looked at the garage mess and realized he had absolutely nothing else to do. He would only end up driving around thinking about her or heading back to his parents' house. Even Google wasn't there. He'd left him out at the mansion with the Ryans for now.

Several sweaty hours later, one corner of the garage

was cleaned and organized. Louie slung another armful of old boards onto the pile to go to the dump. "Did your father save everything?"

Tom brushed his hands down his jeans as he dropped a few old lawn chairs onto the same pile. "Everything. And hauled stuff home from other people's places."

"My father and yours must have gone on scavenger hunts together. Some of this looks like the same crap I tossed out of their house when they moved."

Tom chuckled. "Yep, I think you're right."

A car door slammed and a voice that took his breath away drifted from the front yard. He froze. He wanted to see her so bad he ached, and yet, he knew it would be a whole new hell.

"There're my girls," Tom said and a smile split his face. He practically sprinted towards the front of the house.

Louie followed at a slower pace. Callie launched herself at Tom as if she'd been away from him for days instead of just overnight.

The girls saw Louie and came running. "Uncle Louie!" Emma hollered and he opened his arms to catch the little blonde.

"Hey, angel, what have you girls been up to today?" He hugged her close and inhaled. "Hmmm, I smell cookies." He nibbled her neck and she giggled.

"Aunt Becky has them in the back seat. We've been baking for Grandma Maggie's wedding."

He lifted his eyes and watched Becky lift a small tray out of the back seat. He waited for her to look at him, but as always, she acted as if he wasn't even there. Louie set Emma back on her feet again.

"Come on out back and look how much junk we've gotten rid of," Tom said, sliding his arm around Callie's shoulder.

"Nice Car, Lou." Callie grinned as she walked past.

"I'll take you guys for a spin in a bit if you want," he said.

Amber and Hannah were all over it and he unlocked the door for them to climb inside.

Hannah tossed her hair and slid behind the wheel. "How do I look, Uncle Louie?"

He shook his head. Hannah and Amber already had that look that women had about them. The secret that men weren't privy too. The little girls were still there, but more and more they were morphing into those mysterious creatures. "You look like someone who's going to give me a heart attack in a few years."

She smiled and giggled to Amber who sat in the passenger seat.

Out of the corner of his eye, he watched Becky go through the front door rather than follow her friends out back.

Louie hesitated, but like someone who can't stop themselves from running into a burning fire to try to save something that means the world to them, he followed her.

Chapter Sixteen

The inside of the house was as torn apart as the garage, and Louie passed various piles of furniture that were obviously heading to the local thrift store. He didn't envy Tom the job he had in here, but he sure envied his friend the end result. The woman he loved and three beautiful daughters to fill the rooms with laughter and love.

Becky stood on a step ladder, lining a shelf with contact paper. It reminded him of the months they'd worked together on the house and his guts twisted. The plate of cookies sat on the kitchen table and he walked over to help himself.

"Those are for dessert tonight, leave them alone."

Louie pulled his hand back. "What's tonight?"

She didn't answer and he walked over to where she was setting new dishes into the cupboard. He picked up the stack of plates and handed them to her. She gave him a look of contempt, but took the dishes.

"I said, what's tonight?"

She shook her hair. "My mother and Michael and Callie's folks are coming over for a cookout."

And it was more than obvious that he wasn't invited, something in the past he would have been welcome to join.

"So that's how this will go."

She turned her head to look down at him and he automatically handed her the stack of bowls. "How what will go?"

"You and me."

"There is definitely no you and me."

Her voice was as cold as the beer he'd drank. He was ticked. Not only had he lost her, but now she was making their friends choose between them. Why did he suddenly feel like he was in the middle of a bad divorce? "You've

237

forced them to choose between us, haven't you?"

She snorted and ignored him.

"You have to be childish about this and get your own way, so everyone is uncomfortable and that's why I've been ostracized."

She glared down at him from her perch. "I haven't said a word to them about you. I couldn't care less if you were around or not." She picked up a stack of bowls and set them on the second shelf.

He shook his head. "You still think you're the victim in all this, don't you? Do you ever for one minute stop and think what I've lost?"

She continued to set glasses on the shelf and ignored him.

"Damn it, Becky, I love you. I've always loved you and even more than that, we were friends. I've lost everything because I didn't happen to let you know the size of my bank balance."

Becky stared at the cupboard. He wanted her to talk to him so desperately that he was even willing to fight with her to get her to pay attention to him.

"I don't give a damn about any of that and you know it. You lied to me, you used me, and you broke my trust. I can't forgive you for that and I don't want to."

Something inside him snapped and he reached out and plucked her off the stool. She struggled, but he held tight until she stopped. She glared at him as if he was the nastiest bug she'd ever seen and she couldn't wait to squash him under toe.

"Up until you made the big discovery of who Mr. Mystery was, you were this close to admitting that you loved me and that maybe we had something going for us." He lowered his voice and lifted his hand to caress her cheek. "You can't tell me that what we shared physically wasn't something special."

She narrowed her eyes and tossed her head. "I keep forgetting how incredibly inexperienced you are. That was sex. Nothing else. You are so naïve."

"I see. So you've slept around so much that a night like that is a regular occurrence?"

She shrugged.

"Knock it off, Becky. We both know your reputation is

ninety percent talk, and for some reason you want everyone to believe that you're this worldly woman who takes it where she wants it and walks away. You need to get over yourself."

"I think its you that needs to get over me." Her voice was laced with disgust and Louie couldn't take it anymore. He snaked his hand out and cupped the back of her head, pulling her to him. He kissed her hard and waited for her claws to pierce his skin. But when her arms lifted, they simply wrapped around his waist and then her palms flattened on his back as she leaned into him. She opened her mouth and kissed him back as if she was just as starved for him as he was for her.

His body came back to life. She was his food, his oxygen. He couldn't feel anything without her. Then she pulled away and he let her go. A tear slid down her cheek and she brushed at it.

She looked at him through tortured eyes. "You really are an ass, you know that?"

She spun away and out the back door and he heard her call out to Callie. "I'm going to go over and get those other boxes from your front porch."

She was gone before he got outside. Callie looked at him and shook her head, but he wasn't in the mood for one of her 'talks'.

"Who wants to ride in the Jag?" he invited.

All three girls ran towards him. As he pulled out of the driveway, he caught sight of Tom and Callie racing towards the front steps and laughing. *Guess I better make this ride a bit longer than I was going to.* Somehow, that made him feel even worse than he already did.

****

The bridal march began and the audience rose to their feet. Louie looked up as Becky, dressed in the most beautiful gown he'd ever seen, slowly floated down the aisle. She carried a bouquet of white roses, interlaced with green shamrocks and on her head a tiny wreath of the same. Directly behind her walked Callie dressed in an identical gown. Amber and Hannah followed, and Emma was the last to come down as she tossed rose petals for the bride to walk on.

Louie's heart swelled at the sight of Margaret

holding Callie's father's arm. She was dressed in a floor length white gown with a long train and veil. She'd told him a few weeks ago she felt silly wearing a young girl's bridal outfit, but everyone insisted since it was, in fact, her first wedding. Louie couldn't have agreed more, and in no way did Michael's Lassie look silly. She looked stunning. He stole a glance at Becky as her mother took Michael's hand at the altar. What was she thinking? Not only had she gained a father this month, but she had also met her uncles and their wives and kids. The family he knew she'd always longed for was suddenly all here packed in the church pews watching the ceremony.

As the priest talked about the long journey this couple had been on and the amazing miracle that had brought them to today, Louie let his mind drift. After the scene in the kitchen a week ago, he'd stayed as far away from Becky as he could. He'd buried himself in his computers at work and gone back to wearing his old black glasses and comfortable clothes. The days when he would look up from the counter and find her in his shop or bringing him lunch were long gone. He'd also started making calls to try to get the rest of his life moving forward.

He knew one thing for sure. He couldn't stay in Oakdale. After Callie and Tom's wedding next month, he was going to seriously begin looking for somewhere else to live. The priest began the familiar vows and he jerked his head back to the couple. Maggie had never looked so radiant and so happy. The newlyweds planned to honeymoon on the island where Michael lived. After the initial shock and understanding anger from Michael's brothers had worn off, the entire family insisted that the long lost brother share in the Ryan family fortune even though money was the last thing that Michael or Maggie cared about. Margaret had also sold her beauty shop business to one of her long time employees and seemed to be ready to embark on a whole new life with her first love.

Michael's family held no animosity towards Maggie about keeping Becky a secret from them. Everyone was in a forgiving mood once they saw the couple and how much in love they were. Louie glanced at Becky who smiled as her father slipped the ring on her mother's hand. Maybe in time, she'd...

No. He had to stop thinking like that. It was much better that he just move away and let her live her life and maybe he could find some peace.

****

Becky felt Louie's stare. He'd been watching her almost the entire ceremony. What he was thinking was anyone's guess. He hadn't spoken a word to her since the kiss in Tom's kitchen. She told herself that was good, that's how she wanted it, but inside, she felt a little twinge at her heart. If he loved her as much as he kept insisting, would he have given up? Was that really what she wanted? Him to crawl before she could forgive him? Was she that shallow?

She chewed her bottom lip and shifted the flowers in her hand. He looked incredibly handsome today. The dark tuxedo reminded her of the night of the ball. As much as she tried to block out that night, the memories washed over here at the oddest times. She shifted her feet, remembering what they'd done in the gazebo, the kisses in the moonlight, and in the master bedroom while the party played on downstairs. For some odd reason, now that she'd figured out he was the man behind the mask, the whole thing seemed even hotter and sexier. But hot as it was, it didn't make it right. He lied. He could have pulled off his mask in the gazebo after the first kiss and they could have laughed about it.

She looked at him again and caught his eye. She didn't look away at first, but then in the end she had to. No matter how much chemistry there was between them, he'd let her down in the worst possible way. He'd deceived her and she couldn't get over it.

With a start, she realized her parents...her parents!...were kissing and the audience in the church was applauding. The priest announced the new couple and they floated up the aisle on a cloud of happiness. Becky took the arm of her Uncle Patrick who was the best man and smiled when he lifted her hand to his lips. It was an odd feeling to have all these relatives, but she was getting used to it real quick.

Outside, she accepted the hugs and congratulations of the wedding guests. Louie's parents were in town for the big event and his mother sought her out.

"Rebecca." Mrs. Hansen hugged her tight. "You look absolutely radiant. Next to Maggie, I can't imagine there's anyone happier today than you."

"Thank you. Yes, I'm so happy for them both. Michael loves her and that's what matters to me."

The other woman squeezed her hand. "I heard you did a lot of work out at the Ryan House, I mean, Louie's house. Oh, I don't know what to call it anymore, but the place is beautiful. You definitely have a way with interior decorating."

"Thank you. It was a fun project, of course, I had no idea, well, you know."

"Yes, my dear, I do know and I know what you're saying. Don't think we were too happy with his little story. But of course, he's our only child, a mother can stay angry only so long."

Becky looked up as Louie and his father approached. She accepted a hug from Burt and tried to avoid Louie's gaze, but soon his parents drifted away to talk to more old friends and she was left alone with him.

"Your folks seem to be enjoying being back in town," she said to fill the awkward silence.

Louie nodded. "Yeah, they're talking about moving back." He shook his head. "Five years ago, they couldn't get out of here fast enough and now it's all, 'Well, you know, maybe the snow wasn't so bad'."

She smiled. "People always want what they don't have I suppose." Then realizing what she'd said, she fiddled with her flowers, feeling heat rush to her cheeks. "I probably should find the photographer." She gave an awkward laugh. "It's weird, but suddenly, there're a lot of family pictures to be taken."

She couldn't seem to walk away, though. Louie shoved his hands in his pockets, the way he always did when he was nervous or uncomfortable. She almost felt bad for him...almost.

"You look beautiful, Becky. The flowers in your hair truly make you look like a princess in a fairy tale."

Becky looked up at him and saw pain in his eyes. She was tempted to reach out and take it away, but she couldn't bring herself to. "It's my mother's fairy tale, she's the princess today."

"Actually it's yours too. You always believed that your father was a jerk who left your mother. Instead, you found out that he loved her and never even knew about you."

"Yes, but remember, too, that if my father had stood up to his family and told them he loved my mother, none of this would have happened. They'd have married and had me and we could have lived as a family."

"Your mother forgave him almost as soon as he walked in the door. She loves him that much. Maybe her love is stronger than her anger."

"You're beginning to sound like some Hallmark movie. Don't try to turn this around into some type of lesson for me. I am not my mother."

She turned away and climbed into the limo. The family pictures were being taken in the gardens of the mansion and she dreaded going back there. Louie's words replayed in her mind. Her mother could have easily never forgiven Michael. After all, she'd paid for twenty-five years for him not telling his parents about them. She paid even more by letting the whole town think her husband had left her and her baby.

"There's my baby girl."

Michael Ryan stepped inside the limo and slid across the seat and sat next to Becky.

"You really need to stop calling me that. It makes me feel like I'm five years old." She smiled to soften her words and Michael held lifted his arm, inviting her to move closer. It should feel awkward, she thought, uncomfortable even, for this stranger to hug and kiss her. But as his arm settled around her shoulders, she snuggled into his chest. It felt so right. Her father. Twenty-five years she'd lived without him and now, in less than two months, it was as if he'd always been here. She knew why her mother loved him. Michael had an infectious personality, and everyone he met immediately became his friend.

She lifted her head and he pressed a kiss to her temple.

"I'm going to promise you something right now. No matter where we go or where we end up living for a while,

I will take care of her and I will love her and you will never need to wonder if she's happy. I love your mother more than anything in this world."

Becky's eyes filled with tears and she nodded and kissed his cheek. "I know you do, Michael. She loves you, too."

Tears slipped down her cheeks and she sat back for him to brush them away. He handed her a white handkerchief. "Ahh, baby girl, stop the tears. This is the happiest day of our lives, you and me and Maggie. A family at last. I've something for you."

He shifted in the limo and pulled out a piece of paper. Unfolding it, he glanced at it one more time. "All these years, I was never able to financially support you. I hope to God above you know that if I had known for one second that I had a daughter, I would have given you the moon and all the stars with them."

He handed her the paper. "I calculated how much I might have spent on you over the years. The birthday parties, the proms, the girly things you all seem to need so much, a car for your sixteenth birthday. Then I thought, if Maggie and I had been together all these years, we'd have had a couple more kids, so I took that into account and came up with this number."

Becky's eyes popped out of her head as she looked at the paper. It was a print out from a bank account with her name on it and the figures on it were insane.

"Michael, I can't accept this. I don't want your money."

Michael laughed. "The beauty of this is, you have no choice. I'm your father and I'm telling you that it's your money. You can leave it there and never touch it, and it will be there to take care of you when you are old and gray, or you can use it for some fun, travel, whatever you want. But you, my darling girl, have no choice." He laughed. "Daddy's a rich man, my love, and I'm going to take care of you and your mother whether you want me to or not." He reached behind him to the small shelf in the limo. "I have one more thing for you."

He handed her a familiar box and she shook her head. "No, I can't..."

"Oh yes, this is from your mother and me. Trust me, I

will buy Maggie more jewelry than she can possibly wear, but we want you to have this set."

Maggie lifted the cover to reveal the diamond and emerald necklace and earring set she'd found in the attic last winter. "They are beautiful."

"Yep, and they look much better on you than in the box."

He helped her clasp the necklace, and she took off the pearl earrings he'd already given her earlier in the day and replaced them with the emeralds.

Michael nodded. "Perfect."

Becky leaned over and hugged him. The money didn't mean anything to her, but the fact that he was so determined to spoil her and her mother did. All her life she'd wanted a father to make her feel special, and now she had one. She knew, too, that Michael wasn't just going to take care of her financially. He seemed the type of man who truly wanted to be there for her. The type of guy she could trust. It occurred to her right then, that she'd had no problem at all forgiving him for what he'd done. She loved him too much to let that get in the way of their future.

****

"I'm so nervous that I think I'll get to the door of the church and throw up," Callie announced.

Becky shook her head. She'd been listening to Callie talk about how nervous she was for a week already. She set a glass of diet pop on her dresser and reached for another dress in her closet. "You'll do fine," she answered automatically. She held up a sundress. "What about this one?"

Callie shook her head and Becky sighed and put the red dress back in the closet and reached for another. She'd told Callie to take whatever she wanted out of her wardrobe for her honeymoon, but her friend's taste and hers were so different it wasn't working out.

"Beck, if this marriage doesn't work, we've ruined our kids' lives."

Becky whipped her head around. "What are you talking about? Not working out? You two can't keep your hands off one another."

Callie turned red. "I'm not talking about that part of

it, that part's fine. But there's more to a marriage than what happens in bed."

Becky nodded. "You were married to Stan for seven years, and it wasn't good in that department, but you'd still be married to him if he hadn't died."

Callie sighed. "I know, but Tom is..." She shrugged. "I can't explain it."

Becky came over and sat next to her on the bed. "Listen, I can't begin to explain marriage to you. All I know is that if you love someone, you'll make it work. You and Tom are crazy about each other and each other's kids. It's going to be a great life, and no one is telling you it'll be easy, but you really have something there, Cal, and I know it's going to work out."

Callie nodded. "I guess I get nervous when I think about the every day stuff, the coming home from work and cooking dinner, and getting homework done, and watching TV. I mean, marriage isn't always exciting."

"Again, what do I know? But you have to work to keep it exciting. You can't let it get in a rut. Besides, you've got your parents who love those girls and will take them in a heartbeat if you two need to have a night alone, and you've always got me to do the same. I've got no life and now I've got all this money. I can take them shopping or to the amusement park. Hell, I can take them Disney World every year for you."

Callie looked serious and turned to her. "I don't know if anyone told you, but Louie is leaving Oakdale."

Becky's entire body froze and she couldn't form the words to ask. She stared back at Callie as if she'd just punched in the gut.

"He told us that while we're gone on our cruise, he's going to be relocating to Seattle. I guess he's taken a job with Microsoft as some type of consultant."

"Seattle? Washington? That's the other side of the country."

"That's exactly what he wanted. He said he had to get as far away from here, actually he did say from you, as possible. Have you talked to him at all? He's so miserable."

"I haven't talked to him since my parents' wedding."

But she'd thought of him, every day. The Ryan

relatives had long gone back to their own homes and her parents were still on their island honeymoon. She'd almost driven out to his house a couple of times but didn't know what to say. She ached inside for what had happened and she still was upset with him, but the initial fury had faded to abject misery. Her mother was so happy with Michael, and soon Callie and Tom would be on their honeymoon. A small part of her had started to think maybe she and Louie could find a way to work this out. Maybe she could forgive him, or at least hear him out and maybe start again. She'd see him at the rehearsal dinner on Friday and she'd loosely figured she'd see how things went then before thinking any further ahead.

Callie stood up and began to search through the closet on her own. She pulled out a couple dresses that Becky never wore. "I know what he did was wrong, but I guess I can understand why he did it, a bit. Beck, remember when Tom first came back and I refused to tell him the real reason why I married Stan all those years ago? Remember, I had this idea that if he really loved me, it wouldn't matter."

"I have no idea where you're going with this," Becky said, and folded the couple of dresses that Callie had chosen.

"I think, in time, Louie would have told you he was Mr. Mystery. I don't think he's the type that would have hidden that from you forever, once he knew you loved him. He needed that security first before he could tell you what he did. I needed to know that Tom loved me now and what happened before didn't matter, before I could explain why I never showed up to elope with him that night fifteen years ago."

"So you think that if I hadn't figured it out that morning, if we'd continued on, then he would have told me? I don't think he would have. I think he would have rather I never found out." Becky couldn't picture Louie owning up to that knowing how angry she'd be.

"Let's suppose you were together, in love, making love, having a relationship and six months or a year went by and you discovered what he'd done. Would you throw the whole thing away because of that? I mean, yeah, you'd probably fight with him about it and he'd probably feel bad and you'd get mad and then you'd have this really, really great, hot, make up sex. Knowing you, you'd probably make him put the mask on to make him really pay for his deception."

Becky smirked. She could definitely picture herself doing that. "It was quite the turn on."

"Exactly. So, why don't you give him another chance like Tom gave me, like your mother gave your father, and stop sitting around here looking for ways to spend your fortune on someone else's kids. Go out to the house, scream and yell at him some more, and then jump his bones for the next three days. Just make sure you come up for air in time to be at the rehearsal dinner."

Becky's mind raced. Could she do that? Was Callie right? Was she just waiting for someone to tell her that she needed to forgive him? She chewed her bottom lip.

Callie put her hands on her hips. "Go, before you lose your nerve."

"But you have things you need to get done; this isn't a good time. I should help you with those wedding favors, and..."

But Callie was already hauling her to her feet and shoving her towards the door. "I have three daughters, a mother and a mother-in-law who will be helping me until I'm ready to scream."

Becky smiled and hugged her friend, then flew down the stairs so fast she almost tripped. She stopped to slip on her sandals at the front door and then flung it open.

The mailman stood on her porch about to knock and she almost ran him over.

"Oh, Henry, I'm sorry."

"Not a problem, Miss, I know these are busy days for you girls. I've got a certified letter here you need to sign for." He handed her a pen and the slip of paper and she signed both, wondering what on earth it was. The return address was from a law firm she didn't recognize.

She stepped back inside with the letter and her mail, and Callie came to the top of the stairs. "What did you forget?"

"Nothing, there's a certified letter. I need to see what it is."

She opened the envelope and read the brief note.

"That son of a bitch!" She swore and Callie came racing down the stairs.

Becky handed her the letter without comment. Her chest heaved as if she'd run a mile. Her head felt as if it was going to explode. She hadn't been this mad in a long time. She definitely felt as if she wanted to hit someone.

"Louie signed over the Ryan house to you? With all the contents included? Oh my God."

"I'm going to kill him!"

Callie looked up from the letter. "The man gives you property worth, well, I don't know, maybe a million dollars now, and you are going to kill him? Why does this make no sense to me?"

"He's trying to buy my forgiveness, now. Can't you see that?" She stormed out of the house and her sports car squealed from the abuse she gave it as she backed out of the driveway and headed out to the edge of town.

****

Louie poured the hot water over his tea bag and looked out the large kitchen window. Every day something new popped up in the garden and he had a pang of regret when he realized he wouldn't be around midsummer to see it with everything in full bloom. He strained the tea bag and took the hot mug out to the back patio.

It wasn't even a year ago that he'd stood out here, looked around and wondered how on earth he was ever going to handle the renovations of this place. Now, even though there was a lot to be done inside, the gardens were immaculate. In the distance he could see the gazebo and the greenhouse. He sipped his tea and let himself remember the night of the ball, and how Becky had looked in her gown with her dark hair piled high on her head. *Lady in Red* played again in his mind and he felt the familiar twist in his heart. It wasn't fair. He swallowed hard. It wasn't fair to have been so close to happiness and then have it all come crashing down around him. Then again, he had no one to blame but himself. The Masquerade Ball, the costume, the deception all had been a really bad idea.

Google wound around his feet and Louie sat down on one of the new patio chairs and stroked his grey fur. The cat plopped down and blinked up at him in the sunshine. He hoped Becky would keep him here. The old tomcat had really made the mansion his own. Louie drank his tea. Seattle was definitely going to be a big change. He'd flown out there and even looked into renting a place by the water, but it had seemed so dreary and lonely. Instead, he figured he'd just stay at a hotel until he found what he wanted and then buy something.

His attorney had gone nuts when he signed over the entire property over to Becky, but he knew that was the only thing he could do. He wasn't about to sell it. Michael Ryan didn't want anything to do with it. There was only one person who loved the place the way he did, more than he did for that matter, and it was her.

A car door slammed and he frowned and glanced at his watch. With Tom and Callie's wedding taking place in the gazebo in three days there'd been any number of people coming by and dropping things off. With a sigh, he set his tea cup on the table and headed back inside to let them in.

The last person he expected to see storming into the kitchen was Becky. Her green eyes were flashing and her hair was wild as if she'd had the top of the convertible down and hadn't tied it back. She was furious like he'd never seen her before. He wondered who had messed up. Were the flowers wrong? The harp player not coming? He knew it had to do with the wedding; Becky would never come out here for any other reason. In her hand she waved a letter.

"Good morning, Princess." He tried to sound calm and collected as if everything was fine. He was so happy to have her here again that he really didn't care what the reason, or why she was mad. It was good to just see her.

"You are unbelievable."

He smirked. "So you told me once before."

She walked over to him and her scent wafted through his nostrils, wrapped around his senses and made his knees weak. "I am not for sale."

He nodded. "That's good to know. I think they stopped selling people back in the mid 1800's."

"You can't buy my forgiveness."

"I'm not trying to."

"Yes, you are. Who the hell goes around giving away mansions?"

He stepped away before he touched her. "Can I get you something to drink?"

"Do you really have so much money now that this doesn't matter to you?"

He turned back around. "I don't want the house and you do, so what's the big deal?"

"The big deal is, it isn't some little cottage or a house in town, it's the Ryan House and..."

"And last time I knew, you were a Ryan." He grinned at his own explanation and took a can of diet pop out of the refrigerator. His explanation seemed to render her speechless. He handed her the drink. "You're a Ryan now. Your father doesn't want the house back; your uncles don't want it. I don't want it and you do. What's so complicated about this?"

She lifted her chin. "I'll buy it from you then, but you aren't giving it to me."

"Ok. The sale price is one dollar."

"No, I'm serious. You get an appraiser out here to figure out what its worth and I'll buy it."

"Becky, I do your taxes, I know how much money you make. You can't get a mortgage for this type of house." He knew, of course, from Callie that Michael had gifted Becky with a very large sum of money. But the last thing he wanted was her money.

"My father will co-sign. I'm sure it won't be an issue."

He couldn't argue there. He shrugged. "I told you the sale price, take it or leave it."

She sipped her drink and turned her back on him as she looked out the large picture window. He wondered if she was thinking the same thing he'd been earlier about the gardens. They'd both worked so hard out there.

"I really hate you."

Louie heard the tremble in her voice and his heart sped up. He felt like a heel once again. "You should hate me, I did a rotten thing."

She nodded and he heard her sniffle, but he didn't move towards her. At least she was talking to him. That was a start.

"Now you're trying to make me feel bad about it by

giving me this house."

"No, I'm not. I'm moving and I need to get rid of it and you love it. We've been friends forever, Princess. Why would I do something even more rotten and put it on the market when I know you love this place?" He scanned her dark hair, all tangled from the wind, and longed to finger comb it. He remembered the feel of it on his skin and the scent of the shampoo she always used. He fisted his hands at his side to keep from touching her.

"Why are you moving?" she asked softly.

"You know why."

She turned around and tears pooled in her eyes. "Everyone else has told me why you're moving. I want to hear it from you."

"Why? So you can feel vindicated? So you can know how much I'm hurting? Is that what you need? I know I hurt you. I know you feel like I used you."

"You did use me." Her eyes narrowed and turned cold.

Louie had a hard time keeping up with her emotions. One minute she was furious, then she was almost in tears, now she was furious again. He moved across the room to stand in front of her. "I knew you'd never see me in any other way but as the skinny nerdy buddy you've known since the second grade. I loved you and I wanted you to look at me through new eyes. I thought if for one night, even one hour, I could be somebody else, maybe you'd look at me as a man."

"You went too far."

"Yes. My original idea was to simply share a dance with you, maybe one kiss in the moonlight, then disappear as Mr. Mystery. When we were in the gazebo, it got out of hand. I never intended to do anything more. I wasn't going to meet up with you later even thought we talked about it. That would have been too much, but then you showed up in the bedroom and thought I was Mr. Mystery." He swallowed, remembering the night in perfect clarity. Her lying on the settee, the moonlight washing over her skin. He couldn't stop himself.

"Somehow things blurred and you were in that gown and I was someone else." He raked his hand through his hair. "It was wrong and I know it was, but I couldn't resist you. That's my only excuse."

"You could have taken off the mask and told me the truth."

He nodded. "Yes, but wouldn't you have been just as mad at me? It didn't matter when you found out. You didn't like that you were deceived."

"You made a fool out of me." Her bottom lip trembled.

"Is that what's really behind this whole fight? I never thought of you as a fool. I was the fool. I was the one who wasn't brave enough to tell you what I wanted and how I felt without being someone else."

He took the can of pop from her hand and set it on the window sill, then cupped her face between his hands. Tears fell from her eyes and he brushed them away with his thumbs. "I never meant to hurt you."

She nodded. "I know you didn't."

"And I'm not trying to buy your forgiveness. This house is yours. You know it and I know it. I can't live here without you."

She swallowed. "I can't live here without you, either," she whispered

His heart burst open with hope. "So if neither of us can live here without the other one, what should we do?"

Becky smiled through her tears and lifted her arms to link around him. She sifted her fingers into the hair at the nape of his neck. "I think we should talk some more about this upstairs."

"Upstairs?"

She tipped her head back and looked up at him. "Ok, Nerdman, this is the part where you sweep me up into your arms and make love to me so that I never want to leave your bed."

"Oh, it is?"

She nodded. "Uh, huh."

"Hmm, well I don't know. I have a lot of work to do around here and then I need to pack for Seattle."

Becky pressed her body against him, her breasts cushioned into his chest and her thigh slipped between his. "You're not going to Seattle."

"I'm not?"

Her lips trailed along the side of his neck and nibbled below his ear and his heart raced. "No, I don't like Seattle.

Too cold and rainy."

"I have a job there."

"You don't need a job."

He laughed at that. "I do, because I just gave away most of my fortune to a princess."

She leaned back and looked up at him. "Your princess comes from a very wealthy family and owns a mansion."

"Oh, then I can work for you?" He bent down and scooped her up into his arms.

"I'm pretty sure I can find something for you to do around here, but there is one thing."

"Yes, I'll marry you." He strode down the hall and headed for the den.

"Hey, I said upstairs."

"Do you know how many stairs there are? I'm not Rhett Butler, you know. I'm just a scrawny little Nerdman."

He sank to the sofa with her in his lap. He lowered his head to kiss her.

"Don't you want to now what my stipulation is?"

He leaned back. "I thought it was getting married."

"Hell no, you know I don't care about marriage. But you do need to wear that mask once in a while, just to keep it exciting."

He grinned. "Princess, I have a feeling there will never be a lack of excitement with you around."

He kissed her and captured her breast through her thin t-shirt. Her nipple responded instantly to his touch and he groaned at what it did to his own body. Becky shifted in his arms until she straddled his lap and kissed him hard. She wiggled against him sending jolts of fire through his body. He cupped her hips in his hands and pressed her against him.

"I told you to take me upstairs," she whispered against his neck.

"What's wrong with right here?" He closed his eyes as she trailed her lips down his neck and lifted his t-shirt to place her hands on his bared chest.

"Someone could walk in. I didn't lock the front door," she said.

He opened his eyes and lifted her t-shirt over her

head. She shook out her dark curls and he brushed her hair back as it fell along her bared shoulders. She was the most beautiful woman in the world and he couldn't love her any more than he did right now.

He lifted her breasts in his palms and smoothed the pale skin, marveling at their perfection. Leaning up he captured one rosy tip between his lips and feasted, feeling as if he had finally returned to heaven after a long time away. She arched her back, obviously enjoying his attentions as much as he was. Her chest rose and fell, and her fingers tugged at his hair as he caressed and plucked at one nipple while his mouth plundered the other.

"Nerdman," she moaned.

"Yes, Princess?"

"I love you."

Louie lifted his head to look into her dark eyes. "Say it again."

She smiled. "I love you. I'm sorry I've been such a bitch."

"You are many things, but never a bitch. I deserved it."

She grinned. "Yeah, you did, maybe a little, but right now it seems like it wasn't that big of a deal."

"I'll make it up to you. I promise, every day for the rest of your life."

"Do you really want to marry me?"

"Since the seventh grade."

"Will you buy me a ring?

He laughed. "I think I probably have enough money left to do that."

She looked at him from under lashes, her hands flat on his chest. "I like big rings."

"I know you do."

"You know what else I like?" She leaned forward and whispered in his ear and giggled as he growled.

"Well, then, we probably should take this upstairs."

He chuckled and stood with her wrapped around his waist. She slid to the floor and he kissed her for a long moment before they slipped out of the den and raced upstairs to their bedroom.

A word about the author...

Roni Adams resides in a tiny hamlet in Upstate New York nestled along the Erie Canal. She's been married for 22 years and she and her husband, Scott, have three sons ages 11- 19. Much to her heartache the two older boys will both be leaving the nest this August, one for the Marines and one for an internship at Disney World in Orlando. She thinks the timing for her to get the stories she's worked on for years out has never been better. Escaping into the lives of her characters takes her mind off the fact that her family is growing up.

Roni is an active member of RWA and the San Antonio Romance Authors. She credits many of her published author friends at SARA for helping push her down the right path towards publishing in short stories. She also credits them for help with all her Texas research.

"I have always had a fascination with the state of Texas and horses and cowboys in general. For my 40 th birthday gift I flew to Bandera , TX and stayed on a dude ranch where I could ride horses all day. Until then, I never really knew what John Denver meant when he sang about, "coming home to a place I've never been before." I'd arrived at the home of my heart.

She is also one of the founding members of www.rosescoloredglasses.com a writers community devoted to helping new writers grow and learn.

Roni loves to hear from readers and you can contact her at roni@roniadams.com . You may also visit her web site at www.roniadams.com